RECONSTRUCTION

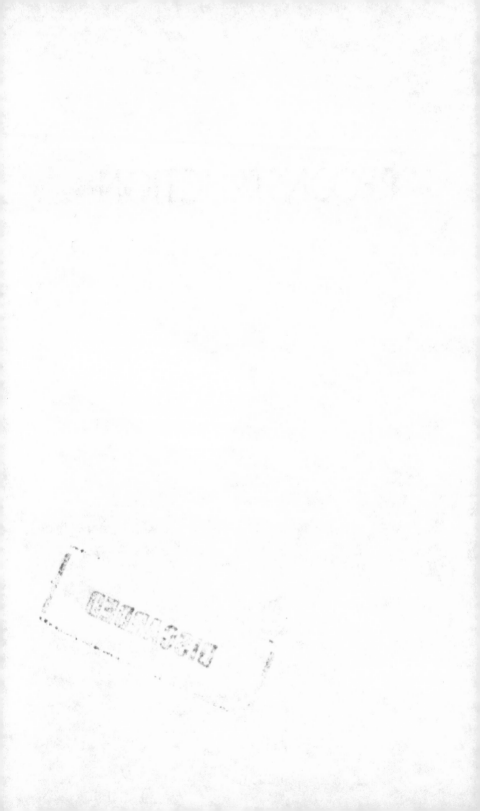

Reconstruction

STORIES

ALAYA DAWN JOHNSON

Small Beer Press
Easthampton, MA

Reconstruction: Stories copyright © 2020 by Alaya Dawn Johnson (alayadawnjohnson.com). All rights reserved. Page 277 is an extension of the copyright page.

Small Beer Press
150 Pleasant Street #306
Easthampton, MA 01027
smallbeerpress.com
weightlessbooks.com
bookmoonbooks.com
info@smallbeerpress.com

Distributed to the trade by Consortium.

Library of Congress Cataloging-in-Publication Data

Names: Johnson, Alaya Dawn, 1982- author.
Title: Reconstruction : stories / Alaya Dawn Johnson.
Description: First edition. | Easthampton, MA : Small Beer Press, [2020] |
    Summary: "Johnson digs into the lives of those trodden underfoot by the
    powers that be: from the lives of vampires and those caught in their
    circle in Hawai'i to a taxonomy of anger put together by Union soldiers
    in the American Civil War, these stories will grab you and not let you
    go"-- Provided by publisher.
Identifiers: LCCN 2020027389 (print) | LCCN 2020027390 (ebook) | ISBN
    9781618731777 (paperback) | ISBN 9781618731784 (ebook)
Classification: LCC PS3610.O315 A6 2020 (print) | LCC PS3610.O315 (ebook)
    | DDC 813/.6--dc23
LC record available at https://lccn.loc.gov/2020027389
LC ebook record available at https://lccn.loc.gov/2020027390

First edition 1 2 3 4 5 6 7 8 9

Set in Centaur MT. Titles in American Typewriter.

Printed on 30% PCR recycled paper in the USA.
Cover art "Marie-Thérèse and Dieunie" copyright © 2020 by Tessa Mars (tessamars.com). All rights reserved.

For Lauren, who read all of the stories that were never published.

Contents

A Guide to the Fruits of Hawai'i

Key's favorite time of day is sunset, her least is sunrise. It should be the opposite, but every time she watches that bright red disk sinking into the water beneath Mauna Kea her heart bends like a wishbone, and she thinks, *He's awake now.*

Key is thirty-four. She is old for a human woman without any children. She has kept herself alive by being useful in other ways. For the past four years, Key has been the overseer of the Mauna Kea Grade Orange blood facility.

Is it a concentration camp if the inmates are well fed? If their beds are comfortable? If they are given an hour and a half of rigorous boxercise and yoga each morning in the recreational field?

It doesn't have to be Honouliui to be wrong.

When she's called in to deal with Jeb's body—bloody, not drained, in a feeding room—yoga doesn't make him any less dead.

Key helps vampires run a concentration camp for humans.

Key is a different kind of monster.

Key's favorite food is umeboshi. Salty and tart and bright red, with that pit in the center to beware. She loves it in rice balls, the kind her Japanese grandmother made when she was little. She loves it by itself, the way she ate it at fifteen, after Obachan

1

died. She hasn't had umeboshi in eighteen years, but sometimes she thinks that when she dies she'll taste one again.

This morning she eats the same thing she eats every meal: a nutritious brick patty, precisely five inches square and two inches deep, colored puce. Her raw scrubbed hands still have a pink tinge of Jeb's blood in the cuticles. She stares at them while she sips the accompanying beverage, which is orange. She can't remember if it ever resembled the fruit.

She eats this because that is what every human eats in the Mauna Kea facility. Because the patty is easy to manufacture and soft enough to eat with plastic spoons. Key hasn't seen a fork in years, a knife in more than a decade. The vampires maintain tight control over all items with the potential to draw blood. Yet humans are tool-making creatures, and their desires, even nihilistic ones, have a creative power that no vampire has the imagination or agility to anticipate. How else to explain the shiv, handcrafted over secret months from the wood cover and glue-matted pages of *A Guide to the Fruits of Hawai'i*, the book that Jeb used to read in the hours after his feeding sessions, sometimes aloud, to whatever humans would listen? He took the only thing that gave him pleasure in the world, destroyed it—or recreated it—and slit his veins with it. Mr. Charles questioned her particularly; he knew that she and Jeb used to talk sometimes. Had she *known* that the *boy* was like this? He gestured with pallid hands at the splatter of arterial pulses from jaggedly slit wrists: oxidized brown, inedible, mocking.

No, she said, of course not, Mr. Charles. I report any suspected cases of self-waste immediately.

She reports any suspected cases. And so, for the weeks she has watched Jeb hardly eating across the mess hall, noticed how he staggered from the feeding rooms, recognized the frigid rebuff in his responses to her questions, she has very carefully refused to suspect.

Today, just before dawn, she choked on the fruits of her indifference. He slit his wrists and femoral arteries. He smeared the blood over his face and buttocks and genitals, and he waited to die before the vampire technician could arrive to drain him.

Not many humans self-waste. Most think about it, but Key never has, not since the invasion of the Big Island. Unlike other humans, she has someone she's waiting for. The one she loves, the one she prays will reward her patience. During her years as overseer, Key has successfully stopped three acts of self-waste. She has failed twice. Jeb is different; Mr. Charles sensed it somehow, but vampires can only read human minds through human blood. Mr. Charles hasn't drunk from Key in years. And what could he learn, even if he did? He can't drink thoughts she has spent most of her life refusing to have.

Mr. Charles calls her to the main office the next night, between feeding shifts. She is terrified, like she always is, of what they might do. She is thinking of Jeb and wondering how Mr. Charles has taken the loss of an investment. She is wondering how fast she will die in the work camp on Lanai.

But Mr. Charles has an offer, not a death sentence.

"You know . . . of the facility on Oahu? Grade Gold?"

"Yes," Key says. Just that, because she learned early not to betray herself to them unnecessarily, and the man at Grade Gold has always been her greatest betrayer.

No, not a man, Key tells herself for the hundredth, the thousandth time. *He is one of them.*

Mr. Charles sits in a hanging chair shaped like an egg with plush red velvet cushions. He wears a black suit with steel gray pinstripes, sharply tailored. The cuffs are high and his feet are bare, white as talcum powder and long and bony like spiny fish. His veins are prominent and round and milky blue. Mr. Charles is vain about his feet.

He does not sit up to speak to Key. She can hardly see his face behind the shadow cast by the overhanging top of the egg. All vampires speak deliberately, but Mr. Charles drags out his tones until you feel you might tip over from waiting on the next syllable. It goes up and down like a calliope—

". . . what do you *say* to heading down there and *sort*ing the matter . . . out?"

"I'm sorry, Mr. Charles," she says carefully, because she has lost the thread of his monologue. "What matter?"

He explains: a Grade Gold human girl has killed herself. It is a disaster that outshadows the loss of Jeb.

"You would not believe the expense taken to keep those humans Grade Gold standard."

"What would I do?"

"Take it in hand, *of* course. It seems our small . . . Grade Orange operation has gotten some notice. Tetsuo asked for you . . . particularly."

"Tetsuo?" She hasn't said the name out loud in years. Her voice catches on the second syllable.

"*Mr.* Tetsuo," Mr. Charles says, and waves a hand at her. He holds a sheet of paper, the same shade as his skin. "He wrote you a *letter*."

Key can't move, doesn't reach out to take it, and so it flutters to the black marble floor a few feet away from Mr. Charles's egg.

He leans forward. "I think . . . I remember something . . . you and Tetsuo . . ."

"He recommended my promotion here," Key says, after a moment. It seems the safest phrasing. Mr. Charles would have remembered this eventually; vampires are slow, but inexorable.

The diffuse light from the paper lanterns catches the bottom half of his face, highlighting the deep cleft in his chin. It twitches in faint surprise. "You *were* his pet?"

Key winces. She remembers the years she spent at his side during and after the wars, catching scraps in his wake, despised by every human who saw her there. She waited for him to see how much she had sacrificed and give her the only reward that could matter after what she'd done. Instead he had her shunt removed and sent her to Grade Orange. She has not seen or heard from him in four years. His pet, yes, that's as good a name as any—but he never drank from her. Not once.

Mr. Charles's lips, just a shade of white darker than his skin, open like a hole in a cloud. "And he wants you back. How do you *feel?*"

Terrified. Awestruck. Confused. "Grateful," she says.

The hole smiles. "Grateful! How interesting. Come here, girl. I believe I shall *have a taste.*"

She grabs the letter with shaking fingers and folds it inside a pocket of her red uniform. She stands in front of Mr. Charles.

"Well?" he says.

She hasn't had a shunt in years, though she can still feel its ridged scar in the crook of her arm. Without it, feeding from

her is messy, violent. Traditional, Mr. Charles might say. Her
fingers hurt as she unzips the collar. Her muscles feel sore, the
bones in her spine arthritic and old as she bows her head, leans
closer to Mr. Charles. She waits for him to bare his fangs, to
pierce her vein, to suck her blood.

He takes more than he should. He drinks until her fingers
and toes twinge, until her neck throbs, until the red velvet of
his seat fades to gray. When he finishes, he leaves her blood on
his mouth.

"I forgive . . . you for the boy," he says.

Jeb cut his own arteries, left his good blood all over the
floor. Mr. Charles abhors waste above all else.

Mr. Charles will explain the situation. I wish you to
come. If you do well, I have been authorized to offer
you the highest reward.

The following night, Key takes a boat to Oahu. Vampires don't
like water, but they will cross it anyway—the sea has become a
status symbol among them, an indication of strength. Hawai'i
is still a resort destination, though most of its residents only go
out at night. Grade Gold is the most expensive, most luxurious
resort of them all.

Tetsuo travels between the islands often. Key saw him do
it a dozen times during the war. She remembers one night, his
face lit by the moon and the yellow lamps on the deck—the
wide cheekbones, thick eyebrows, sharp widow's peak, all frozen
in the perfection of a nineteen-year-old boy. Pale beneath the

6

olive tones of his skin, he bares his fangs when the waves lurch beneath him.

"What does it feel like?" she asks him.

"Like frozen worms in my veins," he says, after a full, long minute of silence. Then he checks the guns and tells her to wait below, the humans are coming. She can't see anything, but Tetsuo can smell them like chum in the water. The Japanese have held out the longest, and the vampires of Hawai'i lead the assault against them.

Two nights later, in his quarters in the bunker at the base of Mauna Kea, Tetsuo brings back a sheet of paper, written in Japanese. The only characters she recognizes are "shi" and "ta"— "death" and "field." It looks like some kind of list.

"What is this?" she asks.

"Recent admissions to the Lanai human residential facility."

She looks up at him, devoted with terror. "My mother?" Her father died in the first offensive on the Big Island, a hero of the resistance. He never knew how his daughter had chosen to survive.

"Here," Tetsuo says, and runs a cold finger down the list without death. "Jen Isokawa."

"Alive?" She has been looking for her mother since the wars began. Tetsuo knows this, but she didn't know he was searching, too. She feels swollen with this indication of his regard.

"She's listed as a caretaker. They're treated well. You could . . ." He sits beside her on the bed that only she uses. His pause lapses into a stop. He strokes her hair absentmindedly; if she had a tail, it would beat his legs. She is seventeen and she is sure he will reward her soon.

7

"Tetsuo," she says, "you could drink from me, if you want. I've had a shunt for nearly a year. The others use it. I'd rather feed you."

Sometimes she has to repeat herself three times before he seems to hear her. This, she has said at least ten. But she is safe here in his bunker, on the bed he brought in for her, with his lukewarm body pressed against her warm one. Vampires do not have sex with humans; they feed. But if he doesn't want her that way, what else can she offer him?

"I've had you tested. You're fertile. If you bear three children you won't need a shunt and the residential facilities will care for you for the rest of your mortality. You can live with your mother. I will make sure you're safe."

She presses her face against his shoulder. "Don't make me leave."

"You wanted to see your mother."

Her mother had spent the weeks before the invasion in church, praying for God to intercede against the abominations. Better that she die than see Key like this.

"Only to know what happened to her," Key whispers. "Won't you feed from me, Tetsuo? I want to feel closer to you. I want you to know how much I love you."

A long pause. Then, "I don't need to taste you to know how you feel."

Tetsuo meets her on shore.

Just like that, she is seventeen again.

"You look older," he says. Slowly, but with less affectation than Mr. Charles.

This is true; so inevitable she doesn't understand why he even bothers to say so. Is he surprised? Finally, she nods. The buoyed dock rocks beneath them—he makes no attempt to move, though the two vampires with him grip the denuded skin of their own elbows with pale fingers. They flare and retract their fangs.

"You are drained," he says. He does not mean this metaphorically.

She nods again, realizes further explanation is called for. "Mr. Charles," she says, her voice a painful rasp. This embarrasses her, though Tetsuo would never notice.

He nods, sharp and curt. She thinks he is angry, though perhaps no one else could read him as clearly. She knows that face, frozen in the countenance of a boy dead before the Second World War. A boy dead fifty years before she was born.

He is old enough to remember Pearl Harbor, the detention camps, the years when Maui's forests still had native birds. But she has never dared ask him about his human life.

"And what did Charles explain?"

"He said someone killed herself at Grade Gold."

Tetsuo flares his fangs. She flinches, which surprises her. She used to flush at the sight of his fangs, her blood pounding red just beneath the soft surface of her skin.

"I've been given dispensation," he says, and rests one finger against the hollow at the base of her throat.

She's learned a great deal about the rigid traditions that restrict vampire life since she first met Tetsuo. She understands why her teenage fantasies of morally liberated vampirism were improbable, if not impossible. For each human they bring over, vampires need a special dispensation that they only receive once or twice every decade. *The highest reward.* If Tetsuo has gotten a dispensation, then her first thought when she read his letter was correct. He didn't mean retirement. He didn't mean a peaceful life in some remote farm on the islands. He meant death. Un-death.

After all these years, Tetsuo means to turn her into a vampire.

The trouble at Grade Gold started with a dead girl. Penelope cut her own throat five days ago (with a real knife, the kind they allow Grade Gold humans for cutting food). Her ghost haunts the eyes of those she left behind. One human resident in particular, with hair dyed the color of tea and blue lipstick to match the bruises under her red eyes, takes one look at Key and starts to scream.

Key glances at Tetsuo, but he has forgotten her. He stares at the girl as if he could burn her to ashes on the plush green carpet. The five others in the room look away, but Key can't tell if it's in embarrassment or fear. The luxury surrounding them chokes her. There's a bowl of fruit on a coffee table. Real fruit—fuzzy brown kiwis, mottled red-green mangos, dozens of tangerines. She takes an involuntary step forward and the girl's scream gets louder before cutting off with an abrupt squawk. Her labored breaths are the only sound in the room.

"This is a joke," the girl says. There's spittle on her blue lips. "What hole did you dig her out of?"

"Go to your room, Rachel," Tetsuo says.

Rachel flicks back her hair and rubs angrily under one eye. "What are you now, Daddy Vampire? You think you can just, what? Replace her? With this broke-down fogey look-alike?"

"She is not—"

"Yeah? What is she?"

They are both silent, doubt and grief and fury scuttling between them like beetles in search of a meal. Tetsuo and the girl stare at each other with such deep familiarity that Key feels forgotten, alone—almost ashamed of the dreams that have kept her alive for a decade. They have never felt so hopeless, or so false.

"Her name is Key," Tetsuo says, in something like defeat. He turns away, though he makes no move to leave. "She will be your new caretaker."

"Key?" the girl says. "What kind of a name is that?"

Key doesn't answer for a long time, thinking of all the ways she could respond. Of Obachan Akiko and the affectionate nickname of lazy summers spent hiking in the mountains or pounding mochi in the kitchen. Of her half-Japanese mother and Hawai'ian father, of the ways history and identity and circumstance can shape a girl into half a woman, until someone— *not a man*—comes with a hundred thousand others like him and destroys anything that might have once had meaning. So she finds meaning in him. Who else was there?

And this girl, whose sneer reveals her bucked front teeth, has as much chance of understanding that world as Key does of understanding this one. Fresh fruit on the table. No uniforms. And a perfect, glittering shunt of plastic and metal nestled in the crook of her left arm.

"Mine," Key answers the girl.

Rachel spits; Tetsuo turns his head, just a little, as though he can only bear to see Key from the corner of his eye.

"You're nothing like her," she says.

"Like who?"

But the girl storms from the room, leaving her chief vampire without a dismissal. Key now understands this will not be punished. It's another one—a boy, with the same florid beauty as the girl but far less belligerence—who answers her.

"You look like Penelope," he says, tugging on a long lock of his asymmetrically cut black hair. "Just older."

When Tetsuo leaves the room, it's Key who cannot follow.

Key remembers sixteen. Her obachan is dead and her mother has moved to an apartment in Hilo and it's just Key and her father in that old, quiet house at the end of the road. The vampires have annexed San Diego, and Okinawa is besieged, but life doesn't feel very different in the mountains of the Big Island.

It is raining in the woods behind her house. Her father has told her to study, but all she's done since her mother left is read Mishima's *Sea of Fertility* novels. She sits on the porch, wondering if it's better to kill herself or wait for them to come, and just as she thinks she ought to have the courage to die, something rattles in the shed. A rat, she thinks.

But it's not rat she sees when she pulls open the door on its rusty hinges. It's a man, crouched between a stack of old appliance boxes and the rusted fender of the Buick her father always meant to fix one day. His hair is wet and slicked back, his white shirt is damp and ripped from shoulder to navel. The skin beneath it is pale as a corpse; bloodless, though the edges of a deep wound are still visible.

"They've already come?" Her voice breaks on a whisper. She wanted to finish *The Decay of the Angel*. She wanted to see her mother once more.

"Shut the door," he says, crouching in shadow, away from the bar of light streaming through the narrow opening.

"Don't kill me."

"We are equally at each other's mercy."

She likes the way he speaks. No one told her they could sound so proper. So human. Is there a monster in her shed, or is he something else?

"Why shouldn't I open it all the way?"

He is brave, whatever else. He takes his long hands from in front of his face and stands, a flower blooming after rain. He is beautiful, though she will not mark that until later. Now, she only notices the steady, patient way he regards her. *I could move faster than you*, his eyes say. *I could kill you first.*

She thinks of Mishima and says, "I'm not afraid of death."

Only when the words leave her mouth does she realize how deeply she has lied. Does he know? Her hands would shake if it weren't for their grip on the handle.

"I promise," he says. "I will save you, when the rest of us come."

What is it worth, a monster's promise?

She steps inside and shuts out the light.

There are nineteen residents of Grade Gold; the twentieth is buried beneath the kukui tree in the communal garden. The thought of rotting in earth revolts Key. She prefers the bright, fierce heat of a crematorium fire, like the one that consumed Jeb the night before she left Mauna Kea. The ashes fly in the wind, into the ocean and up in the trees, where they lodge in bird nests and caterpillar silk and mud puddles after a storm.

The return of flesh to the earth should be fast and final, not the slow mortification of worms and bacteria and carbon gases.

Tetsuo instructs her to keep close watch on unit three. "Rachel isn't very . . . steady right now," he says, as though unaware of the understatement.

The remaining nineteen residents are divided into four units, five kids in each but one, living together in sprawling ranch houses connected by walkways and gardens. There are walls, of course, but you have to climb a tree to see them. The kids at Grade Gold have more freedom than any human she's ever encountered since the war, but they're as bound to this paradise as she was to her mountain.

The vampires who come here stay in a high glass tower right by the beach. During the day, the black-tinted windows gleam like lasers. At night, the vampires come down to feed. There is a fifth house in the residential village, one reserved for clients and their meals. Testsuo orchestrates these encounters, planning each interaction in fine detail: this human with that performance for this distinguished client. Key has grown used to thinking of her fellow humans as food, but now she is forced to reconcile that indelible fact with another, stranger veneer. The vampires who pay so dearly for Grade Gold humans don't merely want to feed from a shunt. They want to be entertained, talked to, cajoled. The boy who explained about Key's uncanny resemblance juggles torches. Twin girls from unit three play guitar and sing songs by the Carpenters. Even Rachel, dressed in a gaudy purple mermaid dress with matching streaks in her hair, keeps up a one-way, laughing conversation with a vampire who seems too astonished—or too slow—to reply.

Key has never seen anything like this before. She thought that most vampires regarded humans as walking sacks of food. What pleasure could be derived from speaking with your meal first? From seeing it sing or dance? When she first went with Tetsuo, the other vampires talked about human emotions as if they were flavors of ice cream. But at Grade Orange she grew accustomed to more basic parameters: were the humans fed, were they fertile, did they sleep? Here, she must approve outfits; she must manage dietary preferences and erratic tempers and a dozen other details all crucial to keeping the kids Grade Gold standard. Their former caretaker has been shipped to the work camps, which leaves Key in sole charge of the operation. At least until Tetsuo decides how he will use his dispensation.

Key's thoughts skitter away from the possibility.

"I didn't know vampires liked music," she says, late in the evening, when some of the kids sprawl, exhausted, across couches and cushions. A girl no older than fifteen opens her eyes but hardly moves when a vampire in a gold suit lifts her arm for a nip. Key and Tetsuo are seated together at the far end of the main room, in the bay windows that overlook a cliff and the ocean.

"It's as interesting to us as any other human pastime."

"Does music have a taste?"

His wide mouth stretches at the edges; she recognizes it as a smile. "Music has some utility, given the right circumstances."

She doesn't quite understand him. The air is redolent with the sweat of human teenagers and the muggy, salty air that blows through the open doors and windows. Her eye catches on a half-eaten strawberry dropped carelessly on the carpet a few feet away. It was harvested too soon, a white, tasteless core surrounded by hard, red flesh.

She thinks there is nothing of "right" in these circumstances, and their utility is, at its bottom, merely that of parasite and host.

"The music enhances the—our—flavor?"

Tetsuo stares at her for a long time, long enough for him to take at least three of his shallow, erratically spaced breaths. To look at him is to taste copper and sea on her tongue; to wait for him is to hear the wind slide down a mountainside an hour before dawn.

It has been four years since she last saw him. She thought he had forgotten her, and now he speaks to her as if all those years haven't passed, as though the vampires hadn't long since won the war and turned the world to their slow, long-burning purpose.

"Emotions change your flavor," he says. "And food. And sex. And pleasure."

And love? she wonders, but Tetsuo has never drunk from her.

"Then why not treat all of us like you do the ones here? Why have con—Mauna Kea?"

She expects him to catch her slip, but his attention is focused on something beyond her right shoulder. She turns to look, and sees nothing but the hall and a closed feeding room door.

"Three years," he says, quietly. He doesn't look at her. She doesn't understand what he means, so she waits. "It takes three years for the complexity to fade. For the vitality of young blood to turn muddy and clogged with silt. Even among the new crops, only a few individuals are Gold standard. For three years, they produce the finest blood ever tasted, filled with regrets and ecstasy and dreams. And then . . ."

"Grade Orange?" Key asks, her voice dry and rasping. Had Tetsuo always talked of humans like this? With such little regard for their selfhood? Had she been too young to understand, or have the years of harvesting humans hardened him?

"If we have not burned too much out. Living at high elevation helps prolong your utility, but sometimes all that's left is Lanai and the work camps."

She remembers her terror before her final interview with Mr. Charles, her conviction that Jeb's death would prompt him to discard his uselessly old overseer to the work camps.

A boy from one of the other houses staggers to the one she recognizes from unit two and sprawls in his lap. Unit-two boy startles awake, smiles, and bends over to kiss the first. A pair of female vampires kneel in front of them and press their fangs with thick pink tongues.

"Touch him," one says, pointing to the boy from unit two. "Make him cry."

The boy from unit two doesn't even pause for breath; he reaches for the other boy's cock and squeezes. And as they both groan with something that makes Key feel like a voyeur, made helpless by her own desire, the pair of vampires pull the boys apart and dive for their respective shunts. The room goes quiet but for soft gurgles, like two minnows in a tide pool. Then a pair of clicks as the boys' shunts turn gray, forcing the vampires to stop feeding.

"Lovely, divine," the vampires say a few minutes later, when they pass on their way out. "We always appreciate the sexual displays."

The boys curl against each other, eyes shut. They breathe like old men: hard, through constricted tubes.

"Does that happen often?" she asks.

"This Grade Gold is known for its sexual flavors. My humans pick partners they enjoy."

Vampires might not have sex, but they crave its flavor. Will she, when she crosses to their side? Will she look at those two boys and command them to fuck each other just so she can taste?

"Do you ever care?" she says, her voice barely a whisper. "About what you've done to us?"

He looks away from her. Before she can blink he has crossed to the one closed feeding room door and wrenched it open. A thump of something thrown against a wall. A snarl, as human as a snake's hiss.

"Leave, Gregory!" Tetsuo says. A vampire Key recognizes from earlier in the night stumbles into the main room. He rubs his jaw, though the torn and mangled skin there has already begun to knit together.

"She is mine to have. I paid—"

"Not enough to kill her."

"I'll complain to the council," the vampire says. "You've been losing support. And everyone knows how *patiently* Charles has waited in his aerie."

She should be scared, but his words make her think of Jeb, of failures and consequences, and of the one human she has not seen for hours. She stands and sprints past both vampires to where Rachel lies insensate on a bed.

Her shunt has turned the opaque gray meant to prevent vampires from feeding humans to death. But the client has bitten her neck instead.

"Tell them whatever you wish, and I will tell them you circumvented the shunt of a fully-tapped human. We have our rules for a reason. You are no longer welcome here."

Rachel's pulse is soft, but steady. She stirs and moans beneath Key's hands. The relief is crushing; she wants to cradle the girl in her arms until she wakes. She wants to protect her so her blood will never have to smear the walls of a feeding room, so that Key will be able to say that at least she saved one.

Rachel's eyes flutter open, land with a butterfly's gentleness on Key's face.

"Pen," she says, "I told you. It makes them . . . they *eat* me."

Key doesn't understand, but she doesn't mind. She presses her hand to Rachel's warm forehead and sings lullabies her grandmother liked until Rachel falls back to sleep.

"How is she?" It is Tetsuo, come into the room after the client has finally left.

"Drained," Key says, as dispassionately as he. "She'll be fine in a few days."

"Key."

"Yes?"

She won't look at him.

"I do, you know."

She knows. "Then why support it?"

"You'll understand when your time comes."

She looks back down at Rachel, and all she can see are bruises blooming purple on her upper arms, blood dried brown on her neck. She looks like a human being: infinitely precious, fragile. Like prey.

Five days later, Key sits in the garden in the shade of the kukui tree. She has reports to file on the last week's feedings, but the papers sit untouched beside her. The boy from unit two and his boyfriend are tending the tomatoes, and Key slowly peels the skin from her fourth kiwi. The first time she bit into one she cried, but the boys pretended not to notice. She is getting better with practice. Her hands still tremble and her misted eyes refract rainbows in the hard noon sunlight. She is learning to be human again.

Rachel sleeps on the ground beside her, curled on the packed dirt of Penelope's grave with her back against the tree trunk and her arms wrapped tightly around her belly. She's spent most of the last five days sleeping, and Key thinks she has mostly recovered. She's been eating voraciously, foods in wild combinations at all times of day and night. Key is glad. Without the distracting, angry makeup, Rachel's face looks vulnerable and haunted. Jeb had that look in the months before his death. He would sit quietly in the mess hall and stare at the food brick as though he had forgotten how to eat. Jeb had transferred to Mauna Kea within a week of Key becoming overseer. He liked watching the lights of the airplanes at night and he kept two books with him: *The Blind Watchmaker* and *A Guide to the Fruits of Hawai'i*. She talked to him about the latter—had he ever tasted breadfruit or kiwi or cherimoya? None, he said, in a voice so small and soft it sounded inversely proportional to his size. Only a peach, a canned peach, when he was four or five years old. Vampires don't waste fruit on Grade Orange humans.

The covers of both books were worn, the spines cracked, the pages yellowed and brittle at the edges. Why keep a book about fruit you had never tasted and never would eat? Why read at all, when they frowned upon literacy in humans and often banned books outright? She never asked him. Mr. Charles had seen their conversation, though she doubted he had heard it, and requested that she refrain from speaking unnecessarily to the *harvest*.

So when Jeb stared at her across the table with eyes like a snuffed candle, she turned away, she forced her patty into her mouth, she chewed, she reached for her orange drink.

His favorite book became his means of self-destruction. She let him do it. She doesn't know if she feels guilty for not having stopped him, or for being in the position to stop him in the first place. Not two weeks later she rests beneath a kukui tree, the flesh of a fruit she had never expected to taste again turning to green pulp between her teeth. She reaches for another one because she knows how little she deserves this.

But the skin of the fruit at the bottom of the bowl is too soft and fleshy for a kiwi. She pulls it into the light and drops it.

"Are you okay?" It's the boy from unit two—Kaipo. He kneels down and picks up the cherimoya.

"What?" she says, and struggles to control her breathing. She has to appear normal, in control. She's supposed to be their caretaker. But the boy just seems concerned, not judgmental. Rachel rolls onto her back and opens her eyes.

"You screamed," Rachel says, sleep-fogged and accusatory. "You woke me up."

"Who put this in the bowl?" Kaipo asks. "These things are poisonous! They grow on that tree down the hill, but you can't eat them."

Key takes the haunted fruit from him, holding it carefully so as not to bruise it further. "Who told you that?" she asks.

Rachel leans forward, so her chin rests on the edge of Key's lounge chair and the tips of her purple-streaked hair touch Key's thigh. "Tetsuo," she says. "What, did he lie?"

Key shakes her head slowly. "He probably only half-remembered. It's a cherimoya. The flesh is delicious, but the seeds are poisonous."

Rachel's eyes follow her hands. "Like, killing you poisonous?" she asks.

Key thinks back to her father's lessons. "Maybe if you eat them all or grind them up. The tree bark can paralyze your heart and lungs."

Kaipo whistles, and they all watch intently when she wedges her finger under the skin and splits it in half. The white, fleshy pulp looks stark, even a little disquieting against the scaly green exterior. She plucks out the hard, brown seeds and tosses them to the ground. Only then does she pull out a chunk of flesh and put it in her mouth.

Like strawberries and banana pudding and pineapple. Like the summer after Obachan died, when a box of them came to the house as a condolence gift.

"You look like you're fellating it," Rachel says. Key opens her eyes and swallows abruptly.

Kaipo pushes his tongue against his lips. "Can I try it, Key?" he asks, very politely. Did the vampires teach him that politeness? Did vampires teach Rachel a word like *fellate*, perhaps while instructing her to do it with a hopefully willing human partner?

"Do you guys know how to use condoms?" She has decided to ask Tetsuo to supply them. This last week has made it clear that "sexual flavors" are all too frequently on the menu at Grade Gold.

Kaipo looks at Rachel; Rachel shakes her head. "What's a condom?" he asks.

It's so easy to forget how little of the world they know. "You use it during sex, to stop you from catching diseases," she says carefully. "Or getting pregnant."

Rachel laughs and stuffs the rest of the flesh into her wide mouth. Even a cherimoya can't fill her hollows. "Great, even more vampire sex," she says, her hatred clearer than her garbled words. "They never made Pen do it."

"They didn't?" Key asks.

Juice dribbles down her chin. "You know, Tetsuo's dispensation? Before she killed herself, she was his pick. Everyone knew it. That's why they left her alone."

Key feels light-headed. "But if she was his choice . . . why would she kill herself?"

"She didn't want to be a vampire," Kaipo says softly.

"She wanted a *baby*, like bringing a new food sack into the world is a good idea. But they wouldn't let her have sex and they wanted to make her one of them, so—now she's gone. But why he'd bring *you* here, when *any* of us would be a better choice—"

"Rachel, just shut up. Please." Kaipo takes her by the shoulder.

Rachel shrugs him off. "What? Like she can do anything."

"If she becomes one of *them*—"

"I wouldn't hurt you," Key says, too quickly. Rachel masks her pain with cruelty, but it is palpable. Key can't imagine any version of herself that would add to that.

Kaipo and Rachel stare at her. "But," Kaipo says, "that's what vampires do."

"I would eat you," Rachel says, and flops back under the tree. "I would make you cry and your tears would taste sweeter than a cherimoya."

_____

"I will be back in four days," Testsuo tells her, late the next night. "There is one feeding scheduled. I hope you will be ready when I return."

"For the . . . reward?" she asks, stumbling over an appropriate euphemism. Their words for it are polysyllabic spikes: transmutation, transformation, metamorphosis. All vampires were once human, and immortal doesn't mean invulnerable. Some die each year, and so their ranks must be replenished with the flesh of worthy, willing humans.

He places a hand on her shoulder. It feels as chill and inert as a piece of damp wood. She thinks she must be dreaming.

"I have wanted this for a long time, Key," he says to her—like a stranger, like the person who knows her the best in the world.

"Why now?"

"Our thoughts can be . . . slow, sometimes. You will see. Orderly, but sometimes too orderly to see patterns clearly. I thought of you, but did not know it until Penelope died."

Penelope, who looked just like Key. Penelope, who would have been his pick. She shivers and steps away from his hand. "Did you love her?"

She can't believe that she is asking this question. She can't believe that he is offering her the dreams she would have murdered for ten, even five years ago.

"I loved that she made me think of you," he says, "when you were young and beautiful."

"It's been eighteen years, Tetsuo."

He looks over her shoulder. "You haven't lost much," he says. "I'm not too late. You'll see."

He is waiting for a response. She forces herself to nod. She wants to close her eyes and cover her mouth, keep all her love for him inside where it can be safe, because if she loses it, there will be nothing left but a girl in the rain who should have opened the door.

He looks like an alien when he smiles. He looks like nothing she could ever know when he walks down the hall, past the open door and the girl who has been watching them this whole time.

Rachel is young and beautiful, Key thinks, and Penelope is dead.

Key's sixth feeding at Grade Gold is contained, quiet and without incident. The gazes of the clients slide over her as she greets them at the door of the feeding house, but she is used to that. To a vampire, a human without a shunt is like a book without pages: a useless absurdity. She has assigned all of unit one and a pair from unit four to the gathering. Seven humans for five vampires is a luxurious ratio—probably more than they paid for, but she's happy to let that be Tetsuo's problem. She shudders to remember how Rachel's blood soaked into the collar of her blouse when she lifted the girl from the bed. She has seen dozens of overdrained humans, including some who died from it, but what happened to Rachel feels worse. She doesn't understand why, but is overwhelmed by tenderness for her.

A half-hour before the clients are supposed to leave, Kaipo sprints through the front door, flushed and panting so hard he has to pause half a minute to catch his breath.

"Rachel," he manages, while humans and vampires alike pause to look.

She stands up. "What did she do?"

"I'm not sure . . . she was shaking and screaming, waking everyone up, yelling about Penelope and Tetsuo and then she started vomiting."

"The clients have another half hour," she whispers. "I can't leave until then."

Kaipo tugs on the long lock of glossy black hair that he has blunt-cut over his left eye. "I'm scared for her, Key," he says. "She won't listen to anyone else."

She will blame herself if any of the kids here tonight die, and she will blame herself if something happens to Rachel. Her hands make the decision for her: she reaches for Kaipo's left arm. He lets her take it reflexively, and doesn't flinch when she lifts his shunt. She looks for and finds the small electrical chip that controls the inflow and outflow of blood and other fluids. She taps the Morse-like code, and Kaipo watches with his mouth open as the glittering plastic polymer changes from clear to gray. As though he's already been tapped out.

"I'm not supposed to show you that," she says, and smiles until she remembers Tetsuo and what he might think. "Stay here. Make sure nothing happens. I'll be back as soon as I can."

She stays only long enough to see his agreement, and then she's flying out the back door, through the garden, down the left-hand path that leads to unit two.

Rachel is on her hands and knees in the middle of the walkway. The other three kids in unit two watch her silently from the doorway, but Rachel is alone as she vomits in the grass.

"You!" Rachel says when she sees Key, and starts to cough.

Rachel looks like a war is being fought inside of her, as if the battlefield is her lungs and the hollows of her cheeks and the muscles of her neck. She trembles and can hardly raise her head.

"Go away!" Rachel screams, but she's not looking at Key, she's looking down at the ground.

"Rachel, what's happened?" Key doesn't get too close. Rachel's fury frightens her; she doesn't understand this kind of rage. Rachel raises her shaking hands and starts hitting herself, pounding her chest and rib cage and stomach with violence made even more frightening by her weakness. Key kneels in front of her, grabs both of the girl's tiny, bruised wrists and holds them away from her body. Her vomit smells of sour bile and the sickly-sweet of some half-digested fruit. A suspicion nibbles at Key, and so she looks to the left, where Rachel has vomited.

Dozens and dozens of black seeds, half crushed. And a slime of green the precise shade of a cherimoya skin.

"Oh, God, Rachel . . . why would you . . ."

"You don't deserve him! He can make it go away and he won't! Who are you? A fogey, an ugly fogey, an ugly usurping fogey and she's gone and he is a dick, he is a screaming howler monkey and I hate him . . ."

Rachel collapses against Key's chest, her hands beating helplessly at the ground. Key takes her up and rocks her back and forth, crying while she thinks of how close she came to repeating the mistakes of Jeb. But she can still save Rachel. She can still be human.

———

Tetsuo returns three days later with a guest.

She has never seen Mr. Charles wear shoes before, and he walks in them with the mincing confusion of a young girl forced to wear zori for a formal occasion. She bows her head when she sees him, hoping to hide her fear. Has he come to take her back to Mauna Kea? The thought of returning to those antiseptic feeding rooms and tasteless brick patties makes her hands shake. It makes her wonder if she would not be better off taking Penelope's way out rather than seeing the place where Jeb killed himself again.

But even as she thinks it, she knows she won't, any more than she would have eighteen years ago. She's too much a coward and she's too brave. If Mr. Charles asks her to go back she will say yes.

Rain on a mountainside and sexless, sweet touches with a man the same temperature as wet wood. Lanai City, overrun. Then Waimea, then Honoka'a. Then Hilo, where her mother had been living. For a year, until Tetsuo found that record of her existence in a work camp, Key fantasized about her mother escaping on a boat to an atoll, living in a group of refugee humans who survived the apocalypse.

Everything Tetsuo asked of her, she did. She loved him from the moment they saved each other's lives. She has always said yes.

"*Key!*" Mr. Charles says to her, as though she is a friend he has run into unexpectedly. "I have some*thing* . . . you might *just* want."

"Yes, Mr. Charles?" she says.

The three of them are alone in the feeding house. Mr. Charles collapses dramatically against one of the divans and kicks off his tight patent-leather shoes as if they are barnacles. He wears no socks.

"There," he says, and waves his hand at the door. "*In the bag.*"

Tetsuo nods and so she walks back. The bag is black canvas, unmarked. Inside, there's a book. She recognizes it immediately, though she only saw it once. *The Blind Watchmaker.* There is a note on the cover. The handwriting is large and uneven and painstaking, that of someone familiar with words but unaccustomed to writing them down. She notes painfully that he writes his "a" the same way as a typeset font, with the half-c above the main body and a careful serif at the end.

> *Dear Overseer Ki,*
> *I would like you to have this. I have loved it very much and you are the only one who ever seemed to care. I am angry but*
> *I don't blame you. You're just too good at living.*
> *Jeb*

She takes the bag and leaves both vampires without requesting permission. Mr. Charles's laugh follows her out the door.

Blood on the walls, on the floor, all over his body.

I am angry but. You're just too good at living. She has always said yes.

She is too much of a coward and she is too brave.

She watches the sunset the next evening from the hill in the garden, her back against the cherimoya tree. She feels the sun's death like she always has, with quiet joy. Awareness floods her:

the musk of wet grass crushed beneath her bare toes, salt-spray and algae blowing from the ocean, the love she has clung to so fiercely since she was a girl, lost and alone. Everything she has ever loved is bound in that sunset, the red-and-violet orb that could kill him as it sinks into the ocean.

Her favorite time of day is sunset, but it is not night. She has never quite been able to fit inside his darkness, no matter how hard she tried. She has been too good at living, but perhaps it's not too late to change.

She can't take the path of Penelope or Jeb, but that has never been the only way. She remembers stories that reached Grade Orange from the work camps, half-whispered reports of humans who sat at their assembly lines and refused to lift their hands. Harvesters who drained gasoline from their combine engines and waited for the vampires to find them. If every human refused to cooperate, vampire society would crumble in a week. Still, she has no illusions about this third path sparking a revolution. This is simply all she can do: sit under the cherimoya tree and refuse. They will kill her, but she will have chosen to be human.

The sun descends. She falls asleep against the tree and dreams of the girl who never was, the one who opened the door. In her dreams, the sun burns her skin and her obachan tells her how proud she is while they pick strawberries in the garden. She eats an umeboshi that tastes of blood and salt, and when she swallows, the flavors swarm out of her throat, bubbling into her neck and jaw and ears. Flavors become emotions become thoughts; peace in the nape of her neck, obligation in her back molars, and hope just behind her eyes, bitter as a watermelon rind.

She opens them and sees Tetsuo on his knees before her. Blood smears his mouth. She does not know what to think when he kisses her, except that she can't even feel the pinprick pain where his teeth broke her skin. He has never fed from her before. They have never kissed before. She feels like she is floating, but nothing else.

The blood is gone when he sits back. As though she imagined it.

"You should not have left like that yesterday," he says. "Charles can make this harder than I'd like."

"Why is he here?" she asks. She breathes shallowly.

"He will take over Grade Gold once your transmutation is finished."

"That's why you brought me here, isn't it? It had nothing to do with the kids."

He shrugs. "Regulations. So Charles couldn't refuse."

"And where will you go?"

"They want to send me to the mainland. Texas. To supervise the installation of a new Grade Gold facility near Austin."

She leans closer to him, and now she can see it: regret, and shame that he should be feeling so. "I'm sorry," she says.

"I have lived seventy years on these islands. I have an eternity to come back to them. So will you, Key. I have permission to bring you with me."

Everything that sixteen-year-old had ever dreamed. She can still feel the pull of him, of her desire for an eternity together, away from the hell her life has become. Her transmutation would be complete. Truly a monster, the regrets for her past actions would fall away like waves against a seawall.

With a fumbling hand, she picks a cherimoya from the ground beside her. "Do you remember what these taste like?"

She has never asked him about his human life. For a moment, he seems genuinely confused. "You don't understand.

Taste to us is vastly more complex. Joy, dissatisfaction, confusion, humility—*those* are flavors. A custard apple?" He laughs. "It's sweet, right?"

Joy, dissatisfaction, loss, grief, she tastes all that just looking at him.

"Why didn't you ever feed from me before?"

"Because I promised. When we first met."

And as she stares at him, sick with loss and certainty, Rachel walks up behind him. She is holding a kitchen knife, the blade pointed toward her stomach.

"Charles knows," she says.

"How?" Tetsuo says. He stands, but Key can't coordinate her muscles enough for the effort. He must have drained a lot of blood.

"I told him," Rachel says. "So now you don't have a choice. You will transmute me and you will get rid of this fucking fetus or I will kill myself and you'll be blamed for losing *two* Grade Gold humans."

Rachel's wrists are still bruised from where Key had to hold her several nights ago. Her eyes are sunken, her skin sallow. *This fucking fetus.*

She wasn't trying to kill herself with the cherimoya seeds. She was trying to abort a pregnancy.

"The baby is still alive after all that?" Key says, surprisingly indifferent to the glittering metal in Rachel's unsteady hands. Does Rachel know how easily Tetsuo could disarm her? What advantage does she think she has? But then she looks back in the girl's eyes and realizes: none.

Rachel is young and desperate and she doesn't want to be eaten by the monsters anymore.

"Not again, Rachel," Tetsuo says. "I *can't* do what you want. A vampire can only transmute someone he's never fed from before."

Rachel gasps. Key flops against her tree. She hadn't known that, either. The knife trembles in Rachel's grip so violently that Tetsuo takes it from her, achingly gentle as he pries her fingers from the hilt.

"*That's* why you never drank from her? And I killed her anyway? Stupid fucking Penelope. She could have been forever, and now there's just this dumb fogey in her place. She thought you cared about her."

"Caring is a strange thing, for a vampire," Key says.

Rachel spits in her direction but it falls short. The moonlight is especially bright tonight; Key can see everything from the grass to the tips of Rachel's ears, flushed sunset pink.

"Tetsuo," Key says, "why can't I move?"

But they ignore her.

"Maybe Charles will do it if I tell him you're really the one who killed Penelope."

"Charles? I'm sure he knows exactly what you did."

"I didn't *mean* to kill her!" Rachel screams. "Penelope was going to tell about the baby. She was crazy about babies, it didn't make any sense, and you had *picked her* and she wanted to destroy my life . . . I was so angry, I just wanted to hurt her, but I didn't realize . . ."

"Rachel, I've tried to give you a chance, but I'm not allowed to get rid of it for you." Tetsuo's voice is as worn out as a leathery orange.

"I'll die before I go to one of those mommy farms, Tetsuo. I'll die and take my baby with me."

"Then you will have to do it yourself."

She gasps. "You'll really leave me here?"

"I've made my choice."

Rachel looks down at Key, radiating a withering contempt that does nothing to blunt Key's pity. "If you had picked Penelope, I would have understood. Penelope was beautiful and smart. She's the only one who ever made it through half of that fat Shakespeare book in unit four. She could sing. Her breasts were perfect. But *her*? She's not a choice. She's nothing at all."

The silence between them is strained. It's as if Key isn't there at all. And soon, she thinks, she won't be.

"I've made my choice," Key says.

"*Your* choice?" they say in unison.

When she finds the will to stand, it's as though her limbs are hardly there at all, as though she is swimming in midair. For the first time, she understands that something is wrong.

Key floats for a long time. Eventually, she falls. Tetsuo catches her.

"What does it feel like?" Key asks. "The transmutation?"

Tetsuo takes the starlight in his hands. He feeds it to her through a glass shunt growing from a living branch. The tree's name is Rachel. The tree is very sad. Sadness is delicious.

"You already know," he says.

You will understand: he said this to her when she was human. *I wouldn't hurt you*: she said this to a girl who—a girl—she drinks.

"I meant to refuse."

"I made a promise."

She sees him for a moment crouched in the back of her father's shed, huddled away from the dangerous bar of light that stretches across the floor. She sees herself, terrified of death and so unsure. *Open the door,* she tells that girl, too late. *Let in the light.*

They Shall Salt the Earth with Seeds of Glass

It's noon, the middle of wheat harvest, and Tris is standing on the edge of the field while Bill and Harris and I drive three ancient combine threshers across the grain. It's dangerous to stand so close and Tris knows it. Tris knows better than to get in the way during harvest, too. Not a good idea if she wants to survive the winter. Fifteen days ago a cluster bomb dropped on the east field, so no combines there. No harvest. Just a feast for the crows.

Tris wrote the signs (with pictures for the ones who don't read) warning the kids to stay off the grass, stay out of the fields, don't pick up the bright-colored glass jewels. So I raise my hand, wave my straw hat in the sun—it's hot as hell out here, we could use a break, no problem—and the deafening noise of eighty-year-old engines forced unwillingly into service chokes, gasps, falls silent.

Bill stands and cups his hands over his mouth. "Something wrong with Meshach, Libby?"

I shake my head, realize he can't see, and holler, "The old man's doing fine. It's just hot. Give me ten?"

Harris, closer to me, takes a long drink from his bottle and climbs off Abednego. I don't mind his silence. This is the

36

sort of sticky day that makes it hard to move, let alone bring in a harvest, and this sun is hot enough to burn darker skin than his.

It's enough to burn Tris, standing without a hat and wearing a skinny strappy dress of faded red that stands out against the wheat's dusty gold. I hop off Meshach, check to make sure he's not leaking oil, and head over to my sister. I'm a little worried. Tris wouldn't be here if it wasn't important. Another cluster bomb? But I haven't heard the whining drone of any reapers. The sky is clear. But even though I'm too far to read her expression, I can tell Tris is worried. That way she has of balancing on one leg, a red stork in a wheat marsh. I hurry as I get closer, though my overalls stick to the slick sweat on my thighs and I have to hitch them up like a skirt to move quickly.

"Is it Dad?" I ask, when I'm close.

She frowns and shakes her head. "Told me this morning he's going fishing again."

"And you let him?"

She shrugs. "What do you want me to do, take away his cane? He's old, Libs. A few toxic fish won't kill him any faster."

"They might," I grumble, but this is an old argument, one I'm not winning, and besides, that's not why Tris is here.

"So what is it?"

She smiles, but it shakes at the edges. She's scared and I wonder if that makes her look old or just reminds me of our age. Dad is eighty, but I'm forty-two, and we had a funeral for an eight-year-old last week. Every night since I was ten I've gone to sleep thinking I might not wake up the next morning. I don't know how you get to forty-two doing that.

Tris is thirty-eight, but she looks twenty-five—at least, when she isn't scanning the skies for reapers, or walking behind a tiny coffin in a funeral procession.

"Walk with me," she says, her voice low, as though Harris can hear us from under that magnolia tree twenty feet away. I sigh and roll my eyes and mutter under my breath, but she's my baby sister and she knows I'll follow her anywhere. We climb to the top of the hill, so I can see the muddy creek that irrigates the little postage stamp of our cornfield, and the big hill just north of town, with its wood tower and reassuring white flag. Yolanda usually takes the morning shift, spending her hours watching the sky for that subtle disturbance, too smooth for a bird, too fast for a cloud. Reapers. If she rings the bell, some of us might get to cover in time.

Sometimes I don't like to look at the sky, so I sprawl belly-down on the ground, drink half of the warm water from my bottle and offer the rest to Tris. She finishes it and grimaces.

"Don't know how you stand it," she says. "Aren't you hot?"

"You won't complain when you're eating cornbread tonight."

"You made some?"

"Who does everything around here, bookworm?" I nudge her in the ribs and she laughs reluctantly and smiles at me with our smile. I remember learning to comb her hair after Mom got sick; the careful part I would make while she squirmed and hollered at me, the two hair balls I would twist and fasten to each side of her head. I would make the bottom of her hair immaculate: brushed and gelled and fastened into glossy, thick homogeneity. But on top it would sprout like a bunch of curly kale, straight up and out and olive-oil shiny. She would parade around the house in this flouncy slip she thought was a dress and pose for photos with her hand on her hip. I'm in a few of those pictures, usually in overalls or a smock. I look awkward and drab as an old sock next to her, but maybe it doesn't matter, because we have the same slightly bucked front teeth, the same fat cheeks, the same wide eyes going wider. We have a nice smile, Tris and I.

Tris doesn't wear afro-puffs any more. She keeps her hair in a bun and I keep mine short.

"Libs, oh Libs, things aren't so bad, are they?"

I look up at Tris, startled. She's sitting in the grass with her hands beneath her thighs and tears are dripping off the tip of her nose. I was lulled by her laugh—we don't often talk about the shit we can't control. Our lives, for instance.

I think about the field that we're going to leave for crows so no one gets blown up for touching one of a thousand beautiful multi-colored jewels. I think about funerals and Dad killing himself faster just so he can eat catfish with bellies full of white phosphorus.

"It's not that great, Tris."

"You think it's shit."

"No, not *shit*—"

"Close. You think it's close."

I sigh. "Some days. Tris. I have to get back to Meshach in a minute. What is going on?"

"I'm pregnant," she says.

I make myself meet her eyes, and see she's scared; almost as scared as I am.

"How do you know?"

"I suspected for a while. Yolanda finally got some test kits last night from a river trader."

Yolanda has done her best as the town midwife since she was drafted into service five years ago, when a glassman raid killed our last one. I'm surprised Tris managed to get a test at all.

"What are you going to do? Will you . . ." I can't even bring myself to say "keep it." But could Yolanda help her do anything else?

She reaches out, hugs me, buries her head in my shirt and sobs like a baby. Her muffled words sound like "Christ" and "Jesus" and "God," which ought to be funny since Tris is a capital-A atheist, but it isn't.

"No," she's saying, "Christ, no. I have to . . . someone has to . . . I need an abortion, Libby."

Relief like the first snow melt, like surviving another winter. Not someone else to worry about, to love, to feed.

But an abortion? There hasn't been a real doctor in this town since I was twelve.

Bill's mom used to be a registered nurse before the occupation, and she took care of everyone in town as best she could until glassman robots raided her house and called in reapers to bomb it five years ago. Bill left town after that. We never thought we'd see him again, but then two planting seasons ago, there he was with this green giant, a forty-year-old Deere combine—Shadrach, he called it, because it would make the third with our two older, smaller machines. He brought engine parts with him, too, and oil and enough seed for a poppy field. He had a bullet scar in his forearm and three strange, triangular burns on the back of his neck. You could see them because he'd been shaved bald and his hair was only starting to grow back, a patchy gray peach-fuzz.

He'd been in prison, that much was obvious. Whether the glassmen let him go or he escaped, he never said and we never asked. We harvested twice as much wheat from the field that season, and the money from the poppy paid for a new generator. If the bell on lookout hill rang more often than normal, if surveillance drones whirred through the grass and the water more than they used to, well, who was to say what the glassmen were doing? Killing us, that's all we knew, and Bill was one of our own.

So I ask Bill if his mother left anything behind that might help us—like a pill, or instructions for a procedure. He frowns.

"Aren't you a little old, Libby?" he says, and I tell him to fuck off. He puts a hand on my shoulder—conciliatory, regretful—and looks over to where Tris is trudging back home. "You saw what the reapers did to my mom's house. I couldn't even find all of her *teeth*."

I'm not often on that side of town, but I can picture the ruin exactly. There's still a crater on Mill Street. I shuffle backward, contrite. "God, Bill. I'm sorry. I wasn't thinking."

He shrugs. "Sorry, Libs. Ask Yolanda, if you got to do something like that." I don't like the way he frowns at me; I can hear his judgment even when all he does is turn and climb back inside Shadrach.

"Fucking hot out here," I say, and walk back over to Meshach. I wish Bill wasn't so goddamn judgmental. I wish Tris hadn't messed up with whichever of her men provided the sperm donation. I wish we hadn't lost the east field to another cluster bomb.

But I can wish or I can drive, and the old man's engine coughs loud enough to drown even my thoughts.

Tris pukes right after dinner. That was some of my best corn-bread, but I don't say anything. I just clean it up.

"How far along are you?" I ask. I feel like vomit entitles me to this much.

She pinches her lips together and I hope she isn't about to do it again. Instead, she stands up and walks out of the kitchen. I think that's her answer, but she returns a moment later with a box about the size of my hand. It's got a hole on one side and a dial like a gas gauge on the other. The gauge is marked with large glassman writing and regular letters in tiny print: "Fetal Progression," it reads, then on the far left "Not Pregnant," running through "Nine Months" on the far right. I can't imagine what the point of that last would be, but Tris's dial is still barely on the left-hand side, settled neatly between three and four. A little late for morning sickness, but maybe it's terror as much as the baby that makes her queasy.

"There's a note on the side. It says 'All pregnant women will receive free rehabilitative healthcare in regional facilities.'" She says the last like she's spent a long day memorizing tiny print.

"Glassmen won't do abortions, Tris."

No one knows what they really look like. They only interact with us through their remote-controlled robots. Maybe they're made of glass themselves—they give us pregnancy kits, but won't bother with burn dressings. Dad says the glassmen are alien scientists studying our behavior, like a human would smash an anthill to see how they scatter. Reverend Beale always points to the pipeline a hundred miles west of us. They're just men stealing our resources, he says, like the white man stole the Africans', though even he can't say what those resources might be. It's a pipeline from nowhere, to nothing, as far as any of us know.

Tris leans against the exposed brick of our kitchen wall. "All fetuses are to be carried to full term," she whispers, and I turn the box over and see her words printed in plain English, in larger type than anything else on the box. Only one woman in our town ever took the glassmen up on their offer. I don't know how it went for her; she never came home.

"Three months!" I say, though I don't mean to.

Tris rubs her knuckles beneath her eyes, though she isn't crying. She looks fierce, daring me to ask her how the hell she waited this long. But I don't, because I know. Wishful thinking is a powerful curse, almost as bad as storytelling.

I don't go to church much these days, not after our old pastor died and Beale moved into town to take his place. Reverend Beale likes his fire and brimstone, week after week of too much punishment and too little brotherhood. I felt exhausted listening to him rant in that high collar, sweat pouring down his temples. But he's popular, and I wait on an old bench outside the redbrick church for the congregation to let out. Main Street is quiet except for the faint echoes of the reverend's sonorous preaching. Mostly I hear the cicadas, the water lapping against a few old fishing boats and the long stretch of rotting pier. There used to be dozens of sailboats here, gleaming creations of white fiberglass and heavy canvas sails with names like *Bay Princess* and *Prospero's Dream*. I know because Dad has pictures. Main Street was longer then, a stretch of brightly painted Tudors and Victorians with little shops and restaurants on the bottom floors and rooms above. A lot of those old buildings are boarded up now, and those that aren't look as patched-over and jury-rigged as our thresher combines. The church has held up the best of any of the town's buildings. Time has hardly worn its stately red brick and shingled steeples. It used to be Methodist, I think, but we don't have enough people to be overly concerned about denominations these days. I've heard of some towns where they make everyone go Baptist, or Lutheran, but we're lucky that no one's thought to do anything like that here. Though I'm sure Beale would try if he could get away with it. Maybe Tris was right to leave the whole thing behind. Now she sits with the children while their parents go to church.

The sun tips past its zenith when the doors finally open and my neighbors walk out of the church in twos and threes. Beale shakes parishioners' hands as they leave, mopping his face with a handkerchief. His smile looks more like a grimace to me; three years in town and he still looks uncomfortable anywhere but behind a pulpit. Men like him think the glassmen are right to require "full gestation." Men like him think Tris is a damned sinner, just because she has a few men and won't settle down with one. He hates the glassmen as much as the rest of us, but his views help them just the same.

Bill comes out with Pam. The bones in her neck stand out like twigs, but she looks a hell of a lot better than the last time I saw her, at Georgia's funeral. Pam fainted when we laid her daughter in the earth, and Bill had to take her home before the ceremony ended. Pam is Bill's cousin, and Georgia was her only child—blown to bits after riding her bicycle over a hidden jewel in the fields outside town. To my surprise, Bill gives me a tired smile before walking Pam down the street.

Bill and I used to dig clams from the mud at low tide in the summers. We were in our twenties and my mother had just died of a cancer the glassmen could have cured if they gave a damn. Sometimes we would build fires of cedar and pine and whatever other tinder lay around and roast the clams right there by the water. We talked about anything in the world other than glassmen and dead friends while the moon arced above. We planned the cornfield eating those clams, and plotted all the ways we might get the threshers for the job. The cow dairy, the chicken coop, the extra garden plots—we schemed and dreamt of ways to help our town hurt a little less each winter. Bill had a girlfriend then, though she vanished not long after; we never did more than touch.

That was a long time ago, but I remember the taste of cedar ash and sea salt as I look at the back of him. I never once thought those moments would last forever, and yet here I am, regretful and old.

Yolanda is one of the last to leave, stately and elegant with her braided white hair and black church hat with netting. I catch up with her as she heads down the steps.

"Can we talk?" I ask.

Her shoulders slump a little when I ask, but she bids the reverend farewell and walks with me until we are out of earshot.

"Tris needs an abortion," I say.

Yolanda nods up and down like a seabird, while she takes deep breaths. She became our midwife because she'd helped Bill's mother with some births, but I don't think she wants the job. There's just no one else.

"Libby, the glassmen don't like abortions."

"If the glassmen are paying us enough attention to notice, we have bigger problems."

"I don't have the proper equipment for a procedure. Even if I did, I couldn't."

"Don't tell me you agree with Beale."

She draws herself up and glares at me. "I don't know *how*, Libby! Do you want me to kill Tris to get rid of her baby? They say the midwife in Toddville can do them if it's early enough. How far along is she?"

I see the needle in my mind, far too close to the center line for comfort. "Three and a half months," I say.

She looks away, but she puts her arm around my shoulders. "I understand why she would, I do. But it's too late. We'll all help her."

Raise the child, she means. I know Yolanda is making sense, but I don't want to hear her. I don't want to think about Tris carrying a child she doesn't want to term. I don't want to think about that test kit needle pointing inexorably at *too fucking late*. So I thank Yolanda and head off in the other direction, down the cracked tarmac as familiar as a scar, to Pam's house. She lives in a small cottage Victorian with peeling gray paint that used to be blue. Sure enough, Bill sits in an old rocking chair on the porch, thumbing through a book. I loved to see him like that in our clam-digging days, just sitting and listening. I would dream of him after he disappeared.

"Libs?" he says. He leans forward.

"Help her, Bill. You've been outside, you know people. Help her find a doctor, someone who can do this after three months."

He sighs and the book thumps on the floor. "I'll see."

———

Three days later, Bill comes over after dinner.

"There's rumors of something closer to Annapolis," he says. "I couldn't find out more than that. None of my . . . I mean, I only know some dudes, Libby. And whoever runs this place only talks to women."

"Your mother didn't know?" Tris asks, braver than me.

Bill rubs the back of his head. "If she did, she sure didn't tell me."

"You've got to have more than that," she says. "Does this place even have a name? How near Annapolis? What do you want us to do, sail into the city and ask the nearest glassman which way to the abortion clinic?"

"What do I want you to do? Maybe I want you to count your goddamn blessings and not risk your life to murder a child. It's a *sin*, Tris, not like you'd care about that, but I'd've thought Libby would."

"God I know," I say, "but I've never had much use for sin. Now why don't you get your nose out of our business?"

"You invited me in, Libby."

"For *help*—"

He shakes his head. "If you could see what Pam's going through right now . . ."

Bill has dealt with as much grief as any of us. I can understand why he's moralizing in our kitchen, but that doesn't mean I have to tolerate it.

But Tris doesn't even give me time. She stands and shakes a wooden spatula under his nose. Bill's a big man, but he flinches. "So I should have this baby just so I can watch it get blown up later, is that it? Don't put Pam's grief on me, Bill. I'm sorrier than I can say about Georgia. I taught that girl to read! And I can't. I just can't."

Bill breathes ragged. His dark hands twist his muddy flannel shirt, his grip so tight his veins are stark against sun-baked skin. Tris is still holding that spatula.

Bill turns his head abruptly, stalks back to the kitchen door with a "Fuck," and he wipes his eyes. Tris leans against the sink.

"Esther," he says quietly, his back to us. "The name of a person, the name of a place, I don't know. But you ask for that, my buddy says you should find what you're after."

I follow him outside, barefoot and confused that I'd bother when he's so clearly had enough of us. I call his name, then start jogging and catch his elbow. He turns around.

"What, Libby?"

He's so angry. His hair didn't grow in very long or thick after he came back. He looks like someone mashed him up, stretched him out and then did a hasty job of putting him back together. Maybe I look like that, too.

"Thanks," I say. We don't touch.

"Don't die, Libs."

The air is thick with crickets chirping and fireflies glowing and the swampy, seaweed-and-salt air from the Chesapeake. He turns to walk away. I don't stop him.

We take Dad's boat. There's not enough gas left to visit Bishop's Head, the mouth of our estuary, let alone Annapolis. So we bring oars, along with enough supplies to keep the old dinghy low in the water.

"I hope we don't hit a storm," Tris says, squinting at the clear, indigo sky as though thunderheads might be hiding behind the stars.

"We're all right for now. Feel the air? Humidity's dropped at least 20 percent."

Tris has the right oar and I have the left. I don't want to use the gas unless we absolutely have to, and I'm hoping the low-tech approach will make us less noticeable to any patrolling glassmen. It's tough work, even in the relatively cool night air, and I check the stars to make sure we're heading in more or less the right direction. None of the towns on our estuary keep lights on at night. I only know when we pass Toddville because of the old lighthouse silhouetted against the stars. I lost sight of our home within five minutes of setting out, and God, how a part of me wanted to turn the dinghy right around and go back. The rest of the world isn't safe. Home isn't either, but it's familiar.

Dad gave us a nautical chart of the Chesapeake Bay, with markers for towns long destroyed, lighthouses long abandoned, by people long dead. He marked our town and told us to get back safe. We promised him we would and we hugged like we might never see each other again.

"What if we hit a jewel?" Tris asks. In the dark, I can't tell if it's fear or exertion that aspirates her words. I've had that thought myself, but what can we do? The glassmen make sure their cluster bombs spread gifts everywhere.

"They don't detonate that well in water," I offer.

A shift in the dark; Tris rests her oar in the boat and stretches her arms. "Well enough to kill you slowly."

I'm not as tired, but I take the break. "We've got a gun. It ought to do the trick, if it comes to that."

"Promise?"

"To what? Mercy kill you?"

"Sure."

"Aren't you being a little melodramatic?"

"And we're just out here to do a little night fishing."

I laugh, though my belly aches like she's punched me. "Christ, Tris." I lean back in the boat, the canvas of our food sack rough and comforting on my slick skin, like Mom's gloves when she first taught me to plant seeds.

"Libs?"

"Yeah?"

"You really don't care who the father is?"

I snort. "If it were important, I'm sure you would have told me."

I look up at the sky: there's the Milky Way, the North Star, Orion's belt. I remember when I was six, before the occupation. There was so much light on the bay you could hardly see the moon.

"Reckon we'll get to Ohio, Jim?" Tris asks in a fake Southern drawl.

I grin. "Reckon we might. If'n we can figure out just how you got yerself pregnant, Huck."

Tris leans over the side of the boat, and a spray of brackish water hits my open mouth. I shriek and dump two handfuls on her head, and she splutters and grabs me from behind so I can't do more than wiggle in her embrace.

"Promise," she says, breathing hard, still laughing.

The bay tastes like home to me, like everything I've ever loved. "Christ, Tris," I say, and I guess that's enough.

———

We round Bishop's Head at dawn. Tris is nearly asleep on her oar, though she hasn't complained. I'm worried about her, and it's dangerous to travel during the day until we can be sure the water is clear. We pull into Hopkins Cove, an Edenic horseshoe of brown sand and forest. It doesn't look like a human foot has touched this place since the invasion, which reassures me. Drones don't do much exploring. They care about people.

Tris falls asleep as soon as we pull the boat onto the sand. I wonder if I should feed her more—does she need extra for the baby? Then I wonder if that's irrational, since we're going all this way to kill it. But for now, at least, the fetus is part of her, which means we have to take it into consideration. I think about Bill with his big, dumb eyes and patchy bald head telling me that it's a *sin*, as though that has anything to do with your sister crying like her insides have been torn out.

I eat some cornbread and a peach, though I'm not hungry. I sit on the shore with my feet in the water and watch for other boats or drones or reapers overhead. I don't see anything but seagulls and ospreys and minnows that tickle my toes.

"Ain't nothing here, Libs," I say, in my mother's best imitation of *her* mother's voice. I never knew my grandmother, but Mom said she looked just like Tris, so I loved her on principle. She and Tris even share a name: Leatrice. I told Mom that I'd name my daughter Tamar, after her. I'd always sort of planned to, but when my monthlies stopped a year ago, I figured it was just as well. *Stupid Bill, and his stupid patchy hair*, I think.

I dream of giant combines made from black chrome and crystal, with headlights of wide, unblinking eyes. I take them to the fields, but something is wrong with the thresher. There's bonemeal dust on the wheat berries.

"Now, Libby," Bill says, but I can't hear the rest of what he's saying because the earth starts shaking and—

I scramble to my feet, kicking up sand with the dream still in my eyes. There's lights in the afternoon sky and this awful thunder, like a thousand lightning bolts are striking the earth at once.

"Oh, Christ," I say. A murder of reapers swarms to the north, and even with the sun in the sky their bombs light the ground beneath like hellfire. It's easier to see reapers from far away, because they paint their underbellies light blue to blend with the sky.

Tris stands beside me and grips my wrist. "That's not . . . it has to be Toddville, right? Or Cedar Creek? They're not far enough away for home, right?"

I don't say anything. I don't know. I can only look.

Bill's hair is patchy because the glassmen arrested him and they tortured him. Bill asked his outside contacts if they knew anything about a place to get an illegal abortion. Bill brought back a hundred thousand dollars' worth of farm equipment and scars from wounds that would have killed someone without access to a doctor. But what kind of prisoner has access to a real doctor? Why did the glassmen arrest him? What if his contacts are exactly the type of men the glassmen like to bomb with their reapers? What if Bill is?

But I know it isn't that simple. No one knows why the glassmen bomb us. No one *really* knows the reason for the whole damn mess, their reapers and their drones and their arcane rules you're shot for not following.

"Should we go back?"

She says it like she's declared war on a cardinal direction, like she really will get on that boat and walk into a reaper wasteland and salvage what's left of our lives and have that baby.

I squeeze her hand. "It's too close," I say. "Toddville, I think you're right. Let's get going, though. Probably not safe here."

She nods. She doesn't look me in the eye. We paddle through the choppy water until sun sets. And then, without saying anything, we ship the oars and I turn on the engine.

Three nights later, we see lights on the shore. It's a glassmen military installation. Dad marked it on the map, but still I'm surprised by its size, its brightness, the brazen way it sits on the coastline, as though daring to attract attention.

"I'd never thought a building could be so . . ."

"Angry?" Tris says.

"Violent."

"It's like a giant middle finger up the ass of the Chesapeake."

I laugh despite myself. "You're ridiculous."

We're whispering, though we're on the far side of the bay and the water is smooth and quiet. After that reaper drone attack, I'm remembering more than I like of my childhood terror of the glassmen. Dad and Mom had to talk to security drones a few times after the occupation, and I remember the oddly modulated voices, distinctly male, and the bright unblinking eyes behind the glass masks of their robot heads. I don't know anyone who has met a real glassman, instead of one of their remote robots. It's a retaliatory offense to harm a drone because the connection between the drone and the glassman on the other side of the world (or up in some space station) is so tight that sudden violence can cause brain damage. I wonder how they can square *potential brain damage* with *dead children*, but I guess I'm not a glassman.

So we row carefully, but fast as we can, hoping to distance our little fishing boat from the towering building complex. Its lights pulse so brightly they leave spots behind my eyes.

And then, above us, we hear the chopping whirr of blades cutting the air, the whine of unmanned machinery readying for deployment. I look up and shade my eyes: a reaper.

Tris drops her oar. It slides straight into the bay, but neither of us bother to catch it. If we don't get away now, a lost oar won't matter anyway. She lunges into our supply bag, brings out a bag of apples. The noise of the reaper is close, almost deafening. I can't hear what she yells at me before she jumps into the bay. I hesitate in the boat, afraid to leave our supplies and afraid to be blown to pieces by a reaper. I look back up and and see a panel slide open on its bright blue belly. The panel reveals dark glass; behind it, a single, unblinking eye.

I jump into the water, but my foot catches on the remaining oar. The boat rocks behind me, but panic won't let me think—I tug and tug until the boat capsizes and suddenly ten pounds of supplies are falling on my head, dragging me deeper into the dark water. I try to kick out, but my leg is tangled with the drawstring of a canvas bag, and I can't make myself focus enough to get it loose. All I can think of is that big glass eye waiting to kill me. My chest burns and my ears fill to bursting with pressure. I'd always thought I would die in fire, but water isn't much better. I don't even know if Tris made it, or if the eye caught her, too.

I try to look up, but I'm too deep; it's too dark to even know which way that is. *God*, I think, *save her. Let her get back home.* It's rude to demand things of God, but I figure dying ought to excuse the presumption.

Something tickles my back. I gasp and the water flows in, drowning my lungs, flooding out what air I had left. But the thing in the water with me has a light on its head and strange, shiny legs and it's using them to get under my arms and drag me up until we reach the surface and I cough and retch and *breathe, thank you, God.* The thing takes me to shore, where Tris is waiting to hug me and kiss my forehead like I'm the little sister.

"Jesus," she says, and I wonder if God really does take kindly to demands until I turn my head and understand: my savior is a drone.

"I will feed you," the glassman says. He looks like a spider with an oversized glassman head: eight chrome legs and two glass eyes. "The pregnant one should eat. Her daughter is growing."

I wonder if some glassman technology is translating his words into English. If in his language, whatever it is, *the pregnant one* is a kind of respectful address. Or maybe they taught him to speak to us that way.

I'm too busy appreciating the bounty of air in my lungs to notice the other thing he said.

"Daughter?" Tris says.

The glassman nods. "Yes. I have been equipped with a body-safe sonic scanning device. Your baby has not been harmed by your ordeal. I am here to help and reassure you."

Tris looks at me carefully. I sit up. "You said something about food?"

"Yes!" It's hard to tell, his voice is so strange, but he sounds happy. As though rescuing two women threatened by one of his reaper fellows is the best piece of luck he's had all day. "I will be back," he says, and scuttles away, into the forest.

Tris hands me one of her rescued apples. "What the hell?" Her voice is low, but I'm afraid the glassman can hear us anyway.

55

"A trap?" I whisper, barely vocalizing into her left ear.

She shakes her head. "He seems awfully . . ."

"Eager?"

"Young."

The glassman comes back a minute later, walking on six legs and holding two boxes in the others. His robot must be a new model; the others I've seen look more human. "I have meals! A nearby convoy has provided them for you," he says, and places the boxes carefully in front of us. "The one with a red ribbon is for the pregnant one. It has nutrients."

Tris's hands shake as she opens it. The food doesn't look dangerous, though it resembles the strange pictures in Tris's old magazines more than the stuff I make at home. A perfectly rectangular steak, peas, corn mash. Mine is the same, except I have regular corn. We eat silently, while the glassman gives every impression of smiling upon us benevolently.

"Good news," he pipes, when I'm nearly done forcing the bland food down my raw throat. "I have been authorized to escort you both to a safe hospital facility."

"Hospital?" Tris asks, in a way that makes me sit up and put my arm around her.

"Yes," the glassman says. "To ensure the safe delivery of your daughter."

The next morning, the glassman takes us to an old highway a mile from the water's edge. A convoy waits for us, four armored tanks and two platform trucks. One of the platform beds is filled with mechanical supplies, including two dozen glass-and-chrome heads. The faces are blank, the heads unattached to any robot body, but the effect makes me nauseous. Tris digs her nails into my forearm. The other platform bed is mostly empty except for a few boxes and one man tied to the guardrails. He lies prone on the floor and doesn't move when we climb in after our glassman. At first I'm afraid that he's dead, but then he twitches and groans before falling silent again.

"Who is he?" Tris asks.

"Non-state actor," our glassman says, and pulls up the grate behind us.

"What?"

The convoy engines whirr to life—quiet compared to the three old men, but the noise shocks me after our days of silence on the bay.

The glassman swivels his head, his wide unblinking eyes fully focused on my sister. I'm afraid she's set him off and they'll tie us to the railings like that poor man. Instead, he clicks his two front legs together for no reason that I can see except maybe it gives him something to do.

"Terrorist," he says quietly.

Tris looks at me and I widen my eyes: *don't you dare say another word.* She nods.

"The convoy will be moving now. You should sit for your safety."

He clacks away before we can respond. He hooks his hind legs through the side rail opposite us and settles down, looking like nothing so much as a contented cat.

The armored tanks get into formation around us and then we lurch forward, rattling over the broken road. Tris makes it for half an hour before she pukes over the side.

———

For two days, Tris and I barely speak. The other man in our truck wakes up about once every ten hours, just in time for one of the two-legged glassmen from the armored tanks to clomp over and give us all some food and water. The man gets less than we do, though none of it is very good. He eats in such perfect silence that I wonder if the glassmen have cut out his tongue. As soon as he finishes, one of the tank glassmen presses a glowing metal bar to the back of his neck. The mark it leaves is a perfect triangle, raw and red like a fresh burn. The prisoner doesn't struggle when the giant articulated metal hand grips his shoulders, he only stares, and soon after he slumps against the railing. I have lots of time to wonder about those marks; hour after slow hour with a rattling truck bruising my tailbone and regrets settling into my joints like dried tears. Sometimes Tris massages knots from my neck, and sometimes they come right back while I knead hers. I can't see any way to escape, so I try not to think about it. But there's no helping the sick, desperate knowledge that every hour we're closer to locking Tris in a hospital for six months so the glassmen can force her to have a baby.

During the third wake-up and feeding of the bound man, our glassman shakes out his legs and clacks over to the edge of the truck bed. The robots who drive the tanks are at least eight feet tall, with oversized arms and legs equipped with artillery rifles. They would be terrifying even if we weren't completely at their mercy. The two glassmen stare at each other, eerily silent and still.

The bound man, I'd guess Indian from his thick, straight hair and dark skin, strains as far forward as he can. He nods at us.

"They're talking," he says. His words are slow and painstakingly formed. We crawl closer to hear him better. "In their real bodies."

I look back up, wondering how he knows. They're so still, but then glassmen are always uncanny.

Tris leans forward, so her lips are at my ear. "Their eyes," she whispers.

Glassman robot eyes never blink. But their pupils dilate and contract just like ours do. Only now both robots' eyes are pupil-blasted black despite the glaring noon sun. Talking in their real bodies? That must mean they've stopped paying us any attention.

"Could we leave?" I whisper. No one has tied us up. I think our glassman is under the impression he's doing us a favor.

Tris buries her face in the back of my short nappy hair and wraps her arms around me. I know it's a ploy, but it comforts me all the same. "The rest of the convoy."

Even as I nod, the two glassmen step away from each other, and our convoy is soon enough on its way. This time, though, the prisoner gets to pass his time awake and silent. No one tells us to move away from him.

"I have convinced the field soldier to allow me to watch the operative," our glassman says proudly.

"That's very nice," Tris says. She's hardly touched her food.

"I am glad you appreciate my efforts! It is my job to assess mission parameter achievables. Would you mind if I asked you questions?"

I frown at him and quickly look away. Tris, unfortunately, has decided she'd rather play with fire than her food.

"Of course," she says.

We spend the next few hours subjected to a tireless onslaught of questions. Things like, "How would you rate our society-building efforts in the Tidewater Region?" and "What issue would you most like to see addressed in the upcoming Societal Health Meeting?" and "Are you mostly satisfied or somewhat dissatisfied with the cleanliness of the estuary?"

"The fish are toxic," I say to this last question. My first honest answer. It seems to startle him. At least, that's how I interpret the way he clicks his front two legs together.

Tris pinches my arm, but I ignore her.

"Well," says the glassman, "that is potentially true. We have been monitoring the unusually high levels of radiation and heavy metal toxicity. But you can rest assured that we are addressing the problem and its potential harmful side-effects on Beneficial Societal Development."

"Like dying of mercury poisoning?" Tris pinches me again, but she smiles for the first time in days.

"I do not recommend it for the pregnant one! I have been serving you both nutritious foods well within the regulatory limits."

I have no idea what those regulatory limits might be, but I don't ask.

"In any case," he says, "aside from that issue, the estuary is very clean."

"Thank you," Tris says, before I can respond.

"You're very welcome. We are here to help you."

"How far away is the hospital?" she asks.

I feel like a giant broom has swept the air from the convoy, like our glassman has tossed me back into the bay to drown. I knew Tris was desperate; I didn't realize how much.

"Oh," he says, and his pupils go very wide. I could kiss the prisoner for telling us what that means: no one's at home.

The man now leans toward us, noticing the same thing. "You pregnant?" he asks Tris.

She nods.

He whistles through a gap between his front teeth. "Some rotten luck," he says. "I never seen a baby leave one of their clinics. Fuck knows what they do to them."

"And the mothers?" I ask.

He doesn't answer, just lowers his eyes and looks sidelong at our dormant glassman. "Depends," he whispers, "on who they think you are."

That's all we have time for; the glassman's eyes contract again and his head tilts like a bird's. "There is a rehabilitative facility in the military installation to which we are bound. Twenty-three hours ETA."

"A prison?" Tris asks.

"A hospital," the glassman says firmly.

When we reach the pipeline, I know we're close. The truck bounces over fewer potholes and cracks; we even meet a convoy heading in the other direction. The pipeline is a perfect clear tube about sixteen feet high. It looks empty to me, a giant hollow tube that distorts the landscape on the other side like warped glass. It doesn't run near the bay, and no one from home knows enough to plot it on a map. Maybe this is the reason the glassmen are here. I wonder what could be so valuable in that hollow tube that Tris has to give birth in a cage, that little Georgia has to die, that a cluster bomb has to destroy half our wheat crop. What's so valuable that looks like nothing at all?

61

The man spends long hours staring out the railing of the truck, as though he's never seen anything more beautiful or more terrifying. Sometimes he talks to us, small nothings, pointing out a crane overhead or a derelict road with a speed limit sign—*55 miles per hour,* it says, *radar enforced.*

At first our glassman noses around these conversations, but he decides they're innocuous enough. He tells the man to "refrain from exerting a corrupting influence," and resumes his perch on the other side of the truck bed. The prisoner's name is Simon, he tells us, and he's on watch. For what, I wonder, but know well enough not to ask.

"What's in it?" I say instead, pointing to the towering pipeline.

"I heard it's a wormhole." He rests his chin on his hands, a gesture that draws careful, casual attention to the fact that his left hand has loosened the knots. He catches my eye for a blink and then looks away. My breath catches—is he trying to escape? Do we dare?

"A wormhole? Like, in space?" Tris says, oblivious. Or maybe not. Looking at her, I realize she might just be a better actor.

I don't know what Tris means, but Simon nods. "A passage through space, that's what I heard."

"That is incorrect!"

The three of us snap our heads around, startled to see the glassman so close. His eyes whirr with excitement. "The Designated Area Project is not what you refer to as a wormhole, which are in fact impractical as transportation devices."

Simon shivers and looks down at his feet. My lips feel swollen with regret—what if he thinks we're corrupted? What if he notices Simon's left hand? But Tris raises her chin, stubborn and defiant at the worst possible time—I guess the threat of that glassman hospital is making her too crazy to feel anything as reasonable as fear.

"Then what is it?" she asks, so plainly that Simon's mouth opens, just a little.

Our glassman stutters forward on his delicate metallic legs. "I am not authorized to tell you," he says, clipped.

"Why not? It's the whole goddamned reason all your glass-man reapers and drones and robots are swarming all over the place, isn't it? We don't even get to know what the hell it's all for?"

"Societal redevelopment is one of our highest mission pri-orities," he says, a little desperately.

I lean forward and grab Tris's hand as she takes a sharp, angry breath. "Honey," I say, "Tris, *please*."

She pulls away from me, hard as a slap, but she stops talk-ing. The glassman says nothing; just quietly urges us a few yards away from Simon. No more corruption on his watch.

Night falls, revealing artificial lights gleaming on the hori-zon. Our glassman doesn't sleep. Not even in his own place, I suppose, because whenever I check with a question his eyes stay the same and he answers without hesitation. Maybe they have drugs to keep themselves awake for a week at a time. Maybe he's not human. I don't ask—I'm still a little afraid he might shoot me for saying the wrong thing, and more afraid that he'll start talking about Ideal Societal Redevelopment.

At the first hint of dawn, Simon coughs and leans back against the railing, catching my eye. Tris is dozing on my shoul-der, drool slowly soaking my shirt. Simon flexes his hands, now free. He can't speak, but our glassman isn't looking at him. He points to the floor of the truckbed, then lays himself out with his hands over his head. There's something urgent in his face. Something knowledgable. To the glassmen he's a terrorist, but what does that make him to us? I shake Tris awake.

"Libs?"

"Glassman," I say, "I have a question about societal redevelopment deliverables."

Tris sits straight up.

"I would be pleased to hear it!" the glassman says.

"I would like to know what you plan to do with my sister's baby."

"Oh," the glassman says. The movement of his pupils is hardly discernible in this low light, but I've been looking. I grab Tris by her shoulder and we scramble over to Simon.

"Duck!" he says. Tris goes down before I do, so only I can see the explosion light up the front of the convoy. Sparks and embers fly through the air like a starfall. The pipeline glows pink and purple and orange. Even the strafe of bullets seems beautiful until it blows out the tires of our truck. We crash and tumble. Tris holds onto me, because I've forgotten how to hold onto myself.

The glassmen are frozen. Some have tumbled from the overturned trucks, their glass and metal arms halfway to their guns. Their eyes don't move, not even when three men in muddy camouflage lob sticky black balls into the heart of the burning convoy.

Tris hauls me to my feet. Simon shouts something at one of the other men, who turns out to be a woman.

"What the hell was that?" I ask.

"EMP," Simon says. "Knocks them out for a minute or two. We have to haul ass."

The woman gives Simon a hard stare. "They're clean?"

"They were prisoners, too," he says.

The woman—light skinned, close-cropped hair—hoists an extra gun, unconvinced. Tris straightens up. "I'm pregnant," she says. "And ain't nothing going to convince me to stay here."

"Fair enough," the woman says, and hands Tris a gun. "We have ninety seconds. Just enough time to detonate."

Our glassman lies on his back, legs curled in the air. One of those sticky black balls has lodged a foot away from his blank glass face. It's a retaliatory offense to harm a drone. I remember what they say about brain damage when the glassmen are connected. Is he connected? Will this hurt him? I don't like the kid, but he's so young. Not unredeemable. He saved my life.

I don't know why I do it, but while Tris and the others are distracted, I use a broken piece of the guard rail to knock off the black ball. I watch it roll under the truck, yards away. I don't want to hurt him; I just want my sister and me safe and away.

"Libs!" It's Tris, looking too much like a terrorist with her big black gun. Dad taught us both to use them, but the difference between us is I wish that I didn't know how, and Tris is glad.

I run to catch up. A man idles a pickup ten yards down the road from the convoy.

"They're coming back on," he says.

"Detonating!" The woman's voice is a birdcall, a swoop from high to low. She presses a sequence of buttons on a remote and suddenly the light ahead is fiercer than the sun and it smells like gasoline and woodsmoke and tar. I've seen plenty enough bomb wreckage in my life; I feel like when it's *ours* it should look different. Better. It doesn't.

Tris pulls me into the back of the pickup and we're bouncing away before we can even shut the back door. We turn off the highway and drive down a long dirt road through the woods. I watch the back of the woman's head through the rear window. She has four triangular scars at the base of her neck, the same as Bill's.

Something breaks out of the underbrush on the side of the road. Something that moves unnaturally fast, even on the six legs he has left. Something that calls out, in that stupid, naive, inhuman voice:

"Stop the vehicle! Pregnant one, do not worry, I will—"

"Fuck!" Tris's terror cuts off the last of the speech. The car swerves, tossing me against the door. I must not have latched it properly, because next thing I know I'm tumbling to the dirt with a thud that jars my teeth. The glassman scrambles on top of me without any regard for the pricking pain of his long, metallic limbs.

"Kill that thing!" It's a man, I'm not sure who. I can't look, pinioned as I am.

"Pregnant one, step down from the terrorist vehicle and I will lead you to safety. There is a Reaper Support Flyer on its way."

He grips me between two metallic arms and hauls me up with surprising strength. The woman and Simon have guns trained on the glassman, but they hesitate—if they shoot him, they have to shoot me. Tris has her gun up as well, but she's shaking so hard she can't even get her finger on the trigger.

"Let go of me," I say to him. He presses his legs more firmly into my side.

"I will save the pregnant one," he repeats, as though to reassure both of us. He's young, but he's still a glassman. He knows enough to use me as a human shield.

Tris lowers the gun to her side. She slides from the truck bed and walks forward.

"Don't you dare, Tris!" I yell, but she just shakes her head. My sister, giving herself to a glassman? What would Dad say? I can't even free a hand to wipe my eyes. I hate this boy behind the glass face. I hate him because he's too young and ignorant to even understand what he's doing wrong. Evil is good to a glassman. Wrong is right. The pregnant one has to be saved.

I pray to God, then. I say, *God, please let her not be a fool. Please let her escape.*

And I guess God heard, because when she's just a couple of feet away she looks straight at me and smiles like she's about to cry. "I'm sorry, Libs," she whispers. "I love you. I just can't let him take me again."

"Pregnant one! Please drop your weapon and we will—"

And then she raises her gun and shoots.

My arm hurts. Goddamn, it hurts, like there's some small, toothy animal burrowing inside. I groan and feel my sister's hands, cool on my forehead.

"They know the doctor," she says. "That Esther that Bill told us about, remember? She's a regular doctor, too, not just abortions. You'll be fine."

I squint up at her. The sun has moved since she shot me; I can hardly see her face for the light behind it. But even at the edges I can see her grief. Her tears drip on my hairline and down my forehead.

"I don't care," I say, with some effort. "I wanted you to do it."

"I was so afraid, Libs."

"I know."

"We'll get home now, won't we?"

"Sure," I say. *If it's there.*

The terrorists take us to a town fifty miles from Annapolis. Even though it's close to the city, the glassmen mostly leave it alone. It's far enough out from the pipeline, and there's not much here, otherwise: just a postage stamp of a barley field, thirty or so houses and one of those large, old, whitewashed barn-door churches. At night, the town is ghost empty.

Tris helps me down from the truck. Even that's an effort. My head feels half-filled with syrup. Simon and the others say their goodbyes and head out quickly. It's too dangerous for fighters to stay this close to the city. Depending on how much the glassmen know about Tris and me, it isn't safe for us either. But between a baby and a bullet, we don't have much choice.

Alone, now, we read the church's name above the door: *Esther Zion Congregation Church, Methodist.*

Tris and I look at each other. "Oh, Christ," she says. "Did Bill lie, Libby? Is he really so hung up on that sin bullshit that he sent me all the way out here, to a *church. . . .*"

I lean against her and wonder how he ever survived to come back to us. It feels like a gift, now, with my life half bled out along the road behind. "Bill wouldn't lie, Tris. Maybe he got it wrong. But he wouldn't lie."

The pews are old but well-kept. The prayer books look like someone's been using them. The only person inside is a white lady, sweeping the altar.

"Simon and Sybil sent you," she says, not a question. Sybil—we never even asked the woman's name.

"My sister," we both say, and then, improbably, laugh.

A month later, Tris and I round Bishop's Head and face north. At the mouth of our estuary, we aren't close enough to see Toddville, let alone our home, but we can't see any drones either. The weather is chillier this time around, the water harder to navigate with the small boat. Tris looks healthy and happy; older and younger. No one will mistake her for twenty-five again, but there's nothing wrong with wisdom.

The doctor fixed up my arm and found us an old, leaky rowboat when it was clear we were determined to go back. Tris has had to do most of the work; her arms are starting to look like they belong to someone who doesn't spend all her time reading. I think about the harvest and hope the bombs didn't reap the grain before we could. If anyone could manage those fields without me, Bill can. We won't starve this winter, assuming reapers didn't destroy everything. Libby ships the oars and lets us float, staring at the deep gray sky and its reflection on the water that seems to stretch endlessly before us.

"Bill will have brought the harvest in just fine," I say.

"You love him, don't you?"

I think about his short, patchy hair. That giant green monster he brought back like a dowry. "He's good with the old engines. Better than me."

"I think he loves you. Maybe one of you could get around to doing something about it?"

"Maybe so."

Tris and I sit like that for a long time. The boat drifts toward shore, and neither of us stop it. A fish jumps in the water to my left; a heron circles overhead.

"Dad's probably out fishing," she says, maneuvering us around. "We might catch him on the way in."

"That'll be a surprise! Though he won't be happy about his boat."

"He might let it slide. Libby?"

"Yes?"

"I'm sorry—"

"You aren't sorry if you'd do it again," I say. "And I'm not sorry if I'd let you."

She holds my gaze. "Do you know how much I love you?"

We have the same smile, my sister and I. It's a nice smile, even when it's scared and a little sad.

Their Changing Bodies

The boy in the lake had achieved some notoriety in camp Ondawalla a week before, when he had been caught rooting through the sanitary pad disposal bucket in the girls' bathroom. The boy was new, and though he had been caught at a rather odd activity, he spent his week-long probationary period the subject of mostly positive gossip. This free afternoon marked his first sighting outside of scheduled activities. The wait had been worth it. The boy in the lake was gorgeous.

Judy had been painfully aware of him since her arrival two weeks ago, when she had seen him across the mess hall. They talked a little, but Judy hadn't been prepared for his appearance or his popularity. She hadn't expected him to change quite so much.

Judy had first met Brandon last summer in the woods of rural Michigan, at an institution the promotional brochures called Better Image! for Teens. The kids sentenced to this energetically punctuated camp had referred to it as the Penitentiary, but Judy's sister Alice had more accurately called it Fat Camp. Judy came home thirty pounds thinner and possessed of a first kiss that had admittedly also encompassed some of her cheek. Still, at sixteen she had finally accomplished several of her goals in life: a) meet a boy, b) talk to the boy, c) impress him with her knowledge of esoteric subjects like grafting apple trees, and, finally, d) mack on him like crazy.

If pressed, Judy admitted that perhaps she still had a slight distance to travel until she fully accomplished d). Even though

71

Brandon had attempted to insert his tongue in her mouth, the reality of it wagging wetly in the air had so disconcerted Judy that she turned at the exact wrong moment, thereupon forcing Brandon's tongue to slither over her cheek until he realized what had happened and put it back in his mouth. How, she asked Alice, does anyone make out with so much spit? Alice just shrugged and said you got used to it.

Judy hoped she would get used to it.

Indeed, she'd spent much of her sophomore year of high school exchanging emails with Brandon, agonizingly clever missives about her latest obsessions: parasitology (when she told him about toxoplasma, he said that explained the counselors at the Penitentiary), figure skating (at her mother's insistence so she could "keep up" with her "progress" at camp, no matter that she was the fattest girl in the class), and her latest: knitting (she was even now working on a blue-and-white garter-stitch scarf that she hoped, at the right time, to give him). Brandon was also an "eclectic dilettante"—his term, which basically meant that they liked lots of things really intensely for a little bit of time.

Because she had hit her "weight loss target" and was a "whole new person" even though she felt like the same old person (being fat didn't matter so much in figure skating, it turned out), her mother had agreed to let her attend Camp Ondawalla with Alice this year. And Brandon—much to her joy, delight, deep confusion, and incipient panic—had written to tell her that he too would be attending this thoroughly normal summer camp, where the kids played capture the flag and ate real ice cream in the mess hall and *there were no scales, anywhere.* If it was curious that out of all the camps in the midwest, Brandon would have chosen this very one for his own normal summer, she hoped the casual hints she had dropped in the last few emails had encouraged him to sign up.

But it was now the end of June, and they had been at Camp Ondawalla for two whole weeks. Fourteen days when they should have been kissing each other's brains out (in the midst of a conversation about neural plasticity, perhaps). Instead, she had barely seen him, barely had a conversation with him, barely *recognized* him because if Judy was a "whole new person" then Brandon had been abducted by aliens over the school year.

"Do you think he had surgery?" Alice asked, squinting past the sun to watch his long, powerful strokes cut a channel through the lake.

"He doesn't have a scar," Judy said. Her hands jerked and she lost the stitch for the fifth time that hour.

"Anyway," said Sonia, Judy's bunkmate, "no surgery gives you muscles like that. I think your crush is a gym bunny, Judy."

Back at the Penitentiary, he hadn't been very big, relatively speaking. Maybe forty pounds overweight. He said his parents sent him because they were Pilates instructors in the San Fernando Valley and he embarrassed them at school functions. He'd only lost sixteen pounds at camp—the fewest of any of the kids—but his emails didn't mention any new diets and she'd just assumed that he would look the same this summer.

Judy surreptitiously lifted her eyes and watched Brandon dive beneath the water and come up, laughing and spluttering. His pectorals glistened; his slicked-back hair revealed the perfectly chiseled jaw that last summer had been hidden beneath an inch of baby fat.

Judy and Alice sighed. Sonia snorted and went back to her book: *Eco-Amazon! Sustainable Living for Modern Women.* Sonia's parents ran their own environmental architectural firm, and Sonia took "harmonious living" very seriously.

"Why won't they just talk to us?" Alice asked. The other boys weren't swimming with Brandon. Instead, they lounged on the pier, wearing the dark, baggy clothing that Pablo and Tom had somehow made cool this summer. Pablo and Tom were the camp heartthrobs, which, according to Sonia, said nothing good about the boys at Ondawalla.

"Maybe they're having a circle jerk?" Sonia said, without looking up from her book.

"Really?" said Judy.

Alice shuddered. "Dude, no more about that ookie cookie rumor. Way too gross to be real. They're boys, not animals."

"Then why don't you go over there?" Sonia asked.

"Cramps," Alice said, stretching. "The sun feels too good to move."

"I got my period last night, but I just take some powdered feverfew first thing, do some morning meditation. Better than a shot of morphine, I'm telling you."

"Feverfew? Could I try some?" Judy said. Around March or April this year Brandon's interests had turned toward female reproductive health. She'd thought it a sign of his unusually forward-thinking nature, and it had been a bit of a thrill to actually be able to discuss things like periods with a boy who wouldn't scream and run away.

Alice snorted. "You're such a hippie, Sonia."

They were startled by a sudden burst of giggles from the girls sipping Cokes and wading in the water a few feet away. Tiffany and her crew had been ignoring them, but now she flipped her scarf over her shoulder.

"A hippie dyke," she said, and her friends all giggled while Sonia swallowed and Alice looked like she wanted to spit on them.

"It's okay," Sonia said, brushing away Judy's arm. She spoke loudly, but refused to look in Tiffany's direction. "She'll have more fun once she's out of the closet."

After an awkward silence, Tiffany went back to ignoring them. Sonia had been out since forever (her parents were very supportive), and she and Tiffany had fooled around for a bit last summer. Judy wondered if Tiffany had been busy with someone else—the scarf around her neck must have been stifling in this July heat.

Sonia shook out her shoulders. "Soon as I graduate, I'll be in New York, hip deep in beautiful women."

Alice whistled a cat call. The sound seemed to carry farther than it had been intended; all the way across the lake, where the black-clad boys lifted their faces and turned toward them in unison.

"Whoa," Sonia said. "That's a little . . . must be those aviator glasses."

Judy agreed. It had an uncanny effect: when all five of them started walking over, Sonia put her hand on Judy's shoulder and Judy had to force herself to breathe.

Maybe it was the baseball caps, with the noon sun casting a deep shadow beneath their curved brims. Like they were being approached by a group of swaggering, faceless, bug-eyed monsters in track suits. Monsters who wanted their blood—

"Hey, Judy!"

She shrieked, just a little, before she recognized the voice from last summer. Brandon must have done a sprint lap across the lake to get to the girls' side so quickly. He was even breathing a little hard as he pulled himself onto the dock, though the effect only seemed to heighten the beauty of his uncanny transformation.

"Hey?"

He glanced behind him, at the posse of black-clad boys even now closing in. "You want to, uh, get some ice cream?"

Judy could hardly breathe. "Really? But the mess hall doesn't open for another hour."

"We can wait out front. All of you."

Now even Sonia looked confused. "You want to get ice cream with all of us?"

"That's Pablo and Tom, isn't it?" Alice asked. She was finger-combing her hair, ogling the approaching boys. Judy couldn't figure it out; they looked like a pack of wolves, way too aggressive to be appealing. And yet Alice still wanted to stick around and talk?

"Sure, ice cream is good," Judy said quickly. Cold food always helped with cramps. "Have you heard of feverfew?" she said, almost tripping over the words with her eagerness to finally have a conversation, to impress him and win him over and make it, finally and forever, through d).

Brandon frowned. "Feverfew? You mean the herb . . . oh, God, Judy, are you on your—"

"Brandon!"

Judy didn't recognize the voice, but she knew it had to be Pablo, identifiable only by the marijuana leaf stitched onto the front of his black baseball cap. Somehow the boys had managed to reach them already.

Brandon cursed under his breath. "Yeah, Pablo?"

Pablo grinned. This close, Judy was struck by the hyper-peroxided pearlescence of his teeth, like a game show host's in an acid bath.

"Trying to steal our girls?"

"We're not your girls," Sonia said.

"Sure we are," Alice said.

"I've heard they've got some nice tampons over in Mrs. Taylor's office," Tom said, which made Tiffany and her crew laugh as they grabbed their things.

"Good luck with that," Tiffany said, fidgeting at her scarf. Judy was struck by the speed with which she and her girlfriends went back down the hill to the cabins.

It was almost like they were running away, Judy thought. From the hottest boys at camp?

"This is weird," Judy said to herself, but the boys all seemed to have heard her whisper like she'd shouted it. Tom flashed his own smile. (Prompting Judy's frantic justification: Maybe it's the shadows? Or the sun? Some optical illusion? How could anyone's teeth be *that white?*)

"We just want to extend an invitation," Tom said.

"Invitation?" Judy repeated.

"You girls want to have some fun later tonight?" Pablo asked. He winked at Sonia as he said this, and Judy put her arm over her friend's shoulders.

Pablo fanned himself. "Even better—"

"Shove it, Pablo," said Alice, and Judy grinned.

"What Pablo is trying to say," said Tom, who had always seemed the nicer of the two, "is that we'd love for you to come down to the pine maze tonight at eleven."

"Yeah," Pablo said, running a pale finger gently up Alice's arm. "We're playing flashlight tag."

"We are?" Judy said.

"*Extra*-extra-curricular, Judy," Alice said, which meant *against the rules* which meant *cool.*

Judy had never been cool before. She wondered if she would like it.

"Well, maybe," Judy said, and then noticed Brandon behind them, still wet from his swim, with a face like he'd seen a ghost. For a moment, she wondered if he might faint right into the lake.

"Hey, Brandon, are you—"

"Yeah, buddy," Pablo said, putting a black arm around Brandon's glistening shoulders. "You don't look so hot."

Brandon swallowed. "I'm fine," he said, firmly, if breathlessly. "See you tonight, Judy."

The boys turned around, Brandon sandwiched between Pablo and Tom up front, the rest of the black-clad boys toddling in eerie, almost ecclesiastical silence behind.

"Boys," Sonia said, somewhere between an observation and a curse.

"Do you think something happened to Brandon?" Judy asked.

"I knew it," Alice said. "Pablo is *totally* in love with me."

The woods were darker than she remembered.

Something rustled in the trees on the left side of the path. Judy raised her arms to cover her face, inadvertently sticking Alice in the back with her knitting needles.

"Dammit, Judy, I think you cut me this time! Those things are dangerous!"

"Sorry!" Judy fumbled to stick her half-finished scarf and the attached pair of giant needles as far as they would squish into her jacket pocket.

"You heard that, too, Judy?" Sonia said.

"Yeah. Do you think it was an animal—"

"Guys," said Alice, "we're in the middle of the woods. Of course there are animals."

Sonia shook her head. "We're damn fools to be going with those freaky boys in the first place."

Judy was inclined to agree with Sonia, but she'd gone along with Alice's determination because of her memory of Brandon's pale face, and they way he'd said, "See you tonight, Judy." She might not understand it, but *something* had happened to him, and maybe if they talked she would find out.

"We are cool, Sonia. Only cool girls get invited to flashlight tag."

"Keep telling yourself that, babe. I'm only here in case you need someone to save your ass."

They tramped along the path in silence for another minute, while Judy thought back to the boys' strange invitation. She recoiled at the memory of Pablo and Tom's smiles. It *had* to have been her imagination, but still . . .

"Did their teeth seem . . . kind of strange to you?" Judy said.

"Their *teeth*? As usual, Judy, you bring on the weird."

Sonia nodded. "No, she's totally right. Pablo and Tom's teeth were all white. Like, denture commercial white. It's weird."

"What, now it's a turn-off for a guy to be into dental hygiene?"

The boys had said to meet at the first intersection of the pine maze. Even though only one path led there, this still felt as eerie as the maze itself, as though the soft crunch of brown pine needles underfoot, the rustling woods beside them, might hide real dangers.

"Hey, Alice?" Judy said.

"Yeah?"

"What's an ookie cookie?"

Sonia snorted and Alice groaned.

"You so don't want to know," said Sonia.

"You so don't," agreed Alice, "but I know you'll bother me forever so here you go: bunch of boys get together around a big cookie. They all jerk off really hard—"

"Wait, wait, *together*? Like, an orgy?"

"They'll say it isn't, but hey."

"It's gross," Sonia said. "Boys are animals."

"What happens after they ejaculate?"

"It's a game," said Alice. "A contest, I guess, 'cause they're boys. They're like bucks in heat."

"Jerking off together."

"Okay, it's not a perfect metaphor. Anyway, the last one to come loses."

Sonia raised the flashlight to her face, turning her chin bloodred and her eye sockets a deep, black shadow. "And then," she said, her voice pitched low, "he has to *eat it!*"

Judy shrieked and covered her face with her half-finished scarf, the knitting needles catching in the beam. Alice choked and then the three of them were laughing and laughing, so helplessly that Judy didn't even notice the vampire until his fangs were an inch from Alice's neck.

"Hey!" Judy yanked him back by the collar of his black shirt. Whatever the vampire might have said was drowned in the volume of Sonia and Alice's screams. Sonia dropped her flashlight and stumbled backward. She might have run if not for the white-knuckled force with which Alice gripped her elbow.

"Jesus Christ!" Sonia said.

The vampire, still bent over awkwardly from Judy's fistful of his shirt, gasped.

Judy kicked him in the shin. "Ow!" said the vampire.

"Knock it off, Pablo," said Judy.

Alice let go of Sonia, who picked up her flashlight.

"Ohmigod, you scared the crap out of us!" Alice said. Her voice still shook, but she smiled.

Pablo grimaced. "Hey, could you tell Super Girl over here to—"

"Judy, let him go!"

Judy wasn't so sure that was a good idea, but Alice's glare could melt polar ice caps. She let him go. At night, apparently, the boys didn't feel the need to wear the same dark clothing that they did during the day. Unfortunately, Pablo's too-pale face in the beam of Sonia's flashlight was hardly more reassuring than his shadowy aviator glasses.

"You didn't tell us this was going to be a costume party, Pablo," Sonia said.

He grinned, and under the illuminating beam of Sonia's flashlight, Judy realized that the terrifying fangs were obvious fakes. The prosthetic overbite prevented him from closing his mouth all the way, so that he had liberally splattered her neck and shoulder with flying spittle.

"It isn't," he said. "It's a game."

"Really?" said Alice, twirling one perfect brown ringlet with her finger and gazing up at him, doe-eyed.

Judy wanted to hit her. "Where's Brandon?" she asked.

Pablo flashed those teeth again, and this time she was sure of it: maybe they were caps, but no way any real teeth looked like that. "Taken care of," he said.

Judy and Sonia shared a worried look. "Didn't he say he'd see us?"

"Guess he'll have to take a rain check," said a deep voice, from the woods behind them. Alice shrieked again. Sonia raised her flashlight like a club. Judy took a deep breath.

But it was just Tom.

He'd also ditched the anonymous track suit and glasses in favor of jeans and a faded t-shirt. His teeth still gleamed that blinding white, even in the oppressive dark of the woods. Judy couldn't help but shudder when his gaze fell on her.

"You girls are late," he said.

"Sorry," Alice said. "We had a hard time sneaking out. Is anyone else coming?"

"It's your turn," said Pablo, still close enough to spray Judy with his spit. Judy thought that if a boy had to spit on her, she wished it could be Brandon.

"We're really glad you showed," Tom said with a smile.

Alice bit her lip and looked away, but not before mouthing "I told you so."

"So, where's the rest of the goon squad?" Sonia asked.

Pablo frowned, but Tom put his hand on his friend's shoulder. "Can I just say you smell delightful this evening," Tom said, with such an insincere smile that Judy tasted the bread pudding she'd had for dessert.

Sonia frowned. "Uh . . . thanks?"

Alice smacked Sonia not-very-surreptitiously. "So, what's this game?"

Tom and Pablo exchanged a look that could have meant anything from "Isn't she hot?" to "Who are these freaks?"

"The game is simple," Tom said.

Pablo opened his mouth, grimaced, and spat out his fangs. In his hand, she could see that they glinted almost like metal, not the plastic she'd originally assumed. But why would he have a pair of prosthetic metal fangs?

"There's only one rule," said Pablo. He looked taller, suddenly. Judy could have sworn he was at least two inches shorter than Tom but now his tousled blond hair rose inches above all of them.

"Oh, fuck," Sonia said, dry-throated and terrified.

Judy understood why a moment later. Pablo wasn't taller, he was *floating*. Judy looked back up. He caught her eye and winked.

"Run," said the boys.

"Alice, if we get out of this alive, you owe me like a thousand carbon credits."

"I do not need to hear about the end of the world right now. I think we're about to die."

"Oh, what made you think that? The serrated *fangs* they put in their mouths? Or maybe it was the *flying through the air?*"

"Oh god, we are so dead."

Alice resumed the snuffling sobs that had punctuated their conversation once they finally stopped running.

"It's okay," Judy whispered, though the words felt painfully fake. Alice cried harder. Sonia gave a shaking sigh: half exasperation, half terror. Judy could hardly feel anything. Even the rough bark of the gnarled tree root in her hand seemed distant, like she was watching someone else's white-knuckled grip and only imagining what it would feel like.

"What do you think they are?" she asked. It was the only question her brain could form. Not, how will we survive? Not, where can we hide? But, what's their taxonomic classification?

Brandon would probably be able to tell her. Brandon would probably be able to explain a lot of things.

"Demons," Sonia said. "It's the effing apocalypse and we're being Left Behind."

Alice stopped snuffling. "Don't you think we'd have, like, *noticed* if half the people on earth disappeared? I think they're zombies."

"Speaking zombies?"

"It's not like they had anything intelligent to say."

The three of them looked at each other. Alice pursed her lips. "As usual, huh?"

They'd stopped at a trench in the middle of a dense thicket of pine trees far off the maze path. It seemed as safe a place as any, and they hadn't heard Pablo, Tom, or any of the not!boys crashing through the woods for a while now. For creatures that could fly, the boys weren't particularly graceful.

Only now, they had no idea where they were and no idea how to get out.

Judy squatted beside her sister and rested her head on her shoulder. If she had to die here, at least she wasn't alone. She thought that this ought to make her cry, but her emotions felt as distant as Alice's hand on hers. Sonia sat beside the two of them, silent and scared. Judy reached for her and they waited like that for what felt like a very long time; there wasn't much else they could do.

Until there was.

A hollow tapping reverberated through the trunk of the tree, too even and rhythmic to be natural. Judy's skin tingled as she tilted her head up; Sonia said "no" over and over and Alice just screamed.

A boy smiled down at them from the highest branches. Not Pablo or Tom, but one of the others. He had slick black hair and apple-red lips that she'd assumed meant he wore lip gloss, but now she wasn't sure.

"We're going to die!" Alice wailed.

Sonia slapped her. "No one is dying!"

The boy smiled, and his acid-bleached teeth glinted in the ambient moonlight. "Sorry," he said, "but I think someone might."

He jumped from the topmost branch and wobbled down like a helicopter seed. The thud when he hit a limb about half-way to their trench released a shower of pine cones. One hit Judy on her nose.

"If it makes you feel better," he said, catching his balance, "think of it like . . . the call of nature."

"You have to go to the bathroom?" Sonia said, eyebrows raised, and Judy could have hugged her.

He frowned. "No, smartass, like *National Geographic.* One of those nature shows, you know, like when the alligator finally catches the gazelle."

Alice gasped and then choked, almost doubling over with the force of her coughing. Even Sonia's hands shook.

Judy remembered the scarf in her pocket.

"Wait, do you know where Brandon is?"

"Tied up," he said, and snorted. "You guys smell *great!* Anyone ever tell you that?"

"Take me first," Judy blurted, and was proud when her voice didn't break.

Alice yanked at her shirt so hard the seam started to rip at the shoulder. "Judy, no!"

"They even line up! Man, Pablo wasn't kidding. This is the shnizzle."

Judy stood, and Sonia quickly followed suit. "What are you doing?" she whispered.

"Trust me."

Sonia shook her head but she didn't stop Judy from climbing out of the trench and walking around to the other side of the tree. The boy wobbled in the air above her, accidentally hit a low-hanging branch and fell the last few feet to the ground.

He licked his apple lips. She was at least three inches taller, and way bigger, which made that bit of her that had been quivering like a Jell-O mold turn solid and sharp, like a knitting needle.

"Hold on," said the boy, his voice cracking. He reached into his pocket and pulled out a pair of those serrated prosthetic fangs. They looked even more ridiculous in his small apple mouth than they had in Pablo's. "Fere," he said, spitting on her, "fats fetter."

Judy tried to look scared. "Will it hurt?" she asked.

The boy blinked. "I don't know," he said. "Fis is my first time."

He fumbled a bit with her shoulders, but his grip was surprisingly strong. His eyes had turned nearly as bright as his teeth by the time he bent over her neck. And Judy didn't have any more experience with this sort of thing than he did, but she'd probably read a lot more, and she decided that this was as far as anyone needed to go.

So she stabbed him in the side, hard, with a steel knitting needle.

Apple-lip boy screamed. Judy was surprised, because she hadn't expected it to work, or for the hole when she withdrew her needle to smoke.

"What . . . it's not suffosed to haffen like fat!"

"Take us to Brandon," Judy said, one needle at his neck and the other below his belt. "Or I'll stick you again."

"Aw, come on, I was just haffing a little fun!"

Judy poked a little harder. "And just so you know, alligators don't eat gazelles."

Brandon was tied to a tree.

He yelled "Judy!" as soon as the three of them came into view with apple-lip boy. The worry with which Brandon infused her name made Judy blush, and started to ease that place inside of her that had gone cold and hard when she thought they were going to die.

Brandon turned to their captive boy. "What did you do, Ben?"

Apple-lip boy glowered and coughed feebly, releasing a bit more of the strange black smoke from the wound in his side. "I'm the victim here, man. I can't even fly. Leaked too much of the good stuff."

Brandon scooted as far forward as the ropes would allow. "Good for you guys," he said, after a moment. "I, uh, wasn't expecting a hostage situation."

"Yeah, about that," said Sonia. "What exactly is going on here? We're split between the four horsemen and a zombie apocalypse."

"I thought you guys might be pulling a really good prank," Alice said, "but that doesn't explain the flying."

"Or the game show host teeth," Judy said, and Alice rolled her eyes.

"We're frakking *vampires*, you nimrods," said apple-lip boy.

Judy jabbed him harder than necessary in the neck. He yelped.

"So not funny," Alice said. She held her arms akimbo, the tangles of her hair silhouetted against the almost-full moon like medusa's snakes.

"I know your zit face from last summer, kid," Sonia said. "Please."

Alice nodded. "Yeah, vampires are, a) hot, b) old, c) not pathetic. Try again."

"No, really! I got turned last week, that's all. I'll get better at it, promise."

"It does explain the fangs," Judy said thoughtfully.

Alice frowned. "Vampires need fake fangs?"

Brandon coughed. It was hard to tell with the distance and the dim light, but Judy could have sworn that he was *blushing*. "He's right."

"No frakking way," said Sonia.

"You watch *BSG?*" said apple-lip boy.

"No, she won't go to the dance with you," said Alice.

"I think that I . . . uh . . . infected them," said Brandon.

Apple-lip boy rubbed his arm. "You smell really great," he said.

Sonia growled. "Will you guys *stop saying that*! What the hell do I look like, a hamburger?"

"You infected them?" Judy said. "But you're not a vampire."

"No. I cured myself." He coughed. "But I guess I was . . . you know . . . uh, like with typhoid and certain other communicable diseases . . . that are transferred through, uh, bodily fluids . . ."

Brandon was definitely blushing. And his near-incoherent speech sounded suspiciously familiar from all their conversations about parasitology and disease vectors last spring. And she couldn't help but think about the one kind of bodily fluid that helped spread too many diseases to count. Maybe even one that she'd thought couldn't exist?

Judy gasped. "Oh, my god."

"You understood that?" Sonia said.

"It's the ookie cookie."

Sonia and Alice stared at her in horror.

"Oh, no," said Sonia. "Oh, no way."

"Are you telling me," said Alice, warming up to her subject with theatrics that Judy thought, for once, were entirely justified, "that we are stuck here in the woods, with horny supernatural *fanboys* out for our blood, all because you just *had* to go and jizz on a cookie and *infect* everyone with some sort of *vampire STD!*"

"Yes?" His response was very soft, almost inaudible. "Just Pablo. He turned the others after losing the first game. I tried to stop them, but Pablo had other ideas. He drugged this girl Tiffany last week and drank from her. I don't think she remembers what happened. But now he isn't even hiding himself. He thinks he's invincible."

Sonia nodded slowly. "I thought Tiffany looked kind of spooked when they came over. Guess we should have run with her."

"But there has to be a way to get out of this," Judy said. "You cured yourself, right, Brandon? How can we cure them?"

"We don't wanna be cured!" wailed apple-lip boy.

Sonia jabbed him. "You wanna leak more smoke?" she said.

"Judy," Brandon said, "you mentioned feverfew earlier. Are you on your period?"

Judy had thought that nothing could surprise her anymore. But even if he'd accidentally turned all the boys in his cabin into vampires, Brandon was still the most surprising guy she'd ever known.

She stammered incoherently until Sonia sighed and waved her hand at him. "Yeah, we all are. Hormonal regulation and all that shit. What about it?"

"That's why they think you smell so good. Vampires are attracted to menstruating women."

"That's . . . unlucky," said Alice.

"Actually," Brandon said, grinning, "it's luckier than you know. Because the only thing that can cure a vampire? Drinking menstrual blood."

"Aw hell, Brandon, you never told us that! It's disgusting!"

Without warning, Sonia twisted apple-lip boy's arm behind him and actually broke his skin a little with the needle. "You are on such thin ice, kid. Don't even start. Periods are not *disgusting*, they are natural and healthy and apparently are going to save your sorry life, so why don't you just play nice and drink up?"

Alice grinned at Sonia. "You are totally my hero, you know that, right?"

"Does that mean I get a kiss?"

Alice looked thoughtful.

Judy moved a little closer to Brandon, who looked torn between excitement and embarrassment. More than anything, that made her think he hadn't changed so much since last summer. "So vampires are attracted to their cure? That's a real evolutionary disadvantage," Judy said. "Maybe that's why we've never seen a vampire before."

Brandon scrunched his nose—his "conundrum face," she'd called it last summer. "The guy who, uh, turned me—anyway, he told me about the cure. He said things got bad if you stayed that way for more than a few weeks."

This excited Judy. "Maybe it's a parasite that can be transmitted more easily in an asymptomatic host, and actually being a vampire is a temporary stage of its development cycle!"

"Hey!" Sonia's voice was sharp. Judy jumped back. "Supportive as I am of geek love, how about we focus on making this stage in their development cycle *very* temporary? So we just smear a little blood . . ."

"It touches his lips," Brandon said, "he turns human again in a few minutes. And he can't ever turn back again."

Apple-lip boy started to cry. Not even Judy could muster compassion.

"Don't worry," Sonia said. "I got this one."

She reached under her sundress and pulled out the brown rubber cup that Judy had seen her rinsing out this morning. Sonia liked it because it had "zero carbon footprint" and was "ecologically harmonious." Apparently, it was also good for curing supernaturally transmitted diseases, because all she had to do was tip the cup into apple-lip boy's screaming mouth for him to choke and then fall to the pine-needle floor in a boneless heap.

"Wow, that was easy," said Alice.

Brandon wriggled against the ropes, but the knots were well tied. "I hope you'll let me help?" he said. Judy knelt and worked at them with a needle until they came undone.

"Can he still transmit?" she asked, gesturing to the groaning, fully human boy.

"Yes," Brandon said, rubbing his wrists. "But only once, and only to another guy, and I'm pretty sure even that wears off after a few months . . ."

"Maybe you should carry him?" Judy said, gesturing to the groaning, fully human boy.

Brandon shrugged and hefted the boy over his shoulder. Sonia handed Alice the knitting needle and held aloft her rubber cup.

"All right, girls," she said, ignoring Brandon. "Let's go slay ourselves some vampires."

They picked a spot in the middle of a maze path with plenty of room on all sides for maneuvering. Brandon hid with apple-lip boy just behind some trees to the side. The three girls sat down in the middle of the clearing.

"You ready?" Judy asked her sister.

Alice took a deep breath, and nodded. "Let's do it."

Judy held her pad, Alice a tampon, and Sonia a half-full rubber cup. They were as ready as they would ever be.

And so Alice started screaming. It was a thing of beauty—ear-piercingly shrill, but full of deep pathos and sadness and despair at the same time. Alice had instantly transformed herself into a hysterical girl. Judy gave her sister a tight, soldierly nod. Judy knew how scared she must be. They all were, stuck in the woods with a bunch of vampire boys out for their blood. But Alice had turned her fear into a weapon, and Judy had never been prouder to be her sister than at that moment.

Judy caught Sonia's eye. "Be ready," she mouthed. Alice had started blubbering, artfully incoherent moans about "mommy" and "being a good girl from now on" and "just get me out of here, please, please, please."

Something rustled in the woods. It took all of Judy's concentration not to jump or whirl around.

See what we want you to see, Judy thought. *Three helpless girls, ripe for the taking. Don't worry about what happened to the other boy. Don't worry that we might hurt you. What can we do, anyway?*

More rustling. Judy made a show of hugging Alice. Sonia dropped to her knees and clasped her hands together, mouthing silent prayers.

Four, maybe five seconds. Alice's sobs drowned out Judy's thudding heartbeat.

And then the woods exploded.

Six boys came at them from all directions, some Judy recognized, some she didn't, but Pablo and Tom clearly in charge. When Pablo was a few feet from Alice and Judy, he paused and held up his hand. The boys all froze, much to Judy's relief.

"Aw . . . begging for your mommy to come find you? Not going to happen, babe."

"Are you really going to kill us?" Judy said. Alice kept burbling; Sonia kept praying; Judy gripped the pad in her pocket.

Tom shrugged. "Maybe. I don't think anyone will notice one way or another with you, will they?"

"She's like Ugly Betty, but less popular," Pablo said. "At least she smells nice."

There was a time when insults like this had made Judy stop speaking for weeks at a time. When she had retreated so deeply into her hobbies that even Alice hardly saw her. At one time, coming from a boy like Pablo, it might have devastated her for life.

Now, she just glared at him.

"You're kind of pathetic," she said. "You don't even have real fangs."

Pablo yanked her up by the roots of her hair. "But I think they'll cut your skin just fine," he said, so close to her face that she could smell the blood on his breath. And more spit, of course.

He lowered his mouth to her neck, but his pearlescent teeth felt about as strong as a set of dentures. "Oh, right," he mumbled, and fumbled at his pocket with his left hand.

"Shit!" he said. "I must have dropped them. Tom, can I borrow yours?"

"Gross, man. No way."

"Come on!"

"You'll, like, give me herpes."

"Bros before hos?"

"Dude, that's . . . I don't even know where to start."

But Judy did. She raised her hands like she was trying to protect her neck and when he turned back to her, she put two fingers, very gently, carefully, into Pablo's mouth.

"Faht the eff . . ." Which was all he had time to say before the blood on her hand did the trick, and he collapsed on top of her, twitching and gurgling.

"Pablo? Are you—"

Brandon sprinted out of the woods, knocking Tom to the ground in a running tackle.

"Goddamn it, Brandon!"

Tom kicked Brandon hard enough to make Judy wince even from her position beneath Pablo. Tom started to float, but

Alice reached him a moment later and stabbed him in the butt with a needle. Tom sank back down like a leaky balloon.

"Will you guys *stop them!*" he yelled, prompting the other four vampire boys to do something more than gape and wince in sympathy.

Judy managed to wrench herself from underneath Pablo (muscle definitely weighed more than fat) around the time that Brandon hauled himself upright.

"Are you okay?" she said, shouting to be heard over the valkyrie screams of her sister and friend, and the moaning gurgles of defeated vampires.

"Yeah. You?"

"The painters are in, buddy!" Sonia shouted, and Judy felt a spatter of blood hit her cheek. She grinned.

Brandon pushed her down in enough time to prevent a tree limb from smashing into her head.

"Sorry, Judy!" Alice hollered. Judy watched Alice wrap her legs firmly around a boy's neck while he gasped and cursed. Alice lifted her tampon, twirled it above her head like a blood-engorged cotton mace, and then thwapped it with wet precision against the boy's lips.

"Listen," Brandon said, "I'm really sorry about this. The whole thing was a mess, and I didn't want to put you in danger—"

"You could have talked to me," Judy said. "I could have helped."

"I . . ."

"Judy!"

But it was too late: Tom gripped her from behind. He held a simple fishing knife against her neck.

"I *told* Pablo those fangs were stupid," he muttered. "Got your attention? Good. Now back away slowly. If I see any of you girls touching yourselves . . ."

"Jackass," Sonia said.

"As for you, Judy," he said, letting the razor bite softly into her skin, "I need some blood. I'll try not to take it all."

Judy was shaking too hard to speak, but she had always been good at thinking. As Tom leaned into her neck, she turned her cheek, like a girl hoping for a kiss. Tom laughed a little and shrugged, as though to say, "Why not?" Except the angles were all wrong—like a certain bumbling attempt on the edge of the woods last year. And just like that time, the boy missed her mouth, landing instead with a wet slobber on her cheek.

The cheek that Sonia had splattered.

Tom dropped with hardly a sound. The helpless twitching that followed a moment later felt particularly satisfying.

"Someone stop me from kicking him," Sonia said.

Alice kissed her.

Well, that's one way of ending an evening, Judy thought.

Judy and Brandon and Sonia and Alice sat by the lake, watching the sun come up. Apple-lip boy had staggered back to his cabin, and Judy didn't much care if the other boys never found their way out.

"You did it to lose weight?" Judy repeated.

Brandon could hardly look at her, but at least he was telling the truth. "Not on purpose. This guy visiting the school glossed over the details. Said it would turn me into a stud. I was . . . you did so well with your weight loss goals and my parents were going to send me back to the Penitentiary and . . ."

"Oh, Brandon," she said, patting his shoulder. "I guess that explains the bathroom raid."

"I hope you can forgive me. I should have said something instead of ignoring you."

"I understand. But maybe your next hobby could be feminism? Sonia has a copy of *The Second Sex.*"

Brandon smiled ruefully. "That sounds like a good idea."

"Oh!" Judy said, blushing. "I meant to show you. It's the garter stitch I wrote about. It's not finished yet, but . . ."

She handed him the half-scarf. The loose ends had unraveled a bit, and the stitching seemed kind of strange in the brightening dawn, but Brandon held it like a golden fleece.

"It's . . . Judy, did anyone ever tell you . . . I mean, back at the Penitentiary . . . I mean, ever since you got here—"

And so Judy grabbed Brandon by the back of his well-coiffed head and crossed d) very thoroughly off her list.

The Score

Don't matter what we sing
Every window we open, they jam another door
They gladhand, pander, lie for the king
It's our song, but their score
                                    —Jake Pray, "What We Sing"
                            (first documented performance:
                        February 15, 2003, at the pre-invasion
                    anti–Iraq War marches in New York City)

Gmail – Inbox – jimmy.sullivan@gmail.com – chat

me: violet, i'm so sorry. if you need someone to come over . . .
Sent at 3:16 PM on Sunday

Violet: he never liked you, you know
Sent at 4:43 PM on Sunday

Violet's new status message—
Two bleeding hearts drank ginger beer / and mocked and stung their gingered fears / to know the future, and still die here. Rahimahullah, Jake.

NEW YORK CITY MEDICAL EXAMINER

NAME: Jacob Nasser	AUTOPSY-NO: 43-6679
SEX: Male	DATE OF AUTOPSY: 3/21/2007
RACE: White (Arab)	TIME OF AUTOPSY: 3:36 p.m.
DOB: 2/1/81	DATE OF REPORT: 4/1/2007
DATE OF DEATH: 3/17/07–3/18/07	

FINAL PATHOLOGICAL DIAGNOSES

I. 25 MICRON TEAR IN CORONARY ARTERY, POS-SIBLE INDICATION OF SPONTANEOUS CORO-NARY ARTERY DISSECTION

II. MINIMAL DRUG INTOXICATION
   A. Probable non-contributory drugs present:
      1. Acetaminophen (2 mg/L)
      2. Cannabis (30.0 ng/mL)

OPINION

Jacob Nasser was a 26-year-old male of Arab descent who died of undetermined causes. The presence of a 25-micron tear in his coronary artery might indicate SCAD (Spontaneous Coronary Artery Dissection), however it was deemed too small to lead to a definitive finding. The presence of cannabis was small and non-contributing.

The manner of death is determined to be: COULD NOT BE DETERMINED.

M. Andy Pilitokis
M.D., LL.B., M.Sc.
Chief Medical Examiner

Andrea Varens, M.D.
Associate Medical Examiner

Jake Pray (Jacob Nasser) prelim autopsy notes [**Recovered**]
Last saved with AutoRecover
4:33 AM Thursday, March 22, 2007

Andrea Varens
3/21/07
The subject was first discovered dead in his holding cell the morning of March 18 in the "Tombs" Manhattan Detention Center. The subject was discovered with a rope in his hand, and so police at first surmised it had contributed in some manner to his death, but there are no consistent contusions on the neck or, indeed, anywhere else on the body.

A preliminary physical examination reveals what looks to be a normal, healthy twenty-six-year-old man with no signs of ill-health or infirmity (beyond the obvious).

Drug interactions? Probably SCAD, poor fucker.

I saw him. I went to the hallway to get a Coke from the machine and I saw him. Leaning against the wall looking out the window. Oh, fuck. Fuck fuck fuck. I've been staring at his sorry face for the last two days, I oughta know. Maybe he has a long-lost twin brother?

Mom was right, I should have gone into

———

The Score

The New York Post
Anti-War Songster "Scored" Dope, Autopsy Says
April 2, 2007

Bad news for the anti-Bush peaceniks who've turned Jake Pray into a martyr: turns out he was stoned on dope (the equivalent of "one joint of strong chronic," according to a well-placed source) when police took him into custody. And he died of a "spontaneous" heart attack. Not police abuse.

Of course, you didn't hear any of that damning data at the packed memorial service in the ultra-liberal Riverside Church this Sunday. In fact, Pray's memorial service sounded more like an anti-war rally.

Violet Omura, a Columbia University grad student who spoke at the memorial, had nothing but contempt for the city's medical examiner. "It's ridiculous," she said. "It's like if you shot me in the head and the autopsy said I had died due to 'spontaneous brain leakage.'"

Pray's fellow protesters were convinced police abuse was responsible. "[The police] really picked on him at the rally," said Billy Davis, a close friend who had been present at the protest. "Guess they saw his skin and hair, you know, and drew their conclusions," Davis said, referring to Pray's Palestinian heritage. "They called him a terrorist. Said ragheads like him were responsible for bringing down the Twin Towers." Davis also accused the officers of using Tasers on the unruly protestors. Conspiracy theories abounded at the memorial of how the nonlethal crowd-control devices could have contributed to his death.

In a statement issued today, the police commissioner denied all accusations of wrongdoing by the officers on the scene and restated the findings of yesterday's autopsy report. "Should any new evidence surface regarding this case, rest assured that we will pursue it with all due diligence."

Rock & Rap Confidential
"What We Still Sing"
Issue 4, Volume 78; May 2007

Jake Pray may never have had a hit song, but to the latest crop of anti-war protestors, "What We Sing" has the same iconic resonance that "Bring the Boys Home" or "Masters of War" had for their parents. And over three hundred youngbloods turned out for the memorial of this iconoclastic musician, held this past March in Riverside Church.

Jake Pray was born as Jacob Nasser to Palestinian immigrants; the family settled in suburban New Jersey when he was just three years old. His father, a professor of linguistics and cultural anthropology at a university in the Gaza Strip, was forced to emigrate after he received death threats for his political positions.

Not surprisingly, Pray became a lightning rod for activists across the world when his life ended in Manhattan's "Tombs" detention facility. He was arrested after an incident with police during the anti-war protests this March. The autopsy report declared its findings inconclusive. The police commissioner, in a written statement, called Pray's death a "tragic incident."

The arresting officer had taunted the twenty-six-year-old man with racial slurs like "raghead." He had shot 50,000 excruciating volts of electricity into his body and then detained him in unspeakable conditions for endless hours. A *tragic incident*? The mind would boggle, if this weren't so painfully predictable.

The larger meaning of Jake's life was best captured by Violet Omura, a twenty-five-year-old graduate student in the physics department at Columbia.

> Perhaps the experiences of his parents in the occupied territories influenced his decision to turn to political activism and the thankless efforts of those who argue from right, not expedience. But I think, perhaps, that he mostly just wanted to tell, he just wanted to sing, he just wanted others to know they had a voice. Our parents were optimists. They gave us "Imagine" and "Blowin' in the Wind." We're not pessimists. God knows Jake wasn't a pessimist. But he wasn't so sure that singing could change anything. Some people complain that "What We Sing" is bleak. I disagree. It's furious, it's strident, and it's real. Jake wanted to change the world, but he couldn't hide from the fact that it might never change.

Billboard Pop 100
Top Ten
Issue Date: 2007-5-19

#1: Beyoncé & Shakira: Beautiful Liar
#2: Gwen Stefani featuring Akon: The Sweet Escape

#3: Fergie featuring Ludacris: Glamorous
#4: Avril Lavigne: Girlfriend
#5: Diddy featuring Keyshia Cole: Last Night
#6: Tim McGraw: Last Dollar
#7: Mims: This Is Why I'm Hot
#8: Jake Pray: What We Sing
#9: Gym Class Heroes: Cupid's Chokehold
#10: Fall Out Boy: This Ain't a Scene, It's an Arms Race

MSNBC TRANSCRIPT
">TUCKER" with Tucker Carlson
Original Air Date: 5/20/07

TUCKER CARLSON: Jake Pray has been in the news a lot lately. After all, the blame-America-firster's mysterious death in police custody, his illicit marijuana use, and his surprise hit song, "What We Sing," have made him the perfect martyr for self-defeating liberal elitists.

But now, one of Pray's own radicals has come out against him. In a damning exposé published in the online fringe-left newsletter *Counterpunch*, James Sullivan has laid bare the despicable anti-Semitic and vitriolic anti-American hate that underlies the rabid far left.

Welcome to the show, Mr. Sullivan.

JAMES SULLIVAN: Thank you very much for having me.

TC: We know you were detained with Jake Pray at the Chelsea Piers before he was taken to the Manhattan Detention Facility. How well did you know him?

JS: Well, when you're as heavily involved in the peace movement as I was, you kind of get to know everyone. Jake was, you know, dedicated. A bit too dedicated. He was a musician, but you could tell it wasn't really about the music for him. It was about the fame. People loved him. I did, too, for a while.

TC: But eventually you realized—

JS: Yeah, you know, he was just full of—sorry, yeah, full of it. A bit of a megalomaniac.

TC: I understand that you're also a musician? Did he ever support you, or...

JS: Never. Jake really resented the presence of another musician in the, well, what he would have called the "inner circle."

TC: Now, I'm going to read a passage from your *Counterpunch* article. It's pretty damning, detailing what happened the afternoon you were both detained by the police. You write: "Pray was furious after the arrest. On the ride down to the pier he just sat in the police truck shaking and clenching his fists. His girlfriend, Violet Omura, tried to calm him down, but he just lashed out at her, called her an 'ignorant bitch' and a few other expressions I'll choose not to print here. He was always like that, in fact, willing—and sometimes eager—to take out his own personal frustrations and failings on others. Billy Davis and Violet and his other cronies are trying to claim that the police officers called him a 'raghead' that day. If they did, I never heard it." And then, further on, you write: "Around the police, Pray was like a rabid dog. At Pier 57 it was like something had popped.

He wasn't quiet anymore. We all heard him: Violet and Billy and the rest who are trying to pretend that it didn't happen."

You go on to list some of the epithets Pray hurled at our men in blue, some of which are not, um, fit for television. Could you share some of the milder ones?

JS: [*Laughter*] Yeah. They're—sure. "Filthy murdering bigots," that was one. He said they were all "closet fags," and accused them of, ah—"practicing on Abner Louima." He just wouldn't stop. Finally, one of the officers tried to get him to calm down. He had dark curly hair, a big nose—you know, obviously Jewish—and Jake nearly tackled him. Said "his kind" was supporting genocide and maybe "they deserved what they got."

TC: "Deserved what they got." What do you think he meant by that?

JS: I think it's obvious. He was saying the Jewish people deserved the Holocaust.

TC: Wow. Now, I hear you're starting to distance yourself from all this and the so-called peace movement.

JS: Yeah. Actually, I'm [*Laughter*] yeah, I'm halfway through *Atlas Shrugged*.

TC: [*Laughter*] How do you like it so far?

JS: Really good. It's giving me a new perspective.

JakePrayTruth.org
Action Statement

Jake Pray, the radical anti-war protestor and singer, died as a result of police abuse on the night of March 17, 2007. This fact, supported by activists present during his arrest and reports from within the holding facility itself, has been systematically covered up by the New York City Police Department and coroner's office. This is just a part of an overall, covert strategy to undermine the vocal anti-war movement with acts of state-sponsored terror. Jake Pray, whose anti-war songs had energized a new generation of protestors, was first on their list because of his growing influence. COINTELPRO had thousands and thousands of pages about John Lennon in their files, because he posed a similar threat. In this age of increasing government control and ongoing illegal wars (one million dead and counting!), Jake Pray's powerful voice and even more powerful message posed an unacceptable threat.

But guess what? So do we. And we resolve to uncover the TRUTH about Jake Pray's murder and bring his message to the world.

—Billy Davis
Founder, JakePrayTruth.org
December 15, 2007

[UPDATE 1/3/08: For our official statement on the allegations made by James Sullivan, please visit our FAQ.]

Just Another (Libertarian) Weblog: Ron Paul 2008!
Rockin' for the Fatherland
Posted January 4, 2008 5:45 pm by BigFish

Well, Billy Davis over at JakePrayTruth has <u>finally</u> <u>responded</u> to the accusations James Sullivan made <u>such a big splash with</u> a few months ago.

Short version: Ole Jimmy is an opportunistic lying asshole.

Still, we have to thank him. "Practicing on Abner Louima" is an expression now enshrined in my soul. Hey, Jake, wherever you are, I never look at a toilet plunger without thinking of you. (Unfortunately none of the <u>inexplicably frequent ghost-sightings</u> of Pray these last few months have involved home plumbing equipment. Though I hear he was spotted outside the Pink PussyCat last Thursday).

In other news, the redoubtable Jimmy Sullivan has <u>made himself a web page</u>! Check out the "latest music" section. And here I had thought right-wing volks-rock had gone out of fashion in the Third Reich.

Oh. Never mind.

Sieg Heil!

To: Professor Violet Omura <vomura12@nyu.edu>
New York University
Department of Applied Physics

From: Zacharias Tibbs <zachknowsthelord@cheese. org>
15 East Rock Way
Topeka, Kansas

March 16, 2015

Dear PROFESSOR Omura:

I hope you are prepared & have sat down to read this letter for I have here enclosed the most ASTONISH-ING and SECRET mathematical formula whereby all events heretofore UNEXPLAINED by the greatest scientists of the world are rendered clear by a simple proof. If you do not believe this, don't trust me, but read on for yourself!

I see from reading your very fascinating articles and biography that you once had the privilege of knowing the great Jake Pray, whose every album I own. Would you believe me if I said that this GREAT MATHE-MATICAL PROOF would even make clear the mystery of the rumors of his ghostly resurrection and spectral warnings of future wars & conflicts? Have I intrigued you? Yes, of course, for you have a keen intellect and open heart and would surely not want to deny your colleagues the benefit of the knowledge I have so HUMBLY stumbled upon.

Merely scroll down to see the world's greatest secret revealed. . . .

$$p(R) = (As * (t(d)/Gw)) * B/V$$

Thus, the probability of any INDIVIDUAL, upon their DEATH & DEPARTURE from this world, becoming a REVENANT is revealed…

Where As = Astrological Sign, with the following values assigned:

Aries = .2
Taurus =.5
Gemini = 1
Cancer = 5
Leo = 1
Virgo = 3
Libra = .7
Scorpio = -1
Sagittarius = 2
Capricorn = 0
Aquarius = 1
Pisces = 2

As determined through intensive STUDY of GOD'S HOLY WORD & observations & deductions of a PERSONAL nature.

$t(d)$ = the time spent in the process of dying

Gw = the number of GOOD WORKS performed in their lives, with the average being 500 for a CHRISTIAN and less than 100 for ALL OTHERS (& in particular those of the apostate MORMON faith)

110

B = that which belongs to BEELZEBUB, otherwise known as SATAN or the DEVIL. The values are assigned thusly:

If the subject is a Mormon, B = 1000, for all MORMONS shall surely walk the EARTH for ETERNITY
For ATHEISTS, B = 500
For CHRISTIANS of pure and godly EVANGELICAL faith, B = 0.1
For ALL OTHERS, B = 1

V = the number of verses in our HOLY BIBLE the departed knew & memorized in life

But perhaps you, in your SECULAR University and GODLESS education, do not understand the true significance of explaining the REVENANTS among us. For do not mistake me, the revenants are responsible for all manner of WEIRD & UNEXPLAINED events. Not merely ghosts (like that of your (sadly GODLESS) REVENANT & FRIEND Jake Pray), but also such sundry as possession by DEMONS, ALIEN ABDUCTIONS, and sightings of UFO'S!

Even the INEXPLICABLE behavior of SUBATOMIC particles through the EXTRA DIMENSIONS is caused by these revenants & of course not to mention the riddle of GRAVITY.

I am sure you can see the potential of this astonishing EQUATION and I will be happy to travel to the GODLESS city of New York to discuss it with you further. Though you are only an Assistant Professor, I feel you are the perfect VESSEL of this KNOWLEDGE.

Yours in RESPECT & ANTICIPATION,

Zacharias Tibbs

From: Violet Omura [vomura12@nyu.physics.edu]
To: zachknowsthelord@cheese.org
Date: March 18, 2015, 4:13 am, EST

Dear Zacharias:

you can bet that I have no aspirations to be the perfect VESSEL for your KNOWLEDGE, or even the person who has to open your crackpotty emails (what, you didn't think I got the first three?)

but I'm drunk and bored and this is definitely the worst day of my year, so I'll bite. taking it as a given that you wouldn't know a quantum theory of gravity from a hemorrhoid, why don't all these horrible sinners and atheists and (!) mormons just go to, you know, hell? seems easier than having billions of revenants wandering the earth like thetans or something. you're not a scientologist, are you?

I don't know what you might have read or whatever about jake and me but you honestly can't believe that a godless intellectual like yours truly believes the woowoo crackpots who say he still shows up at their rallies?

god i wish he did.

(I mean 'god' in a purely rhetorical, godless way, of course).

violet, future revenant

From: zachknowsthelord@cheese.org
To: vomura12@nyu.physics.edu
Date: March 18, 2015, 6:21 pm, CMT

PROFESSOR Omura:

Disregarding your DRUNKEN (and, indeed, Godless) aspersions on my theory & character, you have indeed hit upon the crux of the matter.

For through other EQUATIONS & RESEARCH, I have hit upon the fundamental truth: these revenants do not go to HELL, for we are ALREADY LIVING THERE.

Yes, I say. The present EARTH merged with BEEL-ZEBUB'S kingdom on the night of MARCH 20, 2003.

I trust you recognize the date? Yes, for your friend Jake Pray was present at every RALLY and PEACE MARCH in protest of this war, which I of course included in his calculation for GOOD WORKS.

Contemplate our SINFUL world and tell me that you do not agree. We have been DENIZENS of hell for the last twelve years!

And as a side note, I am of course entirely OPPOSED to all false gods, including the ABSURD teachings of SCIENTOLOGISTS. I must thank you for reminding me of them, for both they AND Mormons should receive a Beelzebub score of 1000…

When would you like to meet?

Zacharias Tibbs

Warp & Weft: An Inclusive Community for Alternative Paradigms and Progressive Politics
Virtual Town Meeting (Excerpt)
Transcript and Audio archived on the community bulletin board
Original event April 1, 2017

[**Rose_Granny**] Thank you all for inviting me here today. I'm Rose, and as my husband used to say, I don't look much like my avatar. [*Laughter*] I've never really believed in ghosts. Oh, I've heard stories and some were eerie enough to make me shiver, but I've lived a long time and I had never seen anything to make me believe that any part of us could survive after death.

When my husband died last year, after a long and painful fight with liver cancer, I was devastated. I decided that it was my duty to make Harold's life count as much as it could, by taking his ideals and courage and using that to further work he would have approved of. So I became, at age 75, a political activist. I attended rallies. I spoke up at virtual town meetings like this one for our local congress members. I made signs, I wrote letters, I organized petitions . . . and I discovered Jake Pray. I'd heard "What We Sing" on the radio years ago, of course, but at the time I hadn't paid any attention to the man or the story behind the song. When I learned of how he died, I was shocked. How could such a young man, with such promise of the future, die so suddenly? He had no serious drugs in his body. There were no signs of violence, self-inflicted or otherwise. He was found dead on the floor of his holding cell, with a bit of rope in his hand.

And then I saw him. Perhaps it will not surprise most of you to learn that I mean this literally. I saw Jake Pray, sitting beside me in the dark early-morning during a sit-in protest in front of the White House. A rope was wrapped around his left hand. He looked very young— the exact image of the twenty-five-year-old I'd seen in all the pictures. Still, I tried to rationalize it as an uncanny coincidence, a kid who happened to look just like him.

"Aren't you cold?" I asked, when I saw his short-sleeved T-shirt. He smiled and shook his head. The cold obviously didn't bother him. That's when I knew he was a ghost: it was at least twenty degrees that morning.

All these questions bubbled inside of me, but I was so nervous I didn't know if I could get them out. "Do you think we'll be able to stop this escalation with China?" I finally asked.

He looked very sad. Just then, a friend tapped me on my shoulder. I glanced away for just a second, but when I turned back, he was gone.

Would it surprise you to learn that I attended that sit-in on March 15? And, yes, India sent the first cruise missiles into Nanjing two days later.

Warp & Weft Message Boards
Topic: Jake Pray was MURDERED and gov't is COVERING it up!
Username: FightAllPwr4
Date: April 2, 2017 – 3:34 EST

Rose_Granny is a government dupe. She says "there were no signs of violence," but how can we trust the coroner's report when it was commissioned by the same government that first marked Pray for assassination?! That's like trusting the tobacco industry to give an accurate autopsy to the Marlboro man! Billy Davis, who was THERE, said the arresting officer called him a "fucking raghead" and "commie" and that he was a "mass murderer" who "flew the planes into the Twin Towers." This jerk couldn't wait to get his hands on Jake. Just consider a few things:

Why is the coroner report dated APRIL 1?! A subtle hint, maybe, that all is not what it seems? APRIL 1, 2007, was a SUNDAY. Who publishes a coroner report on a SUNDAY? This is a fucking ten-year-old April Fools' joke, people!

He had a "spontaneous cardiac artery dissection" but he only had a 25-micron tear? How was that enough to kill him? Do you know how big 25 microns is? Half the width of a STRAND OF HAIR!

Where did this famous rope come from? Violet Omura, a respected physicist, was his lover at the time.

She visited him a few hours before he was discovered dead. She says he seemed distressed by the racist cop's treatment but showed no signs of chest pain or anything that could lead to his "spontaneous" death! Significantly, *she saw no rope anywhere in the cell!* Where did it come from? The forgotten remains of a top-secret government "alternative interrogation" technique, imported from our gulags in Guantanamo, Stare Kjekuty, and Iraq?

Jake Pray was tortured to death by our own government. Maybe the reason he's haunting us, Rose_Granny, is because he wants the truth to come out!

JakePrayTruth.org

Warp & Weft Message Boards
Topic: Re: Jake Pray was MURDERED and gov't is COVERING it up!
Username: SweetGreenOnions
Date: April 2, 2017 – 3:45 EST

omura did it. evidence from "not a factor," the last song he ever wrote:

> The invisible hand blasts the cradle
> Spreading peace by throwing bombs
> We feast beneath the master's table
> Sating growls with salvaged crumbs
> Save the world? It's just a song

she told jake to provoke a fight with those officers.

the NSA <>paid</i> her to be the yoko ono of the antiwar left.

Excerpt from *Real Ghosts: The Warp & Weft Guide to Specters and Revenants of the 21st Century* by Dede Star Flower (New York: HarperPenguin, 2018)

The accuracy of his revenant predictions is quite remarkable. Two days after the New York Medical Examiner saw Pray's ghost in her office building, the Iranians kidnapped fifteen UK soldiers. In 2009, a cocktail waitress sighted Pray in an alley, and that very night the United States dropped the first round of tactical nuclear weapons on Iran. In 2011, Amina Owens was marking the anniversary of John Lennon's death in Central Park when she saw Pray's ghost. The next day the Chinese government shipped one thousand support troops to the Iranian front. The list goes on: thirteen activists see Pray at an antiglobalization rally in Sweden; the next day India tests a nuclear bomb and the cease-fire ends in Kashmir. When San Francisco representative Linda Xiaobo reported seeing Pray during a ceremony in the Mojave desert, we all knew that the talks to bring India into NATO were a certainty. Sure enough, a few days later, the United States honored its obligations under the treaty and declared itself officially at war with China and Pakistan.

As a revenant, Jake cannot stop these horrors from occurring, but he can stand witness to them. He can accuse us, like Hamlet's father, of not doing enough.

Written Communication from Zacharias Tibbs, Topeka, Kansas
To: Violet Omura, NYU, Department of Applied Physics
Date: November 18, 2020 – 10:44 pm, EST

[**Sender:** Verified]

Professor Omura:

Perhaps you have wondered why I have not yet responded to your Communication which you sent to me this past April. In fact it is because I have UNDER-TAKEN to follow your kind & SAGE ADVICE and read those very ERUDITE & SCHOLARLY works by the great Einstein, Feynman, & Chatterjee. I found the latter's work on M-THEORY and the QUANTUM GRAVITY SYNTHESIS most Fascinating, though I must confess that I found a great deal of it Difficult, and indeed, sometimes quite IMPOSSIBLE to understand. GOD, it is clear, has GIFTED her with a great mind. As did HE to YOU.

It's strange, I thought upon my completion of these works, how very CLEAR my errors in the past are to me now. Though I maintain my belief in REV-ENANTS & the HOLY SPIRIT, it is clear that my EQUATIONS & THEORIES, which I had thought could explain the WORLD, were not worth a Greasy Rag. I see the DEPTH of THOUGHT of those PHYSICISTS exploring the universe, and I feel a small INCHWORM in comparison. I must thank you for your most UNUSUAL & FAITHFUL correspondence over the years. Without it I fear I would never have understood my Gross Errors.

I have also Considered your Strange words to me regarding your SAD & PAINFUL feelings of guilt & regret over some mysterious Life Event. I say to you that your grief GRIEVES ME, for I know that you, too, could find solace in the LORD, if only you would open your heart to HIM. You say you Cannot, because "a scientist does not work from faith, but evidence." This is a Worthy Philosophy, but I say that because I KNOW GOD EXISTS, the EVIDENCE for him will someday be FOUND. Cannot you SEE His HAND in Chatterjee's Equations?

Can you not SEE that the reason your friend Jake still WALKS AMONG US is because he is a Revenant on Earth?

I await your Response with great Eagerness & Anticipation.

Zach Tibbs

Excerpt from "Changing the Score: My Life with Jake Pray"
Vanity Fair, May 2025
by Violet Omura

Before I say anything else, before I tell my story, or what little I'm privileged to know of Jake's, let me make this perfectly clear:

I loved Jake Pray. For a certain period of time he, and the anti-war movement, were my entire life. When he died, that life fell apart so completely that for the first and only time I considered suicide. In some ways, on some nights, that pain has never left me. I could never have harmed Jake. Those who suggest otherwise reveal a lack of understanding about our relationship so profound I can only pity them. To those whose critical faculties have not been addled by baseless conspiracy-mongering, I offer my story.

I first saw him at the West End, in December 2003. I was a senior at Columbia, a physics major so obsessed with quantum mechanical particle interactions and Feynman diagrams that I had only dimly registered our country's illegal invasion of a sovereign state. (Such ignorance was possible, then; over a certain income level, foreign wars didn't touch your daily life.) I gleaned my news from articles my sister sent me, or my suitemates' over-heard conversations. I felt the appropriate outrage and promptly forgot about it. What, after all, does outrage look like at the Planck scale?

Later, while drunk, I would amend that rhetorical question: what does it *sound* like? The bar was packed that night. Some were the typical Friday-night crowd of loud freshmen and bored frat brothers, but others had heard Jake at the big rally in February and were excited to see him again. He didn't even perform "What We

Sing," the song that was already turning into an anthem. It didn't matter. Jake had a voice that stuck you to your chair and forced you to listen. Almost gentle, with an ironic bite. "Like fresh ginger," a simile-inclined local reviewer once called it (and Jake and I laughed until we had to stop to breathe; we ate in Chinatown that night, and he bought me ginger beer). His falsetto was eerie; his bass rough. Sometimes his vibrato wavered so wildly you thought he might lose the note, but he never did. His lyrics were passionate and only sometimes political. He had thick, wavy brown hair; a high forehead; wide eyes with camel's lashes; and a chin that dimpled when he smiled. He was young, talented, and beautiful. I was twenty-two, and I felt as though I'd just crawled from Plato's cave.

I introduced myself after the set. He bought me a drink. We talked, I don't remember about what. For all I know I babbled about brane theory and quantum gravity all night. I had never been very good at talking to people. But he didn't seem to mind me. He told me a little about himself. He had graduated from NYU that year as a film major, but he didn't want to make movies. And the usual: he was appalled by the Iraq War, President Bush, our foreign policies. He quoted Chomsky, which was familiar, and Said, which surprised me. He said he had met Edward Said as a child, when his parents had first moved to the States from Palestine. I asked him if he was Muslim; he said he was a "closet atheist." He asked me if I was religious; I said I was a physicist.

He took me back to my dorm that night; my philosophy of alcohol consumption at the time did not include moderation. He kissed me as he pressed the call button for the elevator, as though I might not notice if he were doing something else.

"Do I get your number?" he asked.

What odd syntax, I thought, many years later. Like it was a game show and my number was the all-expense-paid trip to the Bahamas.

My good friend Billy Davis, who died last year, spent his life advocating for a full inquiry into Jake's death. I find it ironic that even now, in the midst of our global war with China and Iran, the relatively insignificant Iraq War has so much cultural relevance. Perhaps because it is the first moment when our generation, collectively, began to realize that something had gone terribly wrong in our political and social system. Jake's death symbolized too much of that moment for us to ever let it go.

They took us to Pier 57, that detention-center-turned-toxic-waste-dump where they liked to herd activists during overcrowded demonstrations. Jake was furious that day, on a manic high. He was no stranger to racism—was any Arab living in New York City after 9-11?—but the arresting officer that day reveled in a particularly nasty brand of invective. "Raghead" was the least of it (and if Jimmy Sullivan can even tell the difference between his mouth and his lower orifice, I've yet to see the evidence). After they arrested us, Jake could hardly sit still. The floor was covered in an unidentifiable sludge that slid beneath our shoes and smelled like decomposing tires. We were all chilly and desperate to get out. Jake went to ask the officers when they would release us. I never heard what they said to him, and I never got to ask. Jake started yelling and shouting. His hands trembled as he gesticulated, like a junkie coming off a high, though I knew that he hadn't had more than half a joint. I remember being terrified, afraid that they would shoot him. When they set off the taser, he dropped to the floor like a marionette loosed of its strings. He groaned, but he couldn't even seem to speak. The police officers laughed, I remember.

What did he yell? "Pigs," certainly. But Jake hated few things more than he hated the ongoing Palestinian/Israeli conflict, and he would have *never* used the despicable anti-Semitic tripe certain opportunistic faux-rock musicians attribute to him. We had been unlawfully detained and verbally abused. Did Jake's behavior represent a failure to turn the other cheek? Of course. But he never meant to be a martyr.

I went to the Tombs late that night, after they released us from the Pier and arrested him. His lawyer said the police insisted on detaining him for questioning and were charging him with "disorderly conduct." Jake was happy to see me. The police had confiscated his guitar, and one of the officers conducting the interrogation was a real (to put it more genteelly than Jake) ignorant racist. I asked Jake if he was okay. He said he was, but he couldn't wait to get out of there. There was no rope in the cell that I can recall.

He was acting a little more restless than normal. Tapping his fingers against the bars and rocking back on his heels like a drinker with the DTs. It didn't seem remarkable at the time, and it might be that I am merely creating false positives, searching for a clue where none exists.

He held my hand before I left and kissed my palm. He liked romantic gestures.

"There's something happening here," he sang softly. Buffalo Springfield.

I kissed him. "I'll get Neil Young and the gang down here tomorrow."

"I'll see you, Angel."

It was the last thing he ever said to me.

But he had never called me "Angel" before.

Written Communication from Violet Omura, NYU, Department of Applied Physics
To: Zacharias Tibbs; Topeka, Kansas
Date: December 25, 2025 – 1:05 am, EST

[**Sender:** Verified]

I woke up twenty minutes ago and couldn't fall asleep. Chatterjee has posted a new paper on the public archives. Did you see it?

It's been a while. Hope you're doing okay.

Merry (godless) Christmas, Zach.

Written Communication from Zacharias Tibbs, Topeka, Kansas
To: Violet Omura, General Communications Inbox, Columbia University Physics Department
Date: March 18, 2027 – 6:01 pm, EST

[Hi! This message has been approved by your filters, but contains some questionable material. Would you like to proceed?]

[Okay! Message below.]

Professor Omura:

Though I know you have not heard from me these past two years, I hope you do remember our long correspondence and will still read my messages despite your new Tenured Position at the venerable Columbia University.

I have not Written due to increased Problems with my Health and also, perhaps more importantly, a crisis with my Faith. You might think that facing Death & the Great Beyond, as I am (a persistent Cancer, which no medicine can treat) would drive one in to the Bosom of their Lord, but I find myself instead Contemplating the letters you have sent me over the twelve years of our correspondence.

You have presented to me a mind steeped in rationality, who does not even let deep grief over personal loss sway her to the side of a comfort that she does not feel has a basis in reason. Is Faith a Good Thing? I ask myself. As a child, I loved mathematics. At the library, I read books about Pythagoras and Newton and Einstein. But in the end I preferred Money to Knowledge, as any Ignorant eighteen-year-old might. I passed over my chance at College. My Father got me a good job as an auto mechanic in his Cousin's shop. Last year, I retired. I had worked there for Sixty-Five Years. I had kept my Faith and raised children. I had read the Bible and tried to use Math to Prove the Beauty of it.

I have wondered why I still Wrote to you, Professor, when you so Clearly held my Views in Disdain. I think now that I Respected the Knowledge you held. The Mathematics that I had loved in Childhood are your Life's Work. I thought if I could Convince you of the Truth of my Faith then it would not be Faith any longer but Reason.

And now, I think I have failed. I face death without the solace of Christ and I think it is not as Hard as I imagined in my youth, but hard enough.

With My Thanks and Respect,

Zacharias Tibbs

Written Communication from Violet Omura; Brooklyn, New York
To: Zacharias Tibbs, Topeka, Kansas
Date: March 19, 2027 — 3:20 am, EST

Zach,

Call me Violet. Would you like to meet for lunch some-time soon? I know of a great fondue place on Flatbush Avenue (that's in Brooklyn, where I live).

Violet

Audio-Visual Transcript of U.S. Internal Investigations files Originally archived on the diffuse-network, proprietary Global-Net, intercepted and transcribed by Chinese Intelligence
Subject: Omura, Violet; U.S. Scientific Authority and Academic;
Status: Dissident
Date: September 12, 2027 – 2:22 am, EST

The subject's apartment is dark. She walks to the window over-looking the street. She removes her shoes and stockings (a run in the back: 4.2 cm). The subject's hair is styled in an elaborate bun. She removes several bobby pins and tosses them to the floor. The subject empties a small, gold purse onto her coffee table.

Contents:
One (1) funeral program. The cover reads: *Zacharias Tibbs: He was Right with Our Lord*
One (1) small rolled marijuana cigarette.

The subject lights the cigarette with a match. Upon completing half the joint, she extinguishes it on the windowsill.

OMURA: [*Soft laughter*]
OMURA: [*Inaudible*]

The subject turns from the window. She abruptly ceases almost all movement. Her breathing resumes after 2.4 seconds. It is at this point that the subject begins to behave very erratically. Her eyes are fixed at a point in the room, as though she is interacting with a person, though motion sensors and audio bots indicate she is alone. The subject has no known history of mental illness. [NOTE: However, our own psychiatrist has stated that her behavior here strongly indicates a psychotic break possibly triggered by the marijuana usage. Hearing voices is common in such incidences.]

OMURA: What . . . Jesus Christ. Jesus Fucking Christ, what's going on?

The subject pauses. Her body relaxes and her head movements are consistent with someone listening to someone else in conversation.

OMURA: Jake? Holy fuck, what was in that pot?

The subject takes two steps forward. [NOTE: The consulting psychiatrist has determined that the person to whom she believes she is addressing herself is standing between the coffee table and her couch.]

OMURA: What do ghosts look like at the Planck scale . . .

20-second pause.

OMURA: Zack did this?

3-second pause. She shakes her head.

OMURA: Maybe. Yes. In a strange way. He could have changed the world. But he fixed other people's cars.

The subject begins to cry. Her hands have a pronounced tremble.

OMURA: Jake, oh fuck. Fucking God, why are you . . . why now? I never believed, not once, and fuck do you know how much I wanted to? I could kill you! Christ, Jake, 30 nanograms of *pot* and not a fucking drop of lithium!

12-second pause. A siren is heard in the background.

OMURA: I knew that. You think it makes me feel better? I should have known! The DTs, I said. Like you were manic. I saw it all then. I've known it all for years. 30 nanograms of pot, 2 milligrams of Tylenol. 0 nanograms of your fucking life.

The subject steps closer.

OMURA: Then why did you? Oh, you came back from the grave for me? God, my maudlin subconscious.

11-second pause.

OMURA: Like Hamlet's father? Did the ghost love?

2-second pause.

OMURA: Like me. Jake . . . if you're real and not my own degenerating brain . . . I'm sorry I asked you taunt—no, listen, I should have known what you were going through. I shouldn't have put you in that position. Not with those trigger-happy assholes. Engineer a conflict? Get it on the news? What a fucking cunt I was.

The subject is silent for nearly one minute and thirty seconds (1:30). Halfway through this period, she closes her eyes and shudders. [NOTE: From the heat patterns in her body, it appears as though she is having a sexual reaction.]

OMURA: The last thing you said to me, what did it mean? Why did you call me Angel?

The subject opens her eyes and looks around. Apparently, the room now appears empty to her. She staggers backward and sits on the couch. After a minute (1:00) she begins to cry with audible sobs.

OMURA: I don't know either.

Associated Press
War Desk: For Immediate Release

September 14, 2027 (SEOUL): Accounts of Chinese warships equipped with long-range nuclear warheads heading into the Hawaiian archipelago have been confirmed, and evacuations of major targets on the United States West Coast will begin within the hour.

A Song to Greet the Sun

Will her brothers mourn
the loss of their jeweled seed?
Her mother has baked all night
dead silent in the kitchen.
The ashes are bitter as cacaotl grounds
But give no liminal visions.
Sunrise: the bread is dense, each slab gray as evening moss.
The father will not eat his slice—
It's salted with his tears.

He used the natleoc, the stick of thorns covered in dust and spores above his doorway, for that was what the priests pre-scribed, and he would have this done as the gods demanded. She did not cry when the sharp points broke her skin, and so he hit her a second time. They both stared at the blood coursing down her arm and breast, astonished and a little afraid at the beauty of the forbidden liquid.

"Father?" she said, just like that. Mild and trusting, and he recalled when she had been younger, a child, not the disobedi-ent strumpet before him, and a red cormorant had stolen the choicest wood-ear from her basket.

"Father?" she had said, and he'd given her two of his own, and she'd smiled.

As she'd smiled for that barbarian? That bare-chested druze?

The sun god shalt not suffer a disobedient daughter to live. And his priests shalt not suffer her father to receive the twelfth district tax appointment, the one for which he had slaved these more than twenty years, without extreme repentance.

"Father?" she said again, as the blood dripped onto his floor, marking his house with his spilled honor. Condemning her to death. There had been spores on the natleoc, more than enough to poison her blood, even without the miasma of river air. But she didn't seem to understand.

He must finish it. They said he must, to reclaim his family's honor.

But he could not speak. So he hit her again, across her cheek. The thorns bit deep, and this time she did cry out. She stumbled to her knees.

"Is this about Colqi?"

The whole district already knew. He was a laughingstock. His friend Ollin, the twelfth district constable, had told him of his daughter's disobedience and recommended he see the priests. "Your daughter has been seen by the river, holding hands with a druze. The one who plays reeds in the cacaotl house."

And the priests had given him a feather, yellow for vengeance, and told him to break her skin. He would dye it red with her blood and bring the proof back to them, and by such measures would his shame be expiated.

He killed her then, closed his eyes to the sight of her blood, his ears to the sound of her sharp breaths.

"Father," she said, "you have killed me."
So he shattered her jaw and she could not speak.
So he crushed her windpipe and she could not weep.

And in her lips, he put a wizened wood-ear, because he remembered she had loved them, and went off to fetch his wife. His sons were good boys; they had held back their mother long enough.

ii.

His legs are long, lithe with unearned grace
His fingers dance like caterpillar legs
Over the reeds of his pipes
He hides from the sun
But the river hears—it loves him as she does.
She, the sun's daughter, by conquering fathers forbidden
To keep her heart in the basket of his reeds—
Fragile beneath the one-eyed god's stare.

Constable Ollin is out traveling. So the girls whisper and laugh at Number 12, the cacaotl house where he and the other petty bureaucrats of the twelfth district like to partake in the evening. Kava regards him with mild curiosity between her sets. It's not like the dour constable to order such fine mushroom grounds in his cacaotl—he is known to enjoy less stupefying brews.

She's dressed in little but her cochineal hair and clacking castanets. When she dances, Ollin stares along with the rest, but who knows what music he sees, or what rainbows he hears.

"Her hair sounds just like morning," Ollin says, late in the night. Another patron, deep into Number 12's legendary Quetzal brew, nods in complete understanding.

The rumor of what happened to that girl, that daughter of the crabbed tax collector Mazatlin, spreads through the tavern like the bitter resin of grounds steeped overlong in a brew. She hadn't been very pretty, Kava remembers, but she had a smile that could coax the sun to love the moon.

An honor killing? That little man? That beautiful smile? "Old Miq had better retire soon, else Mazatlin might honor kill him too!" one passably bold wit offers, but the constable merely nods his head to unseen music. The others laugh nervously. Old Miq, the twelfth district comptroller whose job Mazatlin so violently desires, has been known to deny favors to those with indiscreet tongues.

Halfway through the night, the piper Colqi seems to choke on his reeds. He's druze, but it's a lax crowd at Number 12, more concerned with the potency of the brew and the tapestry of the music than the fickleness of imperial policy. That's just their day job. Still, the jeers as he stumbles off the stage have a cruel aftertaste, a privileged savor.

"Your mother teach you to suck like that?"

"What can you expect? Bunch of lazy monkeys."

"Leave him be!" shouts Kava, and they all do. Cochineal hair commands respect.

The music resumes, absent silent pipes. The druze goes traveling, hunkered down in the shadows like a wood-ear on the underside of a rotting log.

"From the muddy banks of the Nanacoal," says the constable, a vague quotation, involuntarily uttered.

The druze has heard. "*I have gathered the reeds,*" he says, finishing the line.

The constable: "*I wove them tightly enough for a desiccated heart.*"

And, oh, the druze's voice is suddenly like that of his reeds, dark as silt, turbulent as the river:

> "*Not yet have I found you.*
> *And I am left with this basket of the river's weeds*
> *Filled only with my longing*
> *And the one-eyed god's flesh.*"

The constable begins to weep. Everyone sees, but no one makes much of it. He's traveling, after all.

"I saw you smiling by the river," the constable says. "You touched her arm. That smile could greet the sun!"

"That's not how it goes," giggles one of the other girls as she comes up behind him. "Don't you know your Ilticloc? Maybe someone should refresh your memory."

The constable follows her lead, stumbles up the stairs.

The druze travels alone.

iii.

> *The reeds are a safe place to hide a heart*
> *Says Ilticloc, and who are we to argue?*
> *Where can the moon and sun love, but in the shadows?*
> *But she steps beyond their fall*
> *To the one-eyed god's embrace—fierce and fleeting.*
> *My love, says the moon's son*
> *Caterpillar fingers dancing along her breast.*
> *Stay by my side, and we will always sing the brightest colors.*

My love, says the sun's ward
Her smile a tongue of its flame.
I would put the pomegranate seed between your lips,
I would strike my shells to the beat of your heart,
Were my will my own.
Sweeter than any jeweled seed, that kiss
Emboldened by her fickle sun.

High above the riverbank, the constable—
Who has longed for her symphony these many years—
Sees all.

We loved her, never let them say otherwise, in all the ways brothers can love a sister. Every summer, at high sun, she would spend all night gathering wood-ears and glow tongues to weave into wreaths. The best in the district, and she made them for both of us, so the girls would look as we walked along the river, and wonder if we might ask their fathers for permission.

To our mother, she gave the best of all, with the reds of wild soma and the blues of poison nightshade. At night, mother would glow like the empress, and our father was proud.

We loved our little sister, you see, but our father is our family's sun, his word a surrogate for the god's, and she had defied him. We had no choice; there will be war at the end of the rains, and we will make our names in it, so long as we may bear our father's sign and his grace.

Our mother did not understand. We held her arms as she wept and cursed, and though we spoke to cover the sound, we all heard our sister's cries, blue as the poison nightshade she'd once wreathed around our mother's neck.

"Do you remember, mother," we said, "when our sister was ten and father lost her in the streets by the palace? How we all looked for hours, calling her name, peering inside every door? And do you remember that night, after the moon had risen and ascended its heights, a woman leaves the palace by a side gate. Her hair is silver with blight, her eyes reflective as a cat's. And she is holding our sister's hand, and they are talking like the moon to the stars? The woman was princess Xura, mother, do you remember? Before the emperor banished her to that convent."

"Yes," our mother said, when we had thought fury sealed her lips. " 'She's a bold one,' the princess told me. 'I pray the sun won't burn her.' And now I sting at the reproach in her eyes that day, the sorrow of the blight and of each year's first morning."

Our mother fell silent, and in that moment we all three realized the house was still. An ominous absence, colored gray as slate after the rains.

Below us, no one cried. Then our father's footsteps, heavy on the stairs.

"It's done," our mother said, and held us so we could weep.

iv.

> If the sun cannot mourn, the moon will.
> If the moon cannot mourn, the earth will.
> If the earth cannot mourn, may the river?
> And if not the river, at least the hollow reeds
> Whistling along its banks.
> Leave him be, the one who whispers hoarsely there.

You have forsaken his joy,
You have buried his heart in the river's clay.
What is left to him now but the memory of a song
The sweet red seed never tasted?

The years had twisted my husband, my Mazatlin, the way an oak tree will grow gnarled and hard around the persistent flowering of honey mushrooms. But I had always thought of his heart, like that of the oak, as strong and unblemished. I had not thought the rotting threads reached so deep. Now, I recall the heartsblood, the dreaded spore that shoots its threads through our veins, reaching blindly and steadily for the heart. And when it arrives, it takes root. It grips like a choke vine and when it grows, it blooms.

A fortnight, a death's face, the saying goes. And I have never seen the heartsblood bloom, but he had. He told me the misshapen floret of that deadly mushroom does resemble a face, never revealed until the host's life has fled. It bursts through the chest wall at the very end—a stranger's face to bring you to death.

He had seen his uncle die like that, when he was a child. He understood why the gods enjoined us to never break the skin, to never profane our hearths with blood.

And yet he sliced her with the natleoc, he made her bleed before he killed her. The priests told him to, he said, as though I should congratulate him for his careful adherence to their instructions.

I told him I was leaving.

He had not stopped weeping since the moment her cries finally ceased, but he did then, his face frozen with shock.

"You too?" he said, as though our daughter had *wanted* to have her blood spilled, her throat crushed.

I saw our wedding in his eyes, heard the singers' twining harmonies as we walked through the streets. I saw the nun break the pomegranate, scattering its seeds.

"*I put the jeweled seeds between your lips,*" my love had said, because he was no fool or illiterate, ignorant of his Ilticloc.

"*Oh, to be the ruby in your lips,*" I said. "*The longing and the light on your tongue.*"

And so we had kissed, and if the seeds that day were bitter, I did not notice. I named my daughter for them.

"Where can you go, woman?" my husband asked, arm raised as though he would strike me, too. "Who would take in a disobedient wife?"

"The lady Xura," I said, for I remembered the story my sons had told me and held it like one of my daughter's wreaths.

"You will shame me. We could have so much, soon."

I shook my head. "They will never give you that post, Mazatlin. It was always meant for Ollin."

The lady Xura has welcomed me, and lets me share in her cacaotl. Each time, I pray for visions of my daughter, but I see nothing but heartsblood, a man rotting from within.

v.

> The nochtli cactus-pear is orange for a princess
> And white for the gods.
> Merchants hawk their fruit like jewels, this Liminal Night.
> But the girl who walks alone has no care for her belly.

Ayamotli lingers like pepper on her tongue.
What sound is that, what skillful notes
Draw her closer to the shadows?
It is the druze, laughing with his kind,
Feasting on Liminal visions, and each bite a song.
Her questions float between them—

After all,
They are traveling together.

The first time she finds you, it's the Night of Liminal Dream-ing, at the start of carnival. You have never met her before, and she is asking for a song.

"Sweet and sticky and rich, like a pear tart with curds and honey," she says, and because it's the first night, you understand. A few hours ago you too drank the ayamotli, the nectar of the gods, and in a few hours you too will be traveling.

You lift the reeds to your lips, and they are as familiar to you as your fingers and your breath. You play as she asks, a song of your people and of your childhood. *"How far the sun?"* cries the flute. *"Near as your heart, far as your love's."* She doesn't know the tune, but she smiles, for it goes down sweet and sad, just like she wanted.

She is alone this first night, or has slipped away from a parental gaze occluded by visions of gauzy heavens, of powers only annually accessible.

And because it's a Liminal Night, because the ayamotli has turned words to colors, smells to symphonies, songs to braided carpet, you ask her to go traveling with you. You know you shouldn't, that hands so soft and hair so dark could only belong to one of them. *They* have taken your people's land, outlawed your customs, sacrificed your children to their flaming god. They have shunned and exploited you, and they may kill you if they see you corrupting one of their daughters with your song.

But it is carnival, with more powers abroad than even this insatiable empire can constrain. You look at her clear, enchanted eyes—they are like the river, and she floats upon it. Concentrate, and so can you. You touch her hands and you both hover a few impossible inches above the mud brick pavement.

"Will you write a song for me?" she asks. "For the carnival and the river and the forbidden streets where your people live?"

"Now?" you say, startled.

She won't meet your eyes. "I cannot stay long from my family. But songs remember where they were born—even on my side of the river."

Just like one of them, to demand something so precious and pretend to have some right to it. Your fury boils the air around you yellow and green. This means nothing to her. You're the ball in her game; the carnival is her field.

Her sandals smack the pavement. She's lost the ayamotli's grip. "You hate me," she says.

"No." And it hovers somewhere near the truth.

You imagine everything this girl represents, every wrong her people have committed against yours, every barbed boundary between your world and hers.

"What's your name?" you ask.

She tells you as you both float away.

———

vi.

Only the mother wears mourning red.
Within convent walls, she does not see
The father, passed over and lonely
Finding no solace among the colors of the earth.
The brothers have gone to war—
One wears his sister's token against his breast
One will die on the sun god's mountain.
The druze has made a new song:
Yellow, for anger
Blue, for memory
Black, for oblivion.
On the banks of the Nanacoal,
A boar has trampled the reeds.

Father! His beauty is deeper than the sky! He sings, and he will weave a song for me when we marry. His eyes are so light, his hair so sleek. And we have flown through the city, over merchants' courtyards and temple pyramids. We have slept with our heads pillowed on the waves, we have sunk to the bottom of the ocean and seen great volcanoes on the edge of a monstrous lake. We have sat by the river and stared at the sun and I have understood every song ever written.

Oh, Father! May you bless me, for I am his.

Far and Deep

Her mother had never cried, but always closed her eyes when she laughed. Only in death did Pineki seem to weep, her cheeks wet from the ocean. Her eyes joyously closed.

The killer had left Pineki belly-down in the sand. A mottled crab scuttled from the cavity in the back of her head, imperfectly obscured by clumps of dark, bloody hair. Its tiny claw held a gobbet of red flesh.

Just a normal sunrise. Just the normal tides. Just the normal crabs. Leilani's mother was dead. As a pure, rational fact, it was easy enough for her to accept. Pineki's infuriating, unheeding, raw, wild spirit—she swam too far not to be caught in someone's net. Everyone would tell her they'd seen it coming.

Imagining these conversations, Leilani pinched her eyebrows together. She wagged her tongue in the wet, salty early-morning air. She would have to be understanding; she would have to see their sympathy in the context of her mother's life. They would feel bad for Leilani, but they would not keep the smugness from their voices, their unassailable conviction that whoever had smashed in her mother's skull and left her for the crabs and the tides and the beach had righted an imbalance in their world.

Pineki's lips were a lurid purple-red and so full it seemed she had plumped them with straw. They grazed the sand like she was teasing it, like it was the luckiest sand in the world: kissed by a woman still alluring even in death.

"Lei . . . I'm so sorry."

Okilani was not apologizing for her mother's death.

"Not even a diver's funeral?" Leilani had not anticipated this.

"We can't. She hadn't dived in years."

"She did it every day!"

The wind blew back Okilani's graying hair, rattled her mandagah-jewel necklace. "Not with the others, Lei."

Leilani bit her bottom lip, but stopped before she drew blood. She would not throw one of her mother's fits. She would not. "Is that all that matters?" she asked, her tone combative, her posture submissive.

Okilani gestured with her head to the group of elders still seated ceremoniously in the great kukui grove. The five stared straight ahead, but Leilani knew where their attention was riveted.

Okilani did too. "To them," she said. Loudly.

Leilani looked past the one she still loved, to the others she now despised. Leva'ula, the head elder, met her gaze with the same gentle smile she always wore. Leilani had always thought her expression an indication of deep piety, of a mind focused on other, higher matters. Leva'ula gripped her knobbed kukui-wood walking stick like a scepter, she wore her red mandagah jewel like a proclamation. She had been an elder for as long as Leilani had been alive, and Leilani couldn't help but feel a little awe in her presence.

Six elders. Pineki had been the seventh, before the council declared her unworthy, a vow-breaker. Pineki had laughed at the idea of chastity, and now they refused to even burn her body in the grove.

"Whoever did it," Leilani said, "they took her jewel." A shimmering, mesmerizing drop of palest orange, given to Pineki unexpectedly three years ago by a dying mandagah fish. The elders had reluctantly taken this wayward child, older than anyone marked in recent memory, into their collective bosom. And then, one year later, they spat her out again. Pineki had never been to everyone's taste.

Uku, the only male elder and the youngest of the six, stood. "Your mother lost her right to the sacred gift. Hopefully the new owner will make better use of it."

He seemed furious. Leilani stared at him, confused. He had a body like a kukui tree—dark and lean and chiseled as only years of the tides and fishermen's nets could make you. The younger divers would joke about how it was a shame that such a specimen had as much interest in them as the great grove itself. And Pineki would always laugh—eyes shut and so delighted it hurt to watch.

Uku grew more infuriated by Leilani's silence. He took a step toward them. Okilani threw him a sharp look, and he paused. "Lei," she said, a little desperately. "We don't want—"

"Enough." Leilani left the grove.

The body began to stink, and so she rubbed her mother with salt while she waited for the sunset. She did not touch the head, where strange red and pink bruises had begun to tinge the tip of her mother's nose and right cheek. Her skin had turned a sickening almost-gray beneath the deep nut brown that had always been Pineki's joy. Even without the gaping hole in the back of her head, smashed like the egg of a moa, she looked to Leilani like a carcass, a dead body as far from life as a grouper on a stick.

Pineki's leibo were dry now, but they had been wet this morning. At least her murderer had allowed that one concession, a final dive. Leilani looked in the deep pockets of the bone-white diving pants and found three jewels. All were beautiful specimens; Pineki had a knack for only seeking out the healthiest mandagah for their jewels.

The flies came when the sun had just passed its zenith and even the salt could not retard the smell. Leilani peeled off her shirt and swatted at them viciously until her arms burned and she nearly fainted from exertion.

She could hear her mother's laugh. "So much effort. So little result."

Leilani stared at the corpse. "This would never have happened if you had just done as they said!"

But her mother's sweet, mildly mocking delight still echoed in her head, and she sat still. The flies began to feast on the brain. They stayed away from her mother's eyes.

Leilani did not know why she awoke so early this morning, why she had known something was wrong. They lived together, despite everything. Pineki even occasionally spent her nights at home. Yesterday Pineki had given her a pineapple the size of her torso, a fruit so massive that she had been forced to roll it up the stairs like a giant log.

"What is this?" Leilani had asked, when her mother presented it with an air of most uncharacteristic solemnity.

"You used to love them when you were a baby. You would chew my fingers to get at the juice."

"Oh, Piki," she said, using the nickname that could so clearly express simultaneous affection and annoyance, "we left that a long time ago."

Her mother had smiled at her, but so sadly that Leilani nearly burst into tears. Her mother never cried. Her joy seemed to guard against that kind of abject expression, or perhaps even made it redundant. Leilani *almost* never cried, and sometimes the effort to resist was so great it felt like every tearless moment was one bargained for in blood.

Pineki left without another word. Leilani, busy in contemplation of the monstrous fruit, did not even watch her go.

Kapa found her, shaking and dry-eyed.

"I heard," he said, standing back diffidently. Pineki had always intimidated him. Death, as Leilani was discovering, changed little.

Or everything. "It must be all over the island by now." Her voice was very calm. "You're the only one who came."

Kapa looked at the rotting body, the cloud of flies. "We heard the elders refused . . . I think the others are just worried. They'll come."

"Of course." Less than a day ago, Pineki had rolled a giant pineapple up the stairs. Less than a day, and it would stretch until the end of her life.

"Leilani," he said, a little helplessly. He still hadn't touched her. He hadn't even moved close enough for her to smell the fishy scent that always seeped into his clothes after a day's labor.

Alaya Dawn Johnson

Kapa's parents had died years before, drowned on a boat in a storm. He had survived by clinging to a plank of wood. He was a terrible fisherman, but he knew his way around a lute. They had met right after his parents died. Pineki introduced them ("Make this poor child feel better!" she had said, and so commanded, Leilani tried her best).

Kapa began to cry. "Who would do this to her?"

Leilani envied him the ease of his release even as she despised him for it.

"Who wouldn't?" She began to take a deep breath and then thought better of it when the stench from her mother's corpse nearly overwhelmed her. "Who was she sleeping with?"

Kapa looked shocked. "I . . . how would I know?" Recent years had stripped most of the childlike fleshiness from his face. Leilani noted, in dispassionate surprise, that her childhood friend was almost handsome. Not such a paragon of beauty as Uku, but well enough. She wondered, for the first time, if other girls had noticed.

Kapa's questions had given her a goal, a question for which an answer could be sought. Someone had murdered her mother. Their identity had not seemed so very important this morning, but it was a reason to not sit beside her mother's rotting corpse in a stupor.

"What will you do with . . ." Kapa gestured awkwardly to the body.

"Burn her at sunset."

He looked shocked again. Leilani almost laughed. His sensibilities, as Pineki would say, were delicately guarded. "But the elders refused a funeral!"

"I'm burning her at sunset."

150

———

Kapa followed her to the hills in the center of the island, where the slopes and valleys were covered with small plots of land that produced almost all of their food. She rarely ventured here. The divers were a class above the common farmers, and the women of her family had been divers for centuries. She was proud of her legacy, though of course Pineki had viewed this attitude with amused tolerance. She was more inclined to think of the unbroken line of mothers and daughters as the product of "luck, and a knack for holding our breath."

Leilani only saw gentle slopes covered in rich black soil and the flowers of taro plants, but Kapa led her unhesitatingly through the fields and into the valley beyond. It occurred to her that his mother must have farmed, before she died. Perhaps he had spent his childhood in the fruit groves. The farmers—men and women with sunbaked skin and bare torsos glistening with sweat—stopped and stared as the she walked past. They did not whisper. That made it worse.

She rested underneath some orange trees, out of their immediate sight, and just a few feet away from the disappointingly normal pineapple plants. Where had her mother found the monster? Had she conjured it up from a bit of twine and spit, like in the tales? Had the spirits then taken their revenge for her presumption?

A man on the other side of the pineapple plants waved and began walking toward her. He was too far away to recognize.

"Lei," Kapa said, startling her. She had forgotten he was there.

151

In the distance, a pair of moas chortled their deep love song. The trees were heavy with ripe orange-green fruit—she could practically feel its sharp fragrance on her skin. Like the initial shiver of jumping into the morning ocean.

"I've been meaning to ask . . . I mean, I know how hard this must be . . . and now with the elders, and I just wanted you to know that I've always . . ." He paused and cleared his throat. Leilani glanced at him, but kept her gaze focused on the approaching figure. He looked more familiar as he came closer, even through the heat shimmer of late afternoon in the harvest season.

"I make a good income from the fish," he said quietly. "Maybe together—"

"Ukele!" Leilani exclaimed, when the man was close enough to see clearly. Uku's almost-as-handsome farmer brother was crying as he approached them.

"I just heard," he said, embracing her freely. Strange, she thought, and Kapa had yet to touch her. "My sorrow is too great for words."

She looked at him thoughtfully, remembering his brother's obvious hatred earlier this morning. The two were bound by blood, not temperament. And she, after all, should know something of that.

"Did she sleep with you?" she asked.

Kapa grimaced, but Ukele merely laughed and wiped his eyes. "Ah, there's some Pineki in you, then? Yes, I had that pleasure. Only twice, but yes."

Lucky Piki, Leilani surprised herself by thinking. But great Kai, those were two beautiful brothers. His hair was curly and cropped close to his head. His skin was darker than Uku's, which made the sand-brown of his irises stand out like man-dagah jewels.

"Leilani, I swear, if I find out who did this . . ."

She shook her head, and wondered if Ukele and Kapa were the only two people on the island who truly regretted her mother's murder. Pineki had lived to offend, to transgress, to break taboos and laugh at the pleasure. And now she had died for it.

"Ukele, this sounds strange, but yesterday she gave me a giant pineapple. Do you know——"

He put a hand over her lips to stop her question and looked around. Then he motioned silently for them to follow.

They left the shade of the oranges and walked into the full glare of the sun. She could feel the sweat dripping down the back of her neck and under her arms. The salt-smell of the ocean was faint here, overpowered by manure and soil. Already, her breath came out in shallow little bursts. All around her, anonymous figures hacked into the earth to harvest her food. In the distance, a woman raised her voice in an eerie, ululating chant.

If diving was a legacy, what was this?

At first glance, it looked like paradise. A land of the giants, where every seed planted grew vast and plentiful fruit. Deep within the still-unripe coconut groves and hidden by a few steep hills grew pineapples the size of her body, oranges larger than a coconut, plantains fit to feed a family of pygmy elephants, and a taro with a sprout so large she thought it would take five men to pluck the tuber from the earth. An earthworm poked its head out of the ground nearby. Its body was as thick as her handspan, and decorated with red-and-white bands as sharply defined as a layered rock.

"Great Kai," Kapa said reverently.

Leilani's heartbeat sounded like a drum in her ears. This was all so beautiful. And so unnatural. "Did Pineki . . ."

Ukele was crying again. "This was her gift," he said. "To our families."

Last year's harvest had been nearly destroyed by an early rainy season, she recalled. The farmers had, ironically, been the ones least able to afford the remaining food. Pineki had hardly eaten until the rains stopped, much to Leilani's annoyance. Recalling how she had snapped at her mother for what she saw as put-upon martyrdom, Leilani felt almost physically ill.

"Lei . . ."

There was a note in Kapa's voice that made her turn to him immediately. He was pointing to one of the massive coconut trees in the corner of the hidden patch. These, unlike the normal crops surrounding it, were fully ripe. Several of its fruits had been knocked from the branches and something heavy had smashed through both the outer and inner shells. In some cases, the coconuts looked as though they had shattered under the force of multiple blows.

There was nothing overtly disturbing about the scene, and yet the three of them were mute in momentary horror. There were visible dents in the base of the tree trunk where something almost unimaginably strong had struck it. A splatter of juice had dried to a shiny film on the fronds scattered among the fruit. Gobbets of white flesh hung by fibrous tendrils from the inner casing. This was rage and this was satisfaction.

At least no crabs stole the flesh, but she knew the flies would come for it soon. She had, she realized, past experience. Leilani knelt quietly among the carnage. She vomited.

"I'm burning her at sundown."

Quietly, steadily, she said this to everyone she passed. Kapa followed her like a lost moa chick, but she barely noticed his presence. She had two facts now. Two pieces of knowledge that she knew would lead her to an answer. She would force them to.

Fact number one: Someone had murdered her mother. Straightforward and unassailable. Just like when she had come upon the body, alone, this morning. There had been no moment of denial. No frantic calling of her mother's name and pleading for her to be alive. She had seen and she had known.

Fact number two: Her mother had been playing with the spirits, and someone didn't like it.

How else to explain the mythical fruit grove? Nothing could grow so large naturally. Pineki had been an elder, one of the select few who learn the mysteries of geas bindings and the wild earth spirit. And though they had stripped her of her rank after only a year, she was clever enough to learn what she could while she had the chance. The elders thought they had kicked her out, but perhaps Pineki had merely decided to leave.

"Where are you going?" Kapa asked, when they had left the farms.

"What else can a girl do before she burns her mother?"

Kapa just stared at her like he could speak from his pores. She shook her head. "I'm going diving."

"Before sundown? What about the day-eels?"

"You can tell Okilani."

She took off first her sweaty, dusty shirt and then her leibo. Naked, the sun fell on her back like a bonfire. The freshwater eddied around her feet. Kapa had gone, of course, terrified enough of the day-eels to take her advice.

She looked out at the water breaking over the shore, at the innocuously clear ocean surface and felt a shiver of something she had never properly experienced: the delight of anticipating terror. Is this what her mother had loved? Is this why she always sought to offend and to shock—for that frisson of pleasure in the very act of defiance? Leilani had always found her pleasure in tradition, in reason, in fulfilling expectations. When her mother had become an elder, it had never occurred to Leilani that she might not want it. That the strictures against marriage and sex would be as laughable to Pineki as ones against diving or breathing. She hadn't been a bad mother, precisely, but she certainly hadn't embraced the virtues of responsibility either. She would leave Leilani with friends for days at a time while she vanished on some adventure. She first took Leilani diving at age three—dangerously young, according to the elders. The respectable had condemned her for it, but those dives were Leilani's first memories. Their magic still made her breath catch.

Leilani had spent most of her life hating her mother. She had interpreted Pineki's carelessness as not caring, her multiple lovers as not loving.

She had thought a woman who didn't cry never wanted to.

She had not anticipated enigmatic gifts of massive pine-apples. She had not anticipated violent death.

Leilani noted the position of the sun—four hours after noon. The day-eels would be out in force. She took a deep, practiced breath and dove under the surface.

The water slid around her body like the finest cloth from the inner islands—cool and supple. The water was not very deep here, and the sunlight penetrated straight to the coral floor. The mandagah were nowhere to be found at this time of day, but for sheer physical beauty nothing could match their island's natural coral. It rose like a castle from the deep, built by some mad designer with a fetish for bright colors and retractable parts. A massive purple fan waved lazily beneath her until covered by her shadow. It vanished faster than she could blink, leaving nothing but an unremarkable piece of porous gray stone behind. She shook her head in delight, but did not stay to watch its slow re-emergence. *Pineki always swims too far*, the divers would complain to Leilani when their entreaties did not seem to penetrate her mother's laugh. *She dives too deep*. It was unspeakably rude to leave your partner alone on a dive. Even worse, it was dangerous, and Pineki always left anyone behind who couldn't keep up.

"Why can't you just stay with the others!" Leilani screamed once, after another incident. "Even you aren't totally fearless!"

Pineki hadn't laughed, though Leilani could tell she wanted to. "Oh, keika. I'm not fearless at all. Nothing's any fun if you're fearless."

That was before Pineki had refused altogether to dive with the group.

Leilani had made it a point of pride to always dive judiciously and accommodate her partner. Her etiquette had been impeccable, as though she had thought it would make up for her mother's wildness. Pineki had taken a perverse pride in Leilani's conformity. She had once boasted to another diver that her daughter had "never once dipped below thirty feet."

Abruptly, Leilani swam to the surface. Three steadying breaths and she was ready to try again. How strange, to come so close to crying when your eyes are already submerged in water.

The eels were massive, almost worthy of the fruit in Pineki's secret garden. Their heads alone dwarfed her torso. Their unhinged mouths could swallow her in one tiny gulp. Their swiveling bodies looked as long as five of her in a row. She was forty feet under now, with plenty of air in her ears to ease the pressure. She rested very still in the water, and the three eels nearby did not deign to pay her much attention. Their natural prey was the large ahi fish. Fishermen also laid their nets in these waters, and the tales told by the survivors of those on boats unfortunate enough to catch a day-eel had given them a fearsome reputation. As far as she knew, no one but Pineki had ever tested the legend of their taste for human flesh. Their iridescent blue skin that flashed green when they were about to strike, their massive size, and the baleful cast of eyes as big as oranges all conspired to make the worst stories eminently credible. Everyone was terrified of them. Maybe even Pineki. But her mother had stayed in the water and watched the eels for hours. Pineki had realized that so long as she didn't threaten them, they cared about as much for her as the crab scuttling along the sandy floor. She had stayed until sundown, when she saw a lone mandagah fish among the seaweed. Thinking to get

at least one jewel out of her day among the eels, she had gone
to it and received the shock of her life. It deposited two jewels
in her hand. One was white and the other that rare color of the
sun that always marked an elder.

Pineki said she cursed, and then shrugged. She was willing
to try everything at least once.

Leilani decided she was running out of air and slowly
swam to the surface, letting the pressure ease gently. Halfway
there, one of the eels came racing up from below her, its skin
crackling green. She stared at it, frozen in a combination of awe
and terror. It missed her by a mere two inches before falling on
an ahi fish like a living, hungry waterfall. Her skin tingled from
its passage, and she shook from the shock.

She shot to the surface like a cork. No, she would never
match her mother.

Okilani was waiting back at the shore. Leilani tried to smile at
her like she imagined Pineki would have, but it felt so brittle
and terrified instead of calm and daring that she just gave up.

"I hope you enjoyed that," Okilani said. Her voice was
harsh but her eyes were gentle. Okilani was everything she had
always imagined a mother should be.

Leilani took her leibo from the sand and pulled them over
her clammy legs. "It was . . . amazing," she said truthfully. "I'll
never do it again."

Okilani looked into her eyes and then away abruptly.
"Your mother gave you just enough of herself, didn't she? Too
much, and . . ."

Okilani's voice had gotten very tight.

"How much did Piki know? How much power did she have when you tossed her out?"

Okilani looked surprised. "We . . . weren't sure. We didn't teach her anything very explicit, but . . ."

"She's Pineki."

"Oh. I almost forgot. Leva'ula wants to see you."

Her muscles, weak from her dive, burned like alcohol on an open wound after the climb to Leva'ula's tree house. The head elder's home was built into the largest and most ancient of the kukui trees in the sacred grove. Across from it was the tree traditionally reserved for diver and elder funerals of the kind they had refused Pineki.

Leilani was not inclined to be charitable when she knocked on the door, but Leva'ula seemed so much like the same warm but absentminded mystic she had known all her life that it was impossible to maintain her anger. She even smelled familiar, like honeysuckle and coconuts.

"I hear you are going to contravene the council's wishes," she said, when Leilani seated herself on the floor. Leva'ula had taken a chair, forcing Leilani to gaze up at her.

"I'm going to burn my mother at sunset." It was harder, somehow, to say the words in this woman's presence. They seemed so belligerent, and she seemed so benign.

"Well, you know, keika, we forbade her a funeral. She was your mother. I know you must have loved her and seen parts of her hidden from the rest of us, but by her actions she forfeited the right to a consummation, by geas or by fire. You must understand that."

She said "must" as though it were the most natural and reasonable thing in the world. She looked sorrowful at what she had to do, but firm. She spoke like a parent, one who made decisions based on pragmatic rules and bedrock principles.

Leilani found herself nodding. "Yes," she said, "I understand that."

Leva'ula smiled. One side of her mouth curved up a little more than the other, like she had forgotten to smile properly or something had just made her particularly happy.

"So I trust you'll reconsider your decision? I know I cannot force you . . . but you might not like the consequences if you don't. Perhaps a burial would suffice. The farmers always appreciate the fertilizer."

She could hear Pineki's laugh so clearly she nearly covered her ears to block out the sound.

"I'll consider it," she said, her voice wobbling. Why couldn't she just say no? How had her mother defied this woman? How could Leilani? Leva'ula somehow made the entire act of defiance seem childish and just a little disappointing.

"Good," Leva'ula said, rapping the floor with the tip of her walking stick in self-satisfied emphasis. "You can show yourself out, dear. I'm getting a bit old to walk to and from the door like I used to."

I'm going to burn my mother at sunset. But she only thought the words.

Kapa was holding Uku facedown in the sand, his knee on the small of his back, with only a dead woman as witness. Leilani stared at the tableau for a long, uncomprehending moment.

"Kapa, what—"

"I was just paying my final respects to your sweet mother," Uku said, the venom in his voice obvious despite the muffling sand. And to think that Ukele, his brother, had wept.

"He spat on her body, Lei. He says Pineki cursed him." Kapa's voice was quiet, steadying.

"Let him go."

After a moment, Kapa nodded and stood up. Uku scrambled to his feet and looked as though he would take a parting shot at Kapa, but Leilani stood in his way.

"She's dead, Uku. You've dishonored her enough already, don't you think?"

"I could feed her to the worms in my garden and urinate on her every morning and it wouldn't be dishonor enough."

"What did she do to you?" Facts. She needed more. The ones she had now weren't enough.

He laughed. "She was sleeping with my brother. I told her to leave him alone, and she cursed me with the holy powers *we* taught her!"

Life with Pineki had trained her to spot all brands of sexual infatuation. Especially jealousy. "She slept with you."

"She's a whore!"

"Whore." That ugly, inner-island word. It was a concept she knew only from books and hearsay.

"We have no whores on this island," she said.

Hate twisted his face into a hideous mask. Had she ever found him attractive?

"You're right," he said. "She just died."

———

They started to come an hour before sunset, defying the council's ban in twos and threes, until sheer numbers protected them. Leilani was surprised—she had been prepared to do this alone. She had laid the body out on a pile of dry palm and kukui fronds. She removed her mother's leibo and covered her naked body with three fresh leaves. On each of them she put one of the mandagah jewels from her mother's dive this morning. If the elders refused to give her mother the honor she deserved, then Leilani would do as much as she could herself. It had been a remarkably easy decision, after Uku had left. How could she give in to that hate? How could she not honor the spirit of her mother's laughter? She was coming to realize how much pain that carefree sound had always held. How much defiance.

"They could bar you from diving," Kapa said, as the sun began to dip and the silent people approached the body. "I think . . . this is right. But you should know what they'll do."

This time Leilani laughed. "Do you think anyone ever warned Pineki like that? Don't sleep with this man, Piki, he's filled with hate and may bash your skull in with his fist?" *And when he does, no one will punish him, because he's an elder and they think you deserved it?*

Kapa stood very close to her. She almost thought he might take her hand. "Do you think you should have?"

"I think she knew every consequence she risked. I think she liked it that way."

Kapa must have heard something in her voice she wasn't even aware of herself, because he suddenly gripped her shoulders like he could prevent her from falling. *There.* She liked his touch. It was cool, and his fingers were strong.

"Lei," he said, "you can't be your mother. There are other legitimate ways to live."

He was exactly her height. She smiled. "Legitimate . . . but worthwhile?"

Sunset. She let Kapa light the torch. The crowd behind her was huge—a sea of people and she didn't even recognize half. How was that possible? Their island was tiny; she had lived here her whole life. She felt like she had cloistered herself while her mother lived enough for ten people. And still . . . the fading light took the harsh edge off of her mother's stiff, bruised face. She looked young again and beautiful.

"I see you didn't heed my advice." *Leva'ula.* Leilani took a deep breath and turned to face the head elder.

"I didn't think it was worth heeding." Her voice, but Pineki's words. She felt a rush, like her first taste of palm wine or her first dive. Pineki wasn't fearless, but she knew how to use fear.

Leva'ula's smile was almost aggressively forgiving. Leilani wondered if something else lay beneath—vindictiveness rung with tradition and guarded by the authority of her red mandagah jewel.

"I'm afraid I can't vouch for your future as a diver if you go through with this, dear," Leva'ula said. "It would be a shame to see such a good daughter destroyed by such a bad mother."

Okilani had moved silently behind the head elder, and she winced. In the deepening dark, by the light of Kapa's torch, Leilani met Leva'ula's eyes. Even they smiled. Even now. "She was not a bad mother."

"You loved her." Leva'ula said it as though the emotion were a lisp, an unfortunate affliction of the kind some must bear.

"Did you know Uku killed her?"

The elder's lips turned down gracefully, and she sighed. "Yes, I suspected as much. Your mother's wiles were enough to seduce even our proud kukui tree. He had provocation."

Leilani laughed. Great Kai, it felt so good and free that she had to close her eyes to just encompass the absurdity and perverse beauty of it all.

She opened her eyes to see Leva'ula staring like she had seen a ghost.

"I thought you were different from her, Leilani."

Leilani took the torch from Kapa. "Of course I am. But she taught me more than I knew."

Leva'ula drew herself up very straight. "This is my last warning." She gave no hint of kindness anymore. Perhaps this was the true power of Pineki's laughter: it revealed what lay underneath.

She was about to turn from the elder when the light from the torch made something gleam on the top of Leva'ula's walking stick. Slowly, as though she had no inkling of the implied discourtesy, Leilani leaned over and sniffed.

Coconut milk. A few hairs from the outer shell remained stuck in the film.

Leilani looked up. "You washed off the blood, but forgot the coconut."

Leva'ula tried to laugh, but the sound was unconvincing. "You silly girl. I'm much too feeble to go running around bashing grown women's heads in. Even if their favorite pastime is breaking vows and misusing power."

Behind the head elder, Okilani had an expression on her face Leilani couldn't even hope to read. "True," Okilani said, surprising them both. "But you're capable of using a geas to make yourself temporarily stronger."

Leilani understood. "Strong enough to smash a giant coconut with just a stick."

"Giant coconuts? You *have* lost your mind. I trust a fondness for coconut juice is no crime."

"No. Too bad none of the regular trees have ripened yet. The only fruits ripe enough for juice are in my mother's special garden."

Deliberately, hoping her very brazenness would prevent Leva'ula from acting, Leilani put her hand deep in the right-hand pocket of the elder's leibo. They both stared at her discovery for a quiet moment: an iridescent, pale orange jewel, strung on a broken chain.

"Leva'ula." Okilani put a firm hand on her shoulder. "Let the girl send off her mother."

Leilani thought of spitting, or slapping her, or demanding justice from the council. But her mother was still dead. She found she didn't yet have the energy to punish anyone.

Leilani turned away from them, her mother's murderer and her mother's friend. She walked to the pyre.

"Thank you," she said, "for the pineapple."

She tossed the torch on the tinder.

"Kapa," she said, many hours later when the flames had all but vanished, leaving a pile of bone and ashes for the next tide. "Why don't we get married?"

He nearly stumbled to his knees. "Lei!" His voice cracked and he cleared his throat. "Are you serious?"

She laughed at him, but just a little, and not so he would hate her for it later. "Of course."

He closed his eyes and she kissed him.

Home. She hadn't been back here since . . . this morning. She could almost imagine that Pineki would be coming back later that night, her cheeks flushed with wine and love and good conversation. The pineapple was still there, taking up half of their tiny kitchen area.

"Give me your fishing knife."

Kapa obliged, and she used it to hack through the tough, prickly skin to get to the white-gold flesh beneath. She was sweating by the time she succeeded in tearing off a slice, but Kapa prudently didn't ask her if she needed any help. She cut off two bits of flesh as big as her hand and gave one to her husband-to-be.

"Can I eat it?" he asked. His voice wavered just a little. He loved Pineki, too.

"Of course. That's what she made it for. Eating."

She bit into the stringy flesh and held it on her tongue. The juice coated the inside of her mouth, so tart and sweet she had to pucker her lips. She was aware of a perverse desire to imprison this moment forever, to refuse to chew or swallow, to merely exist in this pineapple-induced gustatory orgasm. But habit overcame her. The flesh slid down her throat, passed from joy into memory, and she knew Pineki would understand.

Something occurred to her. "Kapa," she said, "do you know what curse Pineki put on Uku?"

Kapa looked blank for a moment and then began to laugh. "Well . . ." He reached for her hand. "I heard that for about a month, every time he was attracted to a woman, his penis shrunk to the size of a kukui nut."

Leilani began to giggle. "Leva'ula called him a kukui tree. So Piki turned the kukui tree into a kukui nut!"

She threw back her head. She closed her eyes. She laughed until she couldn't breathe, until she had to stop, until the pineapple between her lips was both salty and sweet, with no real difference between them.

Down the Well

"I enjoy watching children," she said. "It comforts me to remember that I too was a child once, and one day they too will be old."

Her shiny olive skin was firm, but even the best youth treatments couldn't hide the purple veins that snaked around her arms like cables. She appeared to be in well-preserved middle age; only I and a few other agents knew the truth. Her eight remaining fingers were casually laced over a knobby walking stick that she carried for show. A particularly knowledgeable observer might have noted that the cherry-red wood was at once lighter and stronger than any known on Earth. Dr. Constance Roya was a scientist in the ancient sense, when that term implied at least as much of a reckless love for adventure as an appreciation of form and method and the furtherance of human knowledge.

I turned my gaze from Dr. Roya to the park below. Children from the nearby ambassador's school scrambled over banyan tree roots, hanging and swinging so adroitly that it suddenly seemed the separation between humans and other apes was not so great as we liked to imagine.

I said as much to Dr. Roya. Her answering smile was brief and indulgent. I had a sudden impression of those dark, full lips breaking me open, holding their silence.

"They're children," she said, her voice incongruously deep and carrying for such a small body. "Ontogeny recapitulates phylogeny . . ."

I stared—was she playing me? She laughed and shrugged.

"... Except when it doesn't, Mr. Smith." I had told her my name. But she insisted on denying me what little individuality I had left. Could I blame her? She saw the agency acronym on my lapel; she knew what I'd come for.

"Dr. Roya, I think it's time you showed me the lab," I said, hoping, like a child, to hurt her with my authority.

She smiled again; I flinched. "A moment, Mr. Smith." I saw her clearly, then: beautiful and terrible, ancient and radical, a goddess as much as any human can be. Killing a hexapedal carnivore with a handmade spear, hiding for two days from a giant amphibious jellyfish desperate for food, surviving alone in the Well for five years before the computers on this side even registered the malfunction—those rumors had floated around the agency for decades. I'd found it impossible to believe that such a small, unassuming woman had done all they said she did.

Now? Evidence acquired, knowledge attained, theory proven. Evolution occurred; Constance Roya could eviscerate me with a glance. QED. I took a step back.

"Do you know what those are?" she said, gesturing again to the park below.

I hesitated. She couldn't be referring to the children. So that left ... *"Ficus benghalensis?"*

She raised an eyebrow. "An invasive species," she said. "Like a bureaucrat."

"I'm not—"

She began walking toward the elevator. She held her spine like a steel rod, her walking stick like a bludgeon. "Of course you are," she said, her voice brittle as fossilized bone. "With just enough knowledge to destroy the world."

———

Dr. Roya flicked on the lights. I expected a clinical fluorescent glow, but the light that filled the room was warm and dappled, as though glancing off summer leaves. It seemed, for a moment, like I could smell the fresh cut grass, evaporating dew, nightsoil fertilizer from the surface a hundred floors above.

"You convinced building services to pump in sunlight?" I said. But you couldn't *smell* sunlight.

Dr. Roya closed her eyes. I could hear the air whistling into her lungs. "It's the only way I can work," she said, after a moment.

I took a discreet sniff. Just normal lab smells: alcohol and preserving chemicals, carpet cleaner, laundered lab coats, disposable gloves. The door to the Well airlock, marked with yellow paint and prominent security touchpads, smelled like nothing at all.

She gave me a quick glance and walked to a recessed door on the far right. To each side hung one of Dr. Roya's legendary illustrations: chimeras and monsters, living fossils and mythic beasts, all drawn to minute anatomical detail. I saw a spray of razor-sharp hairs in the nail bed of a giant flying sloth, perfectly designed to slowly bleed its airborne prey to death before landing. On the other side hung an image that made me shudder, though I had studied it for hours when it first came across the classified feeds. A pair of gigantic red lips, disembodied from any suggestion of a face, washed up on a beach. It had multiple digestive pockets in the lining of its massive mouth, where it could store small sea creatures for weeks like fish in the window of a Chinese restaurant.

Dr. Roya had opened the door, but walked back to where I stood, frozen before her pictures.

"It climbed out of the water," she said, pointing to the mouth. "On its lips. I thought it was going to eat me, but it died. I hacked it open with a stone knife after I drew this." She paused, with a wry smile I supposed she meant for herself. "This creature had a neural net the size of my thumbnail, but it went to a beach to die." She shook her head. "I brought back samples for the lab, but they rotted by the time you fellows rescued me. I've never been able to find it again. Hell, it probably went extinct ten minutes after I left."

I caught something in her voice I recognized, though it took me a moment to place. Some mutant hybrid of envy, wistfulness, and grief. The way I'd felt when I had dropped out of graduate school and taken a post at the agency.

I tried, "It seems like such . . ."

"A waste," she finished. Her voice was uncharacteristically gentle. "Like most treasures."

She let me stare for a few more seconds and then strode back to the open door. "Well, come on. You should at least see everything."

I followed her through. The light here was low and ambient, the temperature a chill ten degrees Celsius. To my right and left rested shelf after shelf of specimens, some preserved in makeshift camp jars and others floating in specially made aquariums that preserved anatomical detail down to the organelles. Standing there, dwarfed by the entire recorded biology of an alien ecosystem, I felt close to hyperventilating. Bug-eyed fish with prehensile fins, meter-thick tree limbs with giant blue leaves for wings and purple fruit for retractable eyes, millipedes as long as my body and thicker than my torso, with each segment differentiated into a cascade of arms.

I had avoided museums since quitting school, though I made a hobby of collecting illustrations. But standing here among thousands of extinct species that were only a fraction of a fraction of the species even now going extinct, old school-day terrors rushed back. I felt as though time itself could crush me. I did not feel awe or joy or any transcendent moment of the scientific understanding of Einstein's god. No, I was a peon again, terrified by the breadth of the universe, by my utterly insignificant place in it, by the eternity of my death and that of everyone I loved. The room swayed. I closed my eyes.

"Oxaloacetate, citrate, cis-aconitate, isocitrate," I whispered, letting my mind go blank.

"The Krebs cycle as catechism?" Her voice was at my elbow. "No wonder they sent you to do this job."

I forced myself to open my eyes. For some reason, her presence was reassuring. Or at least intimidating in a far less existential way. "I begged them," I said. Cracking myself open, hoping she would understand I wasn't just another Mr. Smith.

She touched my sleeve. It was meant for comfort, but my pulse jumped. "So eager to put an old scientist out to pasture?"

I shook my head. "I just wanted to meet you. If *someone* had to do it . . ."

"Better someone who understands my work? I should show you something."

Around the corner from the specimens, a floor-to-ceiling clear plastic wall separated us from a waterless aquarium. Aside from a slime mold growing on the floor, the chamber was empty.

"Now look," Dr. Roya said. Her voice seemed closer to a twelve-year-old girl's, ecstatic with her first discovery of a toad in the garden. She turned down the lights.

Suddenly, the room that had been empty was teeming with life. Ghostly obloid creatures, organs lit up like lights in a Christmas show, swam through the air. They were buoyed by a thick fringe of cilia that beat the air like a broom. Paramecia a handspan across?

Dr. Roya pressed her face against the smudge-proof plastic. In such low light her treated skin was as translucent as tracing paper; I could see a vein throbbing in her forehead. She was eighty-seven years old, give or take a few weeks, according to the agency calculators. But she had been born just ten years before me. The Well extracted its price.

"Single cells," she said, in response to my unvoiced question. "They existed, briefly, in Earth's past. I happened to catch some evolving during phase one."

"In the air?"

"No, no, the project was at least a hundred million years away from getting out of the oceans. I brought them back here, did some old-fashioned genetic engineering. I knocked out genes until my assistants threatened to quit. I took it as far as I could, and what do you know . . ."

One paused before us, shuddered—like a dog shaking off mud—and suddenly split in two.

"Could they . . . do you think they could self-organize?"

She closed her eyes, like the concept almost overwhelmed her. "The oxygen content of the atmosphere might pose technical limitations. But it's possible. Even your bosses can grasp that much."

I knew what she meant. The infinite possibility of time.

"I have some forms," I said, awkwardly, when we went back into the lab.

She laughed. "Of course. 'I hereby agree to sign my life away and bother you no more.' That kind of thing?"

The muscles in my neck felt taut, but I tried to smile. "That's the agency for you. Always signed in someone else's blood."

I had hoped to impress her, but her only response was to take the scroll and quickly tap through the documents. Tediously long, as though they meant to bury their intentions under piles of legalese. And no need for her to pay very close attention, as we both understood what they wanted.

"Oh, look," she said, when she reached the end, "they've already put my pension into a retirement home. India. How thoughtful."

I dimly registered her venom, but she had triggered a memory—fellow agents making joking references to "agency hospitality" and "nurse wards" for certain classes of dissidents. My clearance wasn't high enough to know what exactly happened to these people, but you couldn't work in the agency—even as the humblest clerk in the dullest Science division—without catching the general theme of the proceedings. And that theme was grim, bureaucratic, occasionally cruel and always merciless.

"There, you can tell your masters I cooperated." She tempered it with a smile, but I knew her words were deadly serious. I replaced the scroll in my jacket pocket. She took a few steps away from me, and then began to turn in a circle. Her eyes glittered as they surveyed the room. Her shoulders stiffened. She gripped her stick as though she really would fall down without it.

Then she sighed, a sudden and profound release of tension. "Well then, I guess there's just one thing left. You'll have to decontaminate, of course."

I hadn't expected it. I had *hoped*, like a child hopes for a bicycle on Christmas, but I'd known better than to expect it. No one at the agency had said I needed to inspect the Well. Dr. Roya guarded its access so notoriously I'm sure it never even crossed their minds that she would offer. She gave me no chance to fumble for words of incoherent gratitude. She hadn't used my name, but she would have never shared this with *Mr. Smith*. She understood.

She pressed her finger against the security touchpad and punched in a long string of numbers. Behind us, the seal around the main lab door expanded to create a quarantine-ready lock. It wouldn't open again until the computers confirmed the room was free of dangerous Well contaminants. Dr. Roya held up her right eye for a biometric scan. The door before us slid open with a slight exhalation of compressed air, like a sigh. It shut as soon as we walked inside. We were in the clean room, barely five feet away from the Well's red gate.

She pulled three long pins from her bun and let them plunk to the ground. Her hair, silvered and wavy, settled around her shoulders. She was halfway through unbuttoning her blouse before I realized I had to undress to decontaminate. I'd seen it done before, just not so informally. Hastily, I pulled off my jacket and loosened the strangling tie.

Dr. Roya, naked except for her underwear, clucked her tongue. "The only office in the country that still makes men wear nooses."

Beautiful and terrible. My emotions at the sight of her naked body shocked me. Her skin was taut and painfully thin. I felt as though I could see every corded vein and muscle, every hand-stitched scar, every coffee-stain of age. It should have been grotesque. It wasn't. I'd always thought I understood the difference between admiration and love. But it seemed they shared a common genetic ancestry. I hurriedly disrobed. Naked as a prelapsarian Adam and Eve, we washed in the chemical waters and donned our sterile clothing. I pulled on the supple, practical hiking pants and sweater. Dr. Roya adjusted a knapsack on her slight shoulders. In her left hand she carried her walking stick, in the other a strange metal box that had been waiting in the airlock. I looked at the bright red door ahead of us, surrounded by lights and accompanying touchpad displays. This was the gate. Just beyond: the Well. It was supposedly dangerous to go in without one person waiting Earth-side, but in truth the computers were much quicker at diagnosing problems than humans. I was sure Dr. Roya had done this alone dozens of times. I could tell as much from her alert, almost anticipatory posture.

"Ready?" she asked me, but she meant to go no matter what I said. So I nodded. "Willing, even when terrified. I would have liked you as a graduate student." She grinned.

And suddenly, the clanging inside my head was caused by so much more than arousal and fear. Dr. Roya was the greatest biologist of her age. And I, confronted with the slow-grazing terror of phylogenetic trees, the infinite subtle twistings of evolution's roots, had thrown it all away. Maybe everyone has existential crises. Especially scientists. But I hadn't been strong enough to get through it. And now I was just a dropout. A faceless drone sent to destroy a woman he worshipped.

She handed me a facemask. "Air filters in case the atmosphere's gone toxic again. It shouldn't have. I think I've managed the equilibrium, but better safe. When the doors open, you'll see a ball of red yarn. Grab it and walk through. You'll feel like you're falling off a building. Then we land."

I nodded, too caught up to dare use my voice.

But hers was clear and defiant, like the last rally of a defeated general. "Open the door," she said.

The red parted onto absolute black. The yarn nestled like an egg against the void.

We stepped into the Time Well; we fell off the earth.

Once, one of the fellows from Physics—deeply ambitious but possessed of a quaint fondness for the scientific method—had tried to explain to me how the Time Well worked. You crossed into negative space, he said, into the paper-thin separation of our brane and the next. Then negative energy stabilized a wormhole that opened directly onto another planet. But time in the brane-universe moved faster. I had the vague idea that this had something to do with relativity: despite the fact that information from the brane-universe could travel here almost instantaneously, it took thousands of years for us to communicate back. Twenty-three Earth days for every million brane years, to be precise.

The physicists hadn't known what to do with the useless hunk of Venus-like rock when they first mapped the path through the wormhole. So they turned it over to Science

Administration. And Constance Roya, who had just received her doctorate from Harvard, heard about the project and had an idea. Just give her access to the rock, she said, and she could turn it into a habitable planet. Only she had recognized the potential of the radical time scale shift. Only she had realized that time could turn this planet into something biologists had only dreamed of for centuries: evolution in a lab.

We landed on red, muddy earth. I stumbled to my knees. Behind me, the yarn seemed to vanish in midair. I fumbled to check my facemask, but stopped when I saw that Dr. Roya had already removed hers.

"Twenty-one percent oxygen," she said, a steward's satisfaction in her voice. She pocketed the tiny chemical scanner.

I stood up slowly. We had landed on some kind of mud flat. In the distance I could make out a smudge of ocean. We were surrounded by bright blue hillocks of slimy, interconnected filaments. I shielded my eyes and looked up: the star was large and reddish orange, the sky silvered white. I had read about this: the planet orbited a relatively hot M-class star. Photosynthetic pigments here absorbed the abundant red light, but reflected blue. Blue trees, I thought, almost dizzy with excitement.

"Come," Dr. Roya said. She started hiking across the mud flats. The metal box seemed heavy, but I didn't dare offer to carry it. I followed her to the gently undulating plain of thigh-high blue grass, unspooling the red yarn as I went. The grass smelled surprisingly similar to earth's, but as she beat it down with her stick I caught a whiff of something sweet and unexpected, like anisette. We hiked to a hill a few hundred yards distant, where the grass grew more sparsely. From this vantage point we could see for several kilometers—the ocean and a distant horizon line on our right and a dense blue forest made of swaying, interlocking trees on our left.

"That's all one plant," she said, pointing. "The trees are actually branches. Similar to our quaking aspen except, I think . . . sentient."

I stared at her. She shrugged. "I haven't made a study of it. But its grandfather saved my life, once."

She sat down abruptly and hauled the metal box between her legs. After a moment's hesitation, I sat beside her. A few yards away, a fist-sized green-and-white ball leaped from the ground and rolled down the hill. Halfway to the tall grass, ten wings popped from its unfolding carapace and it flew away, straight into the forest. Automatically, I tried to catalogue it in my mind: kingdom, animalia; phylum, arthropoda—but how absurd. It was an utter unknown. And, given the timescales involved, unknowable.

"They're going to kill me, aren't they?" she said, her voice so utterly bland that I was shocked back into attention.

I opened my mouth to deny it, but she regarded me with such a steady, piercing calm that I couldn't.

A retirement home. India. How thoughtful.

I could admit whatever I wanted out here. Even the agency couldn't touch me in another universe. So I said, "They might not, but I think . . . they won't take that chance."

The twist of her lips was bitter. "I liked the other corrupt administration better. Less imagination. I suppose they've finally realized the potential of my sandbox. Won't do to keep around a loose cannon who knows too much, right?"

We were silent for nearly a minute. The smell of anisette was more redolent up here, with overtones of copper and earth.

Every few seconds a multi-harmonic buzzing, like cicadas in a trombone, pierced the air.

"I've given them something terrible, haven't I?" she said, her voice barely audible over the natural symphony. "Another planet to destroy." She laughed, a little wildly. "But it was inevitable. We're the ultimate invasive species."

Unthinking, I covered her left hand—the one missing two fingers from those five lost years—with my own. "I've worked out a few of the classification codes," I said. "They're giving access to Defense Development."

She nodded. "Weapons. Of course. Keep a few scientists here for fifty years, see what they come up with. Biological, nuclear, who cares? Instantaneous escalation." She looked down at her box. "I guess it's time."

Wearily, as though she could hardly stand to lift her arms, she typed a code into the tiny touchpad. The top of the box slid backward. About ten of the giant paramecia floated out. They hovered around Dr. Roya for a moment, as if confused, but a wind blew and scattered them like spores. Far away from us, forever.

"How quickly do they reproduce?"

"One division a day."

It wasn't hard to calculate. "They could take over everything. In a million years this could be a giant single-cell monoculture."

"Or they could evolve natural predators," she said mildly.

"But still, that could make the environment toxic to everything. . . ." I trailed off. Her gaze was slightly amused, but mostly sad. I could only imagine, suddenly, what that act must have cost her. "Of course," I said. "I apologize."

She held my gaze for too long, grabbing my hand when I tried to look away. As though she were weighing my soul, or grading my suitability. I had the uncomfortable feeling that I'd come up wanting on both counts.

"You've spent your entire life being sorry, haven't you?" she said, and kissed me.

I wondered what it must have been like a hundred thousand years ago for our ancestors, fulfilling their biological imperative—full of purpose, free of cultural meaning. Was copulation better than sex? Could we, *homo sapiens sapiens*, find our way back to that Hobbesian vacuum, even on another world?

I named the parts of her body as I kissed them: clavicle, scapula, sternum, manubrium. Her breath came in sharp jolts, as though she could only exhale when I forced the air from her lungs. A small, purple insect crawled across her nose. I laughed and brushed it off. My hand shook.

"No," she said, even as she groaned, even as I reached for the waistband of her pants. "One last time. . . ." She caressed my hair. "But it would matter too much to you."

I opened my eyes, but I couldn't look at her.

We walked toward the ocean. I squinted into the sun, an excuse for watery eyes.

"Are you a dualist?" she asked, pulling her foot from a sinkhole.

I was surprised, and then realized that I would always be surprised with her. "You're very direct."

She shrugged. "You seem like the type. God is just a means to an end."

She used her stick to tap one of the hillocks of blue filaments. Nothing happened. She tapped it again. Suddenly it popped up, like a cork from a champagne bottle. It landed five feet away. In the now-vacant mud, a miniaturized version of the lip-creature on her lab wall smacked at the empty air. Its skin was a translucent purple-red, reminding me of her.

I thought I heard her sob. But when I turned, she was smiling: an expression as close to pure joy as any I'd seen. "Adaptation," she said. "Better than heaven."

We watched it roll around before using its disproportionately large lips to burrow into the mud. After a few seconds, it disappeared completely.

"And your bosses never even believed me, Mr.——" I had winced in anticipation, but she paused. "You really hate that. You want me to think you're different." She shook her head. "It's been a long time since my opinion mattered that much to anyone. To my self-appointed executioner, no less."

She kept walking. I stumbled behind, wishing I could think of something to say that didn't involve admiration so deep and desperate it was indistinguishable from love.

"If you could live in a universe with an afterlife but without God," she said, minutes later, "or in a universe in which God exists, but you lack an immortal soul, which would you choose?"

Oxaloacetate, citrate, cis-aconitate. "I'm not sure."

We were closer to the ocean now. I could hear the waves. She glanced over her shoulder; just a flash, but I withered under her contempt. "Come on."

"A soul," I said, God forgive me.

"What was your thesis?"

"Evidence for extra-solar seeding of RNA-like polymers in clay-catalyzing scenarios." The old words came so easily I forgot for a moment that I hadn't said them aloud in over ten years.

She laughed. "Panspermia *and* abiogenesis. You really were looking for God." She paused. "But you never finished your degree, did you?" Her gaze was nearly muscular, so efficiently did it pry open my past. "You abandoned your career. Dualism, souls . . . you loved biology, you just couldn't stand its implications."

"Science can't disprove God," I said, and winced. My professors had tried to rescue me with examples of religious scientists—Ken Miller and Isaac Newton trussed up like wax dolls in a traveling history exhibit. The Pope himself declared no conflict between Christianity and evolution. But what sort of God designs a wasp that can only gestate through the existential suffering of a caterpillar? Why would He create and destroy a billion billion species, only to save cockroaches and humans?

Her smile was disdainful. "Of course it can't. You just managed to find the one job where you wouldn't have to prove anything."

My shopworn apologetics fell away. She was right—the agency merely demanded knowledge, never conviction.

I remembered nights in the college chapel, nearly crying with the weight of those millions of dead species, 99% of all creatures once alive on the earth. What was dualism—the disembodied spirit, the earth-bound brain—to that? A flyswatter of justification in a roomful of flies. I left the church, I left the school. But I was haunted by secular ghosts, by the cruelty of Darwin's Ichneumonidae.

I had expected the ocean to be the same comic-book blue as the plants, but it was silver, like the reflected sky. We stood on a spongy ridge made from thousands of decaying blue hillocks and watched the sun set over the ocean. The sky filled with reds and purples so violent it looked as though the sun was bleeding. In the water, two giant bipedal sea-monsters called to each other in voices like submerged foghorns. They were at least a mile away from us, but when they began crashing against each other, the spray misted our clothes. I licked the water from my hand: less salty than our oceans, and distinctly metallic. *I could get used to this*, I thought.

Sometimes I wonder what would have happened if I had said it aloud.

"You should go back," Dr. Roya said.

I already understood that she would stay here. And that it would hardly matter to the agency if she died of old age in another universe or from a morphine drip in an agency care home. But I hadn't anticipated that she would want me to leave.

"There's an alarm," she said. "It alerts the building if I'm gone longer than five days."

"Then we have five days," I said, like some foolish Shakespearean hero.

She shook her head. "They'll see how long you were gone. They might check the Well too early."

And if they did, they might not give her final, desperate experiment a chance to work. I had to leave so she could destroy the world.

In the end, it was easy enough. Another hole in my heart, another wall. I had spent years inured to disappointment. In many ways, it was my only real expertise. She walked me back to the gate.

"It's okay," she said. I think I was crying. "I'll be okay. I gave birth to this world. It should have my body."

My professors had all been shocked when I abandoned my doctorate. I tried to explain why, tried to convey my crisis of insupportable contradictions within a rational philosophical framework, but it came out garbled and terrified. "Catholic guilt?" one had hazarded. "No," I said, remembering childhood lessons of souls impaled in hell. "Catholic doubt."

If there was a heaven, Constance Roya would have nothing to do with it. She would be in Dante's first ring, with Aristotle and Carl Sagan, discussing underworld politics and whether demons have Hox genes.

But there wasn't a heaven.

The airlock would open automatically when I came back alone, she assured me. "Count to thirty," she whispered, her dark lips brushing against my ear. Her voice was rough, and sometimes I imagine that she was crying, also. "Then I'll be gone."

Back through the rabbit hole, out the other side.

I last saw her kneeling in the mud, one hand in her tangled hair, mouth open. As though she would scream, or say that she was glad I had come, that whatever she felt for me, it wasn't just pity.

Down the Well

———

Thirty seconds. I counted thirty-five to be sure, lying on the carpet of her lab. Her sunlight on my face, anisette in my hair.

Third Day Lights

The mist was thick as clotted cream, shot through with light from the luminous maggots in the sand. And through that mist, which I knew would entrap almost any creature unlucky enough to wander through it, came my first supplicant in over thirty cycles. He rode atop one of the butterfly men's great black deer, which greeted me with a sweep of its massive antlers. His skin was as pale as the sand was black; his eyes were the clear, hard color of chipped jade. A fine, pale fuzz covered his scalp, like the babies of humans. He had full, hard lips and high cheekbones. His nose had been broken several times, and was quite large regardless. His ears protruded slightly from his head.

He was too beautiful. I did not believe it. Oh, I had, in my travels, seen men far more attractive than he. Men who had eagerly accepted me in whatever form I chose, and had momentarily pleased me. But I had never seen this kind of beauty, that of the hard edges and chipped flakes of jade. That aura of bitterly mastered power, and unspeakable grief subdued but somehow not overcome. He gave the impression that he was a man to respect, a man who would understand my own loneliness despite my family, a man who might, perhaps, after so many cycles . . .

But I have not lived for so long away from my Trunk by believing in such things.

Eyes never leaving mine, he touched the neck of the deer, and it knelt for him to dismount. His bare feet should have frozen solid seconds after they touched the sand, and the maggots begun devouring the icy flesh, but instead he stood before my staircase, perfectly at ease. From within the hostile mist, lacy hands and mouths struggled toward him but never quite touched.

That is how I knew he wasn't human.

I anticipated with relish the moment when he would speak and allow me to drop him on the other side of the desert. But he stared at me and I glowered back and then I understood: he knew what I was. He knew *who* I was. At the time, I thought this meant that he was incalculably old. Now, I am not so sure.

"Why do you stand before my gate? Tell me your purpose."

He stayed silent, of course. His impassive expression never wavered, and yet—perhaps from his slightly quivering shoulders or faintly irregular breathing—I had the impression that he was laughing at me.

It had been a long time since I had been the subject of even implied ridicule. Not many willingly mock a demon of the scorched desert. I had chosen one of my more forbidding guises before I opened the door. My skin was black as the sand, my naked body sexually ambiguous and covered with thousands of tiny horns that swiveled in whatever direction I looked. The horns had been one of Charm's ideas—the kind he gets when he's drunk on saltwater. At his request, I wore them on this occasion—the one day each cycle when I accept supplicants. I had thought that my appearance would be appropriately awe-inspiring, and yet from the look in the not-quite-a-man's eyes, I realized that he had not been inspired to awe. I growled to cover my uneasiness—*what creature is this?*

I stormed back inside the house, sulfur gas streaming from between the growing cracks in my skin. The mist groaned when it touched me and then receded. I didn't need to look back at the man to know that he hadn't moved. Inside, door shut, I changed my appearance again. I became monstrous, a blue leviathan of four heads and sixteen impossible arms. I shook my wrists in succession, so the bracelets made of human teeth clacked and cascaded in a sinister echo off the walls of my castle.

Yes, I thought, faces snarling, *this should do.*

I stepped forward to open the door again and saw Mahi's face on the floor beneath me, grinning in two-dimensional languor.

"You look nice," he said. "Some upstart at the door? Drop him in the maw, Naeve. I'm sure it's been some time since she's had a nice meal."

The maw is Mahi's mother, but she rejected him because he can only move in two dimensions. She considered him defective, but I have found his defect to be very useful occasionally. He vents his anger by suggesting I toss every supplicant across the scorched desert into her mouth. I did once, nearly three hundred cycles ago, just for his benefit, but we could all hear the sound of her chewing and mating and screaming in some kind of inscrutable ecstasy for days.

Two of my faces snarled down at him, one looked away, and the fourth just sighed and said, "Perhaps." The maw is all the way on the Eastern border of the desert, but that day her screams pierced as though she were gifting it to our ears—some property of the sand, I suppose. Charm, Top, and I nearly went crazy, but Mahi seemed to enjoy it. My family is closer to me than the Trunk ever was, but I know no more about their previous lives than what they choose to tell me. I often wonder what Mahi's life was like inside the maw.

He faded into the floor, off in some two-dimensional direction I couldn't see. I stepped back outside.

The man was still there, absolutely motionless despite the veritable riot of mist-shapes that struggled to entangle him. My uneasiness returned: *what is he?* When he saw me, his eyes widened. No other muscles moved, and yet I knew. Oh, for that economy of expression. Even my malleable body could not convey with a hundred gestures the amusement and understanding and wary appreciation he expressed with a simple contraction of eye muscles. I did not scare him.

"Who are you?" I used my smallest head and turned the others away—the view of him through four sets of eyes was oddly intense, disconcerting. He didn't answer. "*What* are you?"

I turned my head to the deer who was kneeling peacefully at his side. "Why did you bring him, honored one?" I said in the language of the butterfly men.

The deer looked up, purple eyes lovely enough to break a lesser creature's heart. Before I saw this man, I would have said that only demons and butterfly men could look in the eyes of a deer and keep their sanity.

"Because he asked me," the deer said—gracefully, simply, infuriatingly.

I went back inside. Because I only had one more chance to get rid of him, I stalked the hallways, screaming and summoning things to toss at the walls. Top absorbed them with her usual equanimity and then turned the walls a shimmering orange—my favorite color. Charm screamed from somewhere near the roof that he was attempting to rest, and could I please keep my temper tantrum to myself? I frowned and finished changing—it was a relief to have one set of eyes again. Some demons enjoy multiplicity, but I've always found it exhausting. Top turned that part of the wall into a mirror, so I could see my handiwork.

"It's very beautiful," she said. A hand emerged from the wall and handed me a long piece of embroidered cloth. I wrapped it around my waist, made my aureoles slightly larger and walked to the door.

The corners of his mouth actually quirked up when he saw me this time, and the understanding in his eyes made me ache. I did not believe it, and yet I did. I walked closer to him, doggedly swaying my mahogany hips, raising my arms and shaking my wrists, which were still encircled with bracelets of human teeth. This close I could see that his skin was unnaturally smooth—the only physical indication that he was something other than human.

"Come," I said, my voice pitched low—breathy and seductive in a human sort of way. "Just tell me your name, traveler, and I'll let you inside."

I leaned in closer to him, so our noses nearly touched. "Come," I whispered, "tell me."

His lips quirked again. Bile of frustration and rage choked my all-too-human throat, and I began to lose my grip on my body. I could feel it returning to my mundane form, and after a moment I stopped trying to resist. My skin shifted from glowing mahogany to a prosaic cobalt blue. My hair turned wild and red; my second arms grew rapidly beneath the first, and my aureoles contracted.

My skin tingled with frustration and not a little fear—I didn't *need* anyone else in my family—but I refused to show it as I took a passing glance in his eyes. No triumph there, not even relief.

I walked up the stairs, but I didn't hear his footsteps following.

"Well," I said, gesturing with my left hands, "are you coming?"

The man took a step forward, and then another—he moved as though he were exhausted, or the cold of the maggots and mist had subtly affected him after all.

"Go home," he said to the deer, who had risen beside him. "One way or another, I will not need your help when I leave this place."

His voice made me want to weep tears so large Charm would dance beneath me, singing as though nectar were falling from the sky. It was uncompromisingly strong, yet tender all the same, as though he had seen too much not to grant anyone the tenderness he had been denied.

Do not believe it, I told myself, but I was already losing the battle.

"Are you coming?" I repeated, forced by unexpected emotion into a parody of callous disdain.

"Yes," he said quietly. I do not think I could have stood it if all that unexpected tenderness were suddenly directed at me, but he seemed distracted, watching the mist long after the deer had disappeared.

"What is your name?" I asked, just before I opened the door again. An unlikely gambit, of course, but I had to try.

Amusement suddenly retuned to his eyes. "I'm called Israphel," he said.

Mahi had positioned himself in front of the door in his best impression of three-dimensionality. It nearly worked, if you didn't look at him too critically, or move. He grew indistinct when viewed from oblique angles, until he disappeared altogether. His appearance was, in some ways, even more malleable than my own. For this occasion he had fashioned himself to look like one of the wildly costumed humans we sometimes saw in our travels: decked entirely in iridescent feathers of saffron and canary yellow, strewn together with beads that glinted in an imagined sunlight.

"You let him in?" Mahi shrieked, several octaves higher than normal. I've often wondered how a two-dimensional creature can create such startlingly loud sounds in a multi-dimensional universe.

Something in Israphel's demeanor exuded fascination, though when I looked closely at him I didn't know how I could tell—his expression was still one of polite interest.

"The maw's only son, I presume? I had heard she rejected you, but . . . this is an honor."

Mahi sniffed, put out at having been discovered so quickly. His feathers bristled. "Yes, well. A two-dimensional mouth is not particularly useful for three-dimensional food, is it?" He turned to me, his human mouth stretching and widening as it always did when he was hurt or angry. If it continued to expand, it would settle into a shape even I sometimes found disturbing. Mahi was still, after all, the son of the most feared creature in the scorched desert. He grinned—cruelly—revealing several rows of teeth that appeared to be the silently wailing heads of countless ancient creatures.

"I'm surprised at you, Naeve," he said, his voice a studied drawl. "Confounded by a pesky human? Losing your touch, are you?"

I frowned at him, trying to decide if he was being deliberately obtuse. "He's not a human, Mahi," I said carefully.

Mahi's face had now been almost entirely subsumed by his hideous mouth, but he still managed to look thoughtful. "No . . . he isn't, is he? Well, I trust you'll get rid of him soon." He folded himself into some inscrutable shape and seemed to disappear.

Israphel turned to look at me. He smiled, and I felt my skin turning a deeper, more painful shade of blue. For a calculated moment, his eyes were as transparent as windowpanes: amusement and fascination and just a trace of wonder . . .

By the Trunk, who is this man?

"What is my first task, Naeve?" he asked, very gently.

I turned away and walked blindly down a hall that had not been there a moment before. I didn't look, but I knew he was following.

I could practically feel his eyes resting on my back, radiating compassion and equanimity. Out of sheer annoyance, I shifted my body slightly so a gigantic purple eye blinked lazily on my back and then stared straight at him. I had hoped for some kind of reaction—a shriek of surprise, perhaps—but he simply nodded in polite understanding and looked away. His eyes focused on the indigo walls, and he jerked, ever so slightly, in surprise. For a moment I wished for a mouth as big and savage as Mahi's to grin with. I knew he had noticed the gentle rippling of Top's smooth muscles. Israphel looked sharply at my back, but my third eye was beginning to make me feel dizzy, so I subsumed it back into my flesh. No use, I could still sense him.

I ran my hand along Top's indigo gizzards and silently drew the symbol for where I wanted to go. The walls shivered a little in her surprise—it had been nearly a hundred cycles since I had last visited there. But I needed to get rid of this not-a-man quickly, and it was in Top's second appendix that I had saved my cleverest, most wildly impossible task. Even Israphel, with all of his jade green understanding and hard-won wisdom would not be able to solve it.

A light blue membrane slammed across the corridor a few feet ahead of us, blocking the path. Seconds later, a torrent of unidentifiable waste roared just behind it, smelling of freshly digested nematodes and one-eyed birds. Top tried her best, but it was difficult to keep things clean this deep in her bowels. As soon as the last of the waste had gone past, the membrane pulled back and we continued. I surreptitiously glanced at Israphel, but his expression was perfectly bland. Too bland? I wasn't quite sure. Top shunted her waste past us several more times before we reached the entrance to her second appendix. The air here smelled funny, not quite foul but still capable of coating your throat with a thick, decaying mustiness.

"Are you sure about this, Naeve?" Top asked, just before she opened the membranous gate. "It's taking a lot of energy to shunt the digestive flows around you. I'm having difficulty keeping things up. Charm is complaining that his bed feels like cartilage."

"Charm always complains. Let us in."

Israphel paused before the open membrane. "Are you from the scorched desert?" he asked, addressing the walls as though it were the most natural thing in the world.

I could tell that Top was just as mesmerized by his eyes as I was. Of course, she had always loved eyes—mostly for eating. *Perhaps I'll give his to her as a treat once he fails the task*—but the thought made me unexpectedly ill.

"No," Top said. "I'm the first of Naeve's family. She found me on another world."

Israphel frowned, such an unprecedented expression that it had the impact of a fiery declamation. "Another universe?" he said.

"I'm not sure. It's been many triads. You have quite beautiful eyes."

Israphel must have heard the predatory overtones, but he simply smiled and thanked her. Irrationally annoyed, I stepped through the opening into the chamber. Israphel followed me, glancing at the pulsing yellow walls and then the enormous heaps of bric-a-brac that littered the space. Some, including the one for my impossible task, had been there for countless cycles, but they were all immaculately clean. Dust was one of Top's favorite things to eat, which was one of the many reasons that made her an excellent castle.

I summoned the object to me—a fantastic, mysterious device that I had discovered on my travels and had saved for just this sort of emergency. In the far corner of the room something crashed to the floor as my object began its slow, lumbering way towards us. The humans of whatever place I had found it clearly hadn't designed their objects for summoning—it moved gingerly, as though its stubby wooden legs or wide, dark glass screen were in danger of breaking. It had a dark brown tail made of some strange smooth-shiny material that was forked at the end.

I had wanted to destroy his easy composure, and yet I still wasn't prepared for his reaction when he saw the object laboring toward him. He shook with laughter, his hands opening and closing as though they were desperate to hold onto something. He laughed, and yet his eyes nearly seared me. Top gave a sort of giggle-sigh that made the walls shudder. Was it the pain lurking behind his eyes that had made them so beautiful? But the pain wasn't lurking anymore, it was pouring and splashing and nearly drowning both of us. I looked away—what else could I do?

He stopped laughing almost as abruptly as he started, with a physical wrench of his neck. "Where did you find this?" he asked quietly. It had stopped in front of him and shuddered to a halt.

"I don't really remember. Some human place."

He turned to me and smiled. I coughed. "The first human place," he said.

I tried to mask my dismay. "Do you recognize it?" I asked. None of my tasks were allowed to be technically impossible, but I had hoped that this one would be about as close as I could get.

"Yes. They didn't really look like this, when—yes, I do."

"What's it called?" I asked, intrigued despite myself.

"A tee-vee. Television. Terebi. Many other things in many other dead languages. So what task have you set me, o demon of the scorched desert?"

His voice was slightly mocking, but raw, as though he hadn't quite gotten over the shock.

"You have to make it work," I said.

———

Back through Top's lower intestines, he carried it in his arms—
carefully, almost lovingly, the way I imagine humans carry their
babies. I had often pitied humans because of their static bodies
and entirely inadequate one pair of arms, but Israphel did not
ask for my help and I did not offer. Awkward though he was,
he still managed to look dignified.

By the time we reached the end of her intestine, Top had
managed to redecorate the front parlor. I can't say I was entirely
pleased with the changes—fine, gauzy cloth of all different
shades of green draped gently from the ceiling, rippling in an
invisible breeze. The floor was solid, but appeared to be the surface of a lake. It reflected the sky of an unknown world—jade
green, just like Israphel's eyes.

I could have killed her, only it was notoriously difficult to
kill a castle. Instead, I felt my skin tinting red, like my hair.

Israphel gently set the tee-vee down on the rippling lake
floor and looked around contemplatively.

"It's quite nice," he said to the ceiling. "I thank you."

Top knew how angry I was, so the only response she dared
was a kind of wistful "good luck" that made me turn even
redder. My own family!

Perhaps, after all, they *wanted* a . . .

I didn't even want to think of it.

"You have until first light," I said curtly, and walked straight
into a nearby wall.

Hours later, when twilight had sunk onto the scorched desert
and the maggots were giving their farewell light show as they
burrowed deeper into the sand, Charm found me. I knew he

was there because of the peculiar smell that wafted toward my nose this high in the castle—that tang of fresh saltwater could only mean that Charm had been drinking again.

"He's interesting, that fellow," Charm said in a studied drawl.

"You noticed?" I summoned several balls and began juggling them in intricate patterns—a nervous habit.

"Not really human, but . . . I mean, he doesn't smell like one, he doesn't smell like anything I've ever encountered, but he still *feels* like one. Looks like one. The way he stares at that teevee thing of yours? Very human."

I nearly fumbled my balls and had to create an extra hand just to keep the pattern going. "He's succeeding, then? He'll get it to work?"

"I don't know. He isn't doing anything, just sitting there. But still . . . something's just funny about him. Powerful, that much is obvious." He paused. "Mahi is sulking," he said, after a few moments.

I let out a brief laugh. "Typical. Does he really think I'll let this man succeed?"

"I don't know, will you?"

I lost the pattern of the balls entirely, and glared in the direction I guessed Charm was—a challenge even when he wasn't trying to hide.

"Don't be stupid," I said as the balls clacked and bounced on the floor. "I've lived this long without a . . . why would I need him now?"

Charm laughed, and I caught a strong whiff of saltwater. "Why, indeed? But Top was telling me about your fixation with his eyes, his broken nose—"

"*My* fixation . . ."

"You can't fool us, Naeve. We're your family. Why else do you think Mahi's sulking? Maybe you're lonely."

"But I already have all of you."

"Not that type of lonely, Mother." I felt him lean forward until his breath tickled my ear. "Mahi and I could never have passed the third test." His deep whisper sounded louder than an earthquake. "But he can." His voice grew fainter, and I knew he was vanishing in his own strange way—different parts of him at once.

His voice was the last to leave. "Are you lonely, Naeve?"

I sat frozen at the top of my castle, staring at the blackened desert with its shivering, luminescent sand for several minutes. Then, almost involuntarily, I conjured an image of Israphel.

He was sitting in the parlor where I had left him, a few feet away from the tee-vee. His brows were drawn up in concentration and his fingers occasionally stroked the strange object's forked tail. I stared at him for minutes, then hours— how many, I'm not sure. He never stirred, but once in that long night he whispered someone's name. I couldn't hear him clearly, but I saw his lips move and the pain that briefly flitted across his eyes.

Was I lonely?

I waited for the dawn.

First day light. Mahi awoke me from my trance-like stupor, wiping out the vestiges of Israphel's image with a flick of his two-dimensional tongue. He was all mouth this morning, and his grotesquely abundant teeth were screaming a morning aria that I supposed might be pleasurable to the son of a creature who climaxed while she chewed.

"You seem happy. Charm told me you were sulking."

"Why would I sulk? Our green-eyed intruder has failed!"

I sat up straight and stared at him. "Failed? How do you know?"

He cackled like a magpie and his teeth groaned with him. Positively unnerving, even for me. "He hasn't moved. He's just sat there all night, and the tee-vee hasn't done a thing. Go down and see for yourself."

He compressed himself into a line and started darting around me, giggling even as his teeth wailed like damned souls.

"I knew you wouldn't let him pass, Naeve," he said, flattening himself out again. "Are you coming? I want to see you toss him out."

My throat felt like someone had lit a fire to it. "Soon," I croaked.

After he left, I turned to stare back out at the desert. The maggots had started popping back out of the sand, making crackling noises like the sound of bones being slowly crushed. Light sprayed and twisted in the rapidly thickening air as they emerged. Just from the timbre of the pops, low and crunchy, I could tell that it must be fairly late in the season. In two days, perhaps, the desert would have its lights. I couldn't remember the last time I had been here to see it, but my sudden longing was mixed with dread.

If Mahi was wrong like I thought—hoped?—then in two days we would all see something more than just the lights.

———

By the time I arrived, the others were all there, staring silently at Israphel, who stared just as silently back at them. Even Top had fashioned a body for herself for the occasion—a wide-eyed brown human connected to the wall with an orange umbilical cord. He still sat on the floor, the tail of the tee-vee balanced on the tips of his fingers. It appeared that what Mahi said was true—he had not gotten it to work. The object looked just the same as it had yesterday. I fought a surge of disappointment. After all, why should I be disappointed? Just one less nuisance in my life. I could still stay and watch the lights if I wanted.

Israphel looked up as soon as I appeared, and a smile briefly stretched his hard lips. My nipples hardened, and I felt Charm flit over them with an almost-silent laugh.

"There, I've been waiting for you," he said. The night had brought shadows under his eyes, and he held himself with a dignified exhaustion that made him seem very human.

"I've completed the task," he said, when I didn't respond.

Mahi giggled and then stopped when Top glared at him. "You have?" I said, walking closer. "I don't see anything."

"Watch," he said. The black glass on the tee-vee flickered for a few moments and then seemed to come to life.

Strange shapes darted and moved inside the box. After a second I realized that they were human, but oddly seemed to resemble Mahi more than any humans I had ever encountered.

Mahi shrieked and rushed closer to the glass. "What is this? What is this thing?"

An odd, distorted voice came from inside the television: "What time is it?" I realized that one of the flat humans was speaking.

"It's howdy doody time!" smaller humans with gratingly high-pitched voices shouted in chorus.

I turned to Israphel, whose skin was faintly glowing with a sheen of sweat. "How did you do this?" I asked. But before he could answer, Mahi shrieked again—probably in delight, though it was difficult to tell through the distorted sound on the tee-vee. He had managed to enter the picture.

Israphel watched with every appearance of rapt fascination as the humans scattered from Mahi's giant jaws, screaming and blubbering. He gathered up three small stragglers with one swipe of his bloodred tongue and began mashing them up with his teeth. In fact, his teeth themselves seemed to gobble up the two-dimensional humans, and when they finished they spit the masticated globs deep into Mahi's apparently bottomless throat.

He tore through the humans, screaming as he ate them, like his mother had all those cycles ago, and laughed at their obvious terror. "You're all like me, now," I thought I heard him say, but his mouth was too full of screaming humans for me to be sure.

"Unbelievable," Charm said beside me. "I never knew the kid had it in him."

Minutes later, there were no more humans left on the screen. Mahi had relaxed himself into a vaguely anthropomorphic shape—more like a giant mouth with legs and arms—and was reclining in a steaming vat of blood and still-twitching body parts. He giggled and splashed some of the blood at the screen.

"More . . . want more." His words were slurred, as though he was drunk on the killing. "Give more," he said, and giggled again.

"How odd," Israphel said softly. "It must be a property of this universe."

"Naeve," Top said, sounding torn between disgust and envy, "get him out of there. That many humans at once can't be healthy."

"Can you?" I asked Israphel.

He shrugged and let go of the forked tail. Immediately, the screen went black again and Mahi came hurtling back out. I expected him to wail and throw a tantrum, but he was surprisingly quiet as he turned his mouth toward me.

"Keep him," he said. Then he fell down and drifted straight through the floor.

Israphel stood up gingerly, as though his bones ached. "I take it that I've passed the first test," he said.

I nodded, afraid to even speak. The very novelty of what he had just done terrified me.

"And the second?" he said, very gently, as though he understood my fear and wished to reassure me.

"Tell me who you are. Why are you here?"

He seemed surprised, which I took a perverse pleasure in, considering that I was just as surprised myself. Why had I laid such a simple task? But as any sign of emotion fled his face, I realized that perhaps I had stumbled upon an adequate task after all. He didn't want to tell me, but if he wanted to stay, he would.

"Top, Charm," I said suddenly. "Leave us." They left with hardly a murmur, since of course I could hardly stop them from eavesdropping.

Israphel stared at me silently while I smiled and settled myself against the rippled lake-floor.

"I take it you don't want to tell me," I said.

"You don't want to know."

"I'm waiting," I said. "You have until second day light."

Hours passed in silence. I amused myself by changing my body into various imaginative—and perfectly hideous—forms. A gigantic pair of jaws as close to Mahi's mouth as I could manage emerged from my stomach, growling and sweeping its fleshy tongue over the floor. Israphel, staring with a bizarre intentness at the wall behind me, didn't even flinch. I looked over my shoulder once to see what could possibly be so interesting, but of course the wall was blank. Whatever horrors Israphel witnessed that night, they were of his own creation. A thousand tiny arms sprouted from my face and filled the room with the cascading sound of snapping fingers. That, at least, he acknowledged with a slight upward quirk of his lips.

The night dragged on. I wondered if he would remain silent, if he would choose death over revealing his identity. The implications disturbed me on many levels, none of which I particularly wished to examine.

The floor still looked like a lake, and quite possibly was one, since various fauna periodically swam beneath us. A fish—the color of days-old dung and large as my torso—passed underneath me and paused just before Israphel. Its jagged teeth peeked over its lips and a strange appendage on its forehead gave off an ethereal glow that cast our faces in shadow.

"Isn't it beautiful?" I said, without really meaning to.

He turned to look at me, and I flinched. "Beautiful? In its own way, I suppose. But it's not of this world."

"Maybe from Top's world, then?" But after a moment I realized what he had implied. "No . . . from yours. From the human world." He remained silent, and despite myself I was drawn out. "Time acts strangely in our universe, but something tells me that when you traveled here, your human world had long since been destroyed. So how would you know what creatures once lived on it? Unless . . . are you one of those humans? The ones reborn on the other side of the desert?" The very idea seemed ludicrous. Those humans were barely capable of seeing the desert, let alone crossing it.

The fish dimmed its light and swam away, leaving us again in semi-darkness.

"Can you die, Naeve?" he asked.

I snorted. "Am I alive?"

"But old age can't kill you. Or disease . . . probably not even an atomic bomb."

"I'm not human, so why would I die in a human way?"

He looked at me so intently that I felt my skin begin to shiver and glow in response. If his expression hadn't been so serious and inexplicably sad I would have thought he was courting me—I had only ever seen that kind of stare from a demon of the third sex who wanted to mate.

"What do you think happens when you die?"

"My body will take its final journey, back to the Trunk. The Trunk will crush my bones and my siblings will masticate my flesh and I will be remembered by my etching in the bark."

His eyes narrowed, and I struggled to stop my skin from mottling iridescent ochre and gold. Sex ought to be lovely and ephemeral, but with him I knew it would mean far more. I couldn't afford to reveal my desire.

207

"The prospect doesn't scare you?" he said, as though it would certainly terrify him. "What about an afterlife?"

I gave a disbelieving smile. "Afterlife? You mean, some sort of soul-essence surviving somewhere after death? Who believes that but humans? Though," I said thoughtfully, "I suppose you humans might have a point. Wherever you come from, a few of you are reborn here. Maybe this is your afterlife?"

Israphel clenched his hands so tightly I could hear the constricted blood pounding through his veins. "And what of those humans reborn here? And what of their children? None of them die of old age either, but they can be killed. What do you think happens, Naeve, when you die in your own afterlife?"

I gave up and let my skin explode into whorls and star-bursts of color. In the extra light, I could see how the grief I had only glimpsed before now twisted his face.

"I don't know," I said. "I never thought about it before. But I assume the humans feed the maggots, just like the rest of us. Does this have a point, Israphel? You don't have much time until daylight."

He briefly closed his eyes, and when he opened them again, the pain had nearly left his face.

"Let me tell you a story, Naeve, about a human boy who became a post-human and then became a god."

I looked at him curiously. "Is that what you are?"

He shrugged. "It's what I might as well be. Or an angel. A Nephilim, perhaps?" He smiled bitterly, as though at some private joke. "So I was born on the first human world—Earth, as it was unimaginatively called at the time. After humans had traveled to space but long before we really colonized it. I grew roses—like the ones in this world, only you couldn't use the

thorns for impaling stakes. I had a wife who liked to write stories about monsters and death."

"You're partnered? Then you can't—"

His sudden glare was so inimical that I cut myself short.
"She died," he said, his words clipped staccato, "when she was
thirty-five. An eon later, I discovered that she had been reborn
here and that she died here too—nearly a triad ago, by your
count." He was silent for a few moments and then answered my
unspoken question. "She tried to cross the desert."

"Which is why you're here?"

"Yes. No. Not entirely."

"What else, then?"

"To retrieve the last of the humans, the ones we spent centuries hunting for before we found this strange pocket universe.
Do you know how statistically improbable it is that a universe
so unlike anything ever burped into the cosmos could exist? We
didn't even realize it until the computers showed a discrepancy of
precisely one billionth of a percent between the predicted numbers of retrieved humans and actual ones. But I already knew
something was wrong, because no one could retrieve my wife. So
I came here, and I realized—a person can't exist in two places at
once, and they can't be retrieved if they don't exist at all."

I had spent my life traveling between universes, and yet
what Israphel was implying boggled me. Humans were that
dominant in his time? "This retrieval . . . you mean, you're
trying to revive every human who ever existed?"

"And every one who might have existed. Those are easier.
It's a moral duty."

"But . . . that must be . . . do numbers that large exist?
Where could you possibly get the resources?"

His eyes looked very hard, and the last of my sexual arousal shivered as it left my skin. "You don't want to know," he said. "It will be easier for you if you don't."

"Or you don't want to tell me."

He met my eyes, but twitched as though he longed to look away. Some strange emotion was tearing at him, I could tell that by his posture, but what? "Other universes," he said, his voice rough. "We strip other universes, and then convert them to power sources, and when they burn out, we find other ones."

Of course. Now I understood the elusive emotion: guilt.

"That's why you're here?" I said. My eyes turned glassy and golden as magma with anger. "To save all the humans and then destroy this universe and every other creature in it? What about saving *us?* Does your moral imperative only apply to yourselves?"

He looked away and stared at the lake floor. "It would be a never-ending task. Humans take care of humans." It sounded like a mantra, something recited frequently to stave off doubts or reason.

I snorted in self-fury—I had thought better of him. "I'm sure they told you to believe that. And you call us demons. Of all the monumentally selfish . . . I suppose you came here and petitioned me so you could use my powers to hunt down the stragglers from your project?" I laughed, high and brittle. And I had thought I was too old to feel such bitter disappointment.

I elongated my lower left arm and forced him to meet my eyes. He looked positively tormented, which pleased me. "You would kill me too, wouldn't you? If you get your way, you would use me and then strip this universe and kill me too."

He grimaced and roughly knocked my hand away. "I'll find a way to save you—"

"And my family?"

He remained silent, but met my eyes.

I sighed. "No, of course not. Well," I said softly, leaning in closer and letting my eyes burn so hot he flinched, "lucky for us that you won't succeed."

"Naeve . . . I told you what you demanded. I've passed the second task, and you know it. You can't break your own law."

I smiled. "You want your third task, human? First tell me, you wish to become a member of my family, but which one? I already have three children. Would you be my fourth child? Or someone else?"

"Someone else," he said.

My turn to dance. "Who?"

The unexpected compassion in his smile made me feel like tearing at my skin. "Your partner," he said.

I leaned in so close our noses touched. "Then your task is to pleasure me." Before I could pull away, his eyes caught mine and his fingers gently traced my lips.

Abruptly, I stood up. "You'll have to do better than that," I said, shaking. I turned my back on him and headed toward the nearest hallway.

"Don't let him leave," I said to Top. Even after the wall had solidified behind me, I had the eerie sensation that I could feel those unfathomable eyes on my back.

I lay on the roof, shivering and devouring bits of Trunk bark laced with black sand. Usually this treat comforted me, reminded me of my childhood, but today it merely deepened my loneliness. Oh, I had a family, but I was still lonely. Israphel's presence made me realize it—if only because of how much I had foolishly hoped he would comfort me. He was lonely, too—anyone could sense that—but he had chosen to deal with it by brainwashing himself to a cause whose end result was the complete eradication of the non-human universe.

My hysterical laughter became confused with sobs, and I fell asleep.

When I woke, it was dark. The maggots had buried themselves for the night, but in the final stage of their metamorphosis they glowed so brightly that their light was visible even through the sand. The desert now looked like the skin of a giant black leopard.

The maggots would die too, if Israphel succeeded.

Charm lightly brushed my shoulder and offered me a jug filled with saltwater. I took a swig just to be polite—saltwater didn't affect me the same way. He took it back, and when he drank I could momentarily see the outline of his long neck and squat torso. When he first petitioned I wondered what his face looked like, or if he even knew. Now I figured that he didn't—why else would he drink so much?

"Desert's beautiful," he said. "I think they'll change this morning. It's been a while, hasn't it?"

"Yes," I said. "I remember . . . they were changing the day I cut off from the Trunk . . . I thought all the world would be that beautiful."

Hard to believe we were the same person: that young demon crawling out of her sac, covered in amniotic fluid, staring in mesmerized joy at the swarms of fluttering light . . .

"Will he really destroy all this?" Charm asked.

"I'll kill him in the morning, but others will come. I think there may be too many of them."

Charm took a long pull from the jug. "You know why I like saltwater?" he said. "It tastes like tears. I had some of yours while you were sleeping. I hope you don't mind."

I shook my head. "What did they taste like?" I asked.

"Bitter, like despair. Like disappointed love. I don't think you should kill him."

"What else can I do? Let him kill all of us?"

"He keeps asking a question down there. Top wouldn't disturb you but I thought you should know. He says: 'Do the humans here know that the desert will kill them?'"

I looked sharply at him—or at least, his bottle. "Do the *humans* know? Of course they do. They know jumping off a cliff will kill them too. What kind of a question is that?"

Charm's breath dusted my ear. "His wife, Naeve," he said.

I stood up and started running down the stairs.

Israphel looked startled—almost afraid—when I burst into the room.

"Come," I said, grabbing his elbow. I dragged him to the front doors and pushed them open with my right hands. We stumbled down the steps and onto the sand, where the buried maggots wiggled away from our feet. I bent down and plucked one from its lair. I held its squirming form between us—it was a particularly fine specimen: juicy and fat and bright enough to make him squint. I grew a third arm on the left side of my body—glowing mahogany, just like the human body I had used in my failed attempt to seduce Israphel that first day.

213

"This is a human hand," I said. "Watch what happens."

Steeling myself, I dropped the maggot on my new left palm. Immediately, it started burrowing into my flesh, devouring my skin and blood in great maggot-sized chunks. It chomped through my bones with reckless abandon and I gasped involuntarily. My hand had nearly fallen off by the time it finished gorging and settled itself in the ruined, bloody mass of my palm.

"Do you see?" I said between gritted teeth. I needed to withdraw the nerve endings, but not before Israphel understood. "This is just one maggot. You can find this out without dying. Anyone who lives alongside the desert knows what they do. I've heard the humans even sometimes harvest the maggots for their farms. They all know. How long was your wife here before she went to the desert?"

He swallowed slowly, as though his throat was painfully constricted. "By your count . . . seventeen triads."

"She was older than me . . . time enough to die."

He started to cry, but they were furious tears, and I knew better than to touch him. "What if she didn't know? What if she lived far from the desert, and when she came here no one told her—"

I picked up the maggot—which was by now nearly the size of my palm—and held it in front of his face. "Look! *She knew.* She was older than me, Israphel, and I am very old. She knew." I let the maggot drop into the sand and withdrew my ruined hand back into my body.

He sank to his knees. I knelt down so my face was even with his. "Do you know how demons die?" I said softly.

He shook his head.

"We choose," I said. "If we wanted to, we could live forever, but every demon dies. Some die sooner than others, but we all, eventually, make the choice. Death doesn't scare me, Israphel, but eternity does. Seventeen triads is a very long time."

"We could have been together forever," he said.

"No one wants forever, even if they don't realize it. I imagine that your project hasn't been operating long enough to discover this, but it's true . . . life is sweet because life is finite. Do you *really* want to live forever?"

He met my eyes for a moment and gave a brief, painful smile. My skin started tingling again. "No," he said.

The ground began to shake, softly at first, then more violently. Then came the sound I remembered so well—a low, buzzing hum that gouged my ears and made my spine shiver. The lights under the sand grew even brighter. Israphel looked around—curious, wary, but certainly not scared. It was a good attitude for someone who planned to live with me. I started laughing, first in soft giggles and then in unstoppable peals. I lay down in the sand to get closer to the buzzing. When I felt Israphel touch my cheek, I laughed even more and pulled him on top of me with all four of my arms.

"What is it?" he asked.

"The lights!" I couldn't seem to explain any more. While I laughed he kissed me slowly—first my eyes, then my mouth, then my nipples. I was coming by the time the maggots burst from the sand, metamorphosed from fat little worms to gigantic, glowing moths. They swirled around us, dipping into my hair and alighting on Israphel's fuzzy scalp.

"I'm going to fight you, Israphel," I said. "I won't let you destroy my universe just because you passed the third task."

His laugh was deep, like the buzzing just before the lights. "I wouldn't have expected otherwise," he said.

We held each other as we rolled around on the sand, buffeted on all sides by the glowing moths. The maggot that had eaten my hand had also metamorphosed and now swooped on its gigantic wings down toward our faces, as though to greet us before flying away.

"What happens after you die, Naeve?" Israphel asked—softly, as though he didn't expect an answer.

"Nothing," I said.

And then we laughed and stood and I danced with my husband in the lights.

The Mirages

Lalo hadn't been back to this block of Isabel la Católica for more than a year, not since the affair. Foot traffic was thin for a Friday afternoon, just a farmer in a sacksuit on the corner of Madero, exposed wrists peeling and cracking. She sold jocotes and nanches, sunset colors in straw baskets. In the sun-shaded park by Bellas Artes where Lalo had sometimes met with Lili this past year, any food was sold by approved vendors in laminate stalls, their faces permanently obscured by government-issued dust masks. Lalo hesitated and then approached him.

"The jocotes," he said. "Would you take five hundred?"

It wasn't what they were worth. It was all he had.

The farmer, at least seventy years old and hard in a way that made Lalo seem soft and ready to fall off a bone, gave him a long, steady look. He pivoted to inspect the nanches and his hip bag brushed against the basket of jocotes. One rolled out and the farmer caught it between calloused fingers. Only a few jagged, cloudy splinters remained where her fingernails had been. This one wouldn't be going north. Just like Lalo.

"Five hundred pesos," Lalo said again. She nodded. Lalo's sigh whistled through his mask and he gave her the last of his change.

"It's for my daughter," Lalo said, as he was turning to go. "It's her birthday today." His shoulders jerked. She raised her eyebrows, as though she could see something that he couldn't, as though he were exposed in the sun despite his dust mask and PVC suit. He turned and hurried away.

It was another block to the tunnel access point. The below-ground apartments were solidly fresa, but this entrance still stubbornly held to the memory of the neighborhood's grubby intellectual past. The concrete wall had a new mural, a Tlaloc whose snarling jaws and long fangs made the ancient rain god a feral beast, an avatar of the ancestors' rage. Behind the holes of his mask, tears of blood rained to the earth and evaporated into a fine pink mist. Lalo's lips quirked. A blunt instrument of moral symbolism, but that was to be expected in these intellectually starved times. Not everyone could be Juan O'Gorman. Certainly not now, when the fever to go p'al pinche norte had so consumed the survivors of this desertified rock that artistic endeavor had been left to the degenerates, the sick, the old. At least the cocoliztli could serve some purpose besides class-based death and destruction; like the consumption of the Romantic era, it could inspire those afflicted and those left behind to look beyond imperialism's empty seductions. Lalo shook himself—gently—and stepped closer to the gate. The gatekeeper's image—middle aged, güero, close-lipped smile—resolved on a screen. It startled visibly as if it recognized him, and Lalo was reminded of how much he disliked the human affectations of the latest generation AI. That, at least, he hadn't missed.

"Been a while, hasn't it?" it asked.

"I'm just visiting."

A buzz and the door fell inward with a small sigh.

"Are those jocotes from a local farm? They're not safe, Eduardo, they use sewer water and unfiltered sun—"

Lalo pushed past the screen and moved quickly down the black staircase. The voice stopped as soon as he stepped from its field of vision. "Pinche bots," he muttered to himself. "Inherit the earth along with the cockroaches after we're done screwing it up."

Halfway down he paused for breath. He pushed his mask over his shoulder-length hair, blue and purple this week, Lili's favorite colors. He put his nose in the basket and breathed as deep as he could. Some of the tunnel smell seeped in anyway—mold and concrete and miles of rubber insulation—but mostly it was the heavy citrus perfume of the jocotes and their faint alcoholic aftertaste. Lalo shook his head sharply and checked the time. Then he slipped the mask back on and kept walking, each heavy footstep echoing down the empty tunnels. They wound down and down into the old dry lakebed, filled with apartments and shopping plazas and offices, but Zara's apartment was near surface level, beneath the C storage tower.

Lalo stopped at a door of wrought iron and wood, made for a kinder era. It had been the door to Garibay's sacristy, saved before the church was demolished in the floods, and kept at the university before even that secular shrine to learning was divided like a turkey for market and sold to the north's top three multinational hegemonies. He had been offered a teaching position at the reconfigured Unilever Institute, but he had declined. Perhaps that was when the trouble had started. Zara had lost respect for him. Lili can't live on your *principles*, she had snarled, that withering judgment seared into his memory. He buzzed the intercom and waited while its chime seemed to settle into the corners of this narrow corridor like dust. The chimes stopped, but no one's face appeared on the monitor. From its speaker came the sounds of an argument— "*I'll go—no—*" Spanish mixed with English. Zara had barely been able to order imported beer when she kicked Lalo out.

The rubber gasket released with a tired puff of air. The aromas of sweet dough and frosting assaulted Lalo at the same moment. If Lalo were still living there, it would have smelled of nixtamal and tortillas. Zara was a dutiful child of the city's petit-bourgeoisie, not the sort who would normally look twice at an intellectual moreno of the laboring classes. She had been raised on the street-corner tortillerías, shops whose masa was more cob than corn, but Lalo's mother had migrated to the city from rural Puebla and never lost her taste for fresh-ground corn and the tortillas that inflated like balloons on the griddle. Zara had taken up his mother's tradition with pride in the first years of their marriage. But Zara was going north, and they said that the field corn was bad for you now, just like jocotes.

Zara slid the door the rest of the way open and then stood there in the airlock, mouth open.

"You came," she said.

"It's her birthday."

Zara didn't move.

"Will you let me in?"

Zara stepped back and Lalo crossed the threshold. The two of them slid the door shut again.

"She's getting back from school soon. Jared and I have some things we need to discuss with you beforehand."

"In English or Spanish?" Lalo asked, and laughed as though he had told a joke.

"Now you don't get to puff yourself up over your English, Lalo."

"I never did that."

Zara froze for a second. "You always just pretended that you didn't mean it. Lili's the best in her class now. She came in third in the district migration exams. Jared says that our application is a foregone conclusion."

"Do you expect me to be happy about that?"

They were standing in the airlock, too close. Zara's long hair fell over Lalo's shoulder, and they both closed their eyes.

Zara stepped back. "I expect even an unrepentant narcissist like you to care that our daughter is happy and healthy and successful."

Zara was thinner than the last time Lalo had seen her. The shadows beneath her eyes were deep and purple.

"Jared isn't taking such good care of you, though, is he?"

Zara drew herself up and jammed her finger against Lalo's chest. "Jared is getting us *out*. He's getting Lili out, and that's worth anything to me, Lalo. All this time you've been blaming me, I wish that you could think for one second about your daughter and what's best for her."

"How is it good for her to lose her father?"

"She's gaining another." But even this new, north-evangelized Zara looked a little doubtful.

Lalo snorted. "A better one, your mother would say. Poor lady, she never lived to see her wayward daughter mejorar la raza at last. Two güeros and one beautiful child." He checked the boxes off in the air with his finger. Fucking gabachos and their border nets, their imperialist notions of worthy families. He held out the basket. "I bought jocotes."

"From the *surface*?"

"Lili loves them. If she's really going north, she'll never taste them again."

Zara looked between the sunset basket and Lalo's dry, dry eyes. She nodded. "Let's go inside. Jared will be wondering what we're up to."

"I wish we could give him a good reason to wonder."

Zara didn't turn around. "Shut up, Lalo."

Jared was sitting at the dining room table, at the far side of the small kitchen. He didn't get up to greet him, just watched the two of them together, lips tight with disapproval. But he had always had that acquisitive slant to his eyebrows.

"Hello, Jared," Lalo said civilly, then added, "fancy seeing you here. Looking like you own the place."

Zara sighed. "Don't start, Lalo"

Jared frowned and waved his hand above the three beers sweating on the table.

"An associate of mine just brought them back from Saskatchewan. Black calabash stout."

"Illegal contraband, Jared?" Lalo said in Spanish. "How very gabacho of you."

He frowned again. "English, please. Unless you've forgotten it already, Lalo."

"As the zapatistas would have said, speaking the language of our oppressors weakens our ability to fight them," Lalo said in English, and sat down.

"We need to talk about Lili," Zara said slowly, as though the syllables were hot bricks that someone had told her how to arrange once, impatiently.

"Why? Aren't you all running away without me soon?"

Zara rounded on Lalo. "We have to agree on how to tell her!"

"You haven't yet?" Lalo said at the same time that Jared unstopped a beer with the back end of a lighter and said, with appalling calm: "*English.*"

"We decided," Zara said, fingers dancing lightly in the doughnut puddle left by her rapidly warming beer.

"You decided what?" said Lalo in his perfect English. He had studied harder at anyone at University, far harder than Zara. Sure, she'd been an anomaly there; families like hers scorned the free autonomous university of the people. But it was Lalo who'd had something to prove.

Zara kept laying bricks. "We decided that we need a story for you that you tell Lili. So that the tran-transition . . ."

She looked up to Jared.

"So that the transition goes more smoothly," he finished. "We put the application in next week, but it's just a formality. We already have a unit reserved in the New South Nunavut settlement. State-of-the-art. All the play areas have UV screening and twelve-pass filters. We believe that Lili will be happy there."

"Happy and *healthy* there, Lalo," Zara said, glancing down and then away from Lalo's arm. Lalo had a wound from a month ago that still hadn't healed. The gauze peeked just below the black sleeve of his suit, but Zara had noticed. Even Zara, with her imported beers and strictly filter-grown organic produce, looked brittle as tinder. Her light skin, that lifelong pass to the good opinion of the society that had only measured Lalo for his utility, no longer pretended to beauty; it had curdled to a sour yellow. Jared had lived here for two years, but he had never lost that milky glow, that fat, the clean and manicured nails of p'al pinche norte.

And now they were going to take his Lili there forever.

Zara snatched a swig of Jared's beer. Jared gave her a flat stare and appropriated Zara's untouched bottle

"It's for the best," Jared said. "Do this for your daughter's sake, Lalo."

"Where *do* you find the moral high ground these days, Jared? Do they sell it on Amazon?"

"Stop it, Lalo," Zara said.

Lalo unstoppered his beer without looking down and passed it to the woman he had once sworn to love and cherish for the rest of their lives.

"I think it's time to put the past behind us," Jared said.

"I've been reading," Lalo began, as though he hadn't spoken, "about the psychology of betrayal. About romantic and sexual betrayal in particular. It's fascinating." He dug his fingers into the ridged edges of the bottle cap, dug until it hurt.

Jared and Zara stared. He continued in Spanish. "They say that it's generally an extreme case of narcissism or entitlement that leads one partner to cheat, because an affair of any length requires a fabric of lies and deceptions and half-truths that will always destroy the foundation of a healthy marriage. That's what hurts the most, they say—not the extramarital affairs per se, but the sustained, daily betrayal. Some cheaters get off on it, and they don't feel bad because they don't really, at bottom, think that their partner is as human as they are. They think that they deserve all of the sex and emotional highs and dramatic declarations and that their partner can just make do, and deal with the kids on top of everything."

Zara gripped the table edge so tightly that every swollen knuckle stood out white beneath the full-spectrum sun lamps. Her gaze ought to have nailed Lalo to the wall. Jared was scrambling to take control again, but it was easier to ignore his self-assured English than the perfect recognition in Zara's furious gaze.

"The hardest thing to believe in," Lalo continued, "is the remorse of a person capable of that kind of long-term deceit. Focus on their actions, the experts say, does this seem like a good prospect for a *new* long-term commitment?" Lalo laughed shortly. It sounded like a chest cough. Zara's frown deepened. "Of course not. The cheated-on partner has no idea who the person they married really is. They've been loving and faithful to a mirage."

Zara's voice dripped acid. "Are you quite done, Lalo?"

Lalo's voice was very soft. "Even if, for the sake of argument, the wretched creature behind the mirage truly did regret their actions and truly did love them—well, there would be no way to be sure, would there?"

Zara shook her head, disbelieving. "Now?"

"Now," Lalo agreed, in English. "You were telling me about the lie you want me to tell our daughter on her birthday to explain why she'll never see me again."

Jared reached over and took the beer that Lalo had given Zara. "No need to be dramatic, Lalo. We have very good VR communication tech these days, and of course for Lili's sake I'll do what I can to support your migrant petition when the application period opens up again next year."

"To do what? A doctor of political anthropology scrubbing toilets? They don't believe in our universities up there, do they?"

"Are you teaching at Unilever, Lalo?" Zara asked, her own subtle retaliation.

Lalo winced. "My university no longer exists. In any case, your northern settlements require health checks."

"Eat less unregulated farm produce and you'll be more likely to pass it." Jared nodded at the jocotes.

"We want you to tell Lili just that," Zara said abruptly. "That you are sick. That she has to leave where she will be safe from contamination, and you will come later when you are better."

"And if I die down here in the polluted hell-hole you've left behind, all the better, eh?"

"You can't blame us for the *drought*, Lalo," Jared said. "It's a global phenomenon."

"There's the international spirit! Where was it when you first-world assholes were dumping toxic loads of carbon into the atmosphere for the whole twentieth fucking century?"

Jared slammed the third empty beer bottle down on the table. Zara jerked. "My God, you're just the same, a goddamned overeducated anarchist hippie. And you wonder why the board decided to reorganize your rogue university—"

"It wasn't rogue, it was *autonomous*, a crucial concept in the history of Mexico's social movements—"

"The rogue universities still belaboring the carbon-warming link needed to be reined in. It isn't proven, and in any case it's opened up unprecedented opportunities in the reclaimed arctic—"

Lalo stood up. "And unprecedented opportunities for the cocoliztli to kill off—"

The sound of the airlock opening went off like a gunshot behind them.

226

"Mamá?" Lili called. "Jared?"

Jared looked belligerent and just a little worried. "You'll go along, Lalo? For her sake?"

Lili walked into the kitchen and peeled off her lucha libre dust mask.

"Cocoliztli?" Zara mouthed, glancing at Lalo's fresh bandage again, then at his face.

Lalo grimaced. "You've made—" he started to say, but by then Lili had seen him.

"Lalo!" she cried and ran forward. Lalo caught and lifted his eleven-year-old daughter to kiss her. *Your choice* was the logical end of that sentence, unraveling like the ends of Lili's two plaits.

"Where did your ribbons go, mi amor?" he asked, breathing her in.

"Mamá said they were my birthday ribbons so I gave them to Genaro because it's his birthday too and his dad has the coco."

"English, Lili," Jared said. "We have to practice, remember."

Lalo hugged her tighter. "That was sweet of you, cariño."

Lili froze in his arms and then leaned back so she could meet Lalo's eyes. "Do you want something? Does Mamá owe you money?"

Zara clapped her hands. "Mamá made you tres leches cake and piloncillo cookies, Lili. Do you want to help me get them from the oven?"

Lili squirmed out of Lalo's grip and ran to Zara. They busied themselves by the stove, while Lalo and Jared watched them from beside the dining room table.

"I know you still care about her," Jared said.

"She's my daughter."

"No, I mean Zara. I want you to know I'm serious about this. No matter how things started, I'm going to do this right. We're getting married as soon as we're settled into the development."

"Congratulations."

"And I'll take good care of Lili, too."

"We were taking good care of her here."

Jared laughed. "Zara always says you lack self-awareness."

"Said the pot to the griddle."

Jared stepped closer. He punched Lalo on the arm hard, but not as hard as those cartoonish biceps were capable of. Lalo grunted and just stopped himself from gripping the tender flesh. Jared spoke, sotto voce. "Play this right, Lalo, and I could help you. There are new treatments available at the embassy hospital. They work."

Lili and Zara crossed into the dining room, Zara carrying the cake and Lili with a basket of still-warm cookies.

"They're pig cookies, Lalo," Lili said, handing him one that was still hot enough to singe her hands. "They're your favorite."

Lalo's laugh wobbled. "They're *your* favorite, my little butterfly."

Lili sighed and shook her head, so like Zara. "Oh, Lalo, how do you not even know which is your favorite anymore?"

Lalo bit off the head of the cookie pig. His shoulders jerked. "I've been a little lonely, butterfly. But look, I brought you jocotes."

Lili stared at the basket. "Oh, you mean the ones with the big stone in the middle? Thank you, Lalo," she said politely.

Zara started cutting the cake. "Let's sing mañanitas, okay? Then we can eat dessert for dinner."

"Dessert for dinner," Lili laughed, all forgotten.

They sang mañanitas, which even Jared had managed to learn. Afterward he insisted on singing the gabacho happy birthday and Lili kept smiling. They then ate for a precise five minutes before Zara stood up.

"I just remembered that I haven't changed the filters. No, Jared, stay here. Lalo can come with me."

Zara lifted her mask from the hook by the door and walked back to the airlock. Lalo followed. He moved as though the floor were gently tilting and returning to its center, and that he didn't trust it even when it held steady.

Zara pushed the ladder from the wall beside the air lock and started climbing. Lalo stared at the metal rungs and breathed with a high whistle. He thumped his chest and coughed.

Zara poked her head out from the loft.

"Coming?" she asked.

Lalo started up behind her. He must have been taking too long, because Zara started talking when he was only halfway there.

"Do this right, Lalo," she said, her scorn illuminating a normally hidden fresa nasality, the high rises of Santa Fe here in the heart of the dying city.

"I'm trying."

"Stop fucking trying. Just stop. You always try, and never make it. Don't make this harder for her. If you ever loved us just a little, let us go."

"Of course." Lalo, nearly at the top of the ladder, paused to catch his breath. "Of course I love you. Haven't you been listening? You don't have to go off with him, Zara. You can still save our family. It's not too late."

229

Zara hit the ladder and Lalo slipped down a rung. "I *am* saving our family, cabrón. As always, you make me do the hard shit while you try to soak up all the pity like it's drinking water. Can you imagine what this has been like for me? Do you think I like Jared? Gabacho pretty boy with arms like inflated tires? I bet you tell all your friends about how your crazy ex-wife left you for a fucking gringo. The man who destroyed your precious university. Oh, the fresa in her, selling out her principles for the mirage of the imperialist class, yes, that sounds like you. But you don't tell them why I had to leave! You don't tell them how he was around to save me from the mess you made! Traditional families, traditional values, responsible immigration, assimilation—" She choked the words out. "Do you know how much I hate it? Can you even imagine? They've erased me before I've even taken a step past their wall. I hate them and I can't tell anyone but you."

Lalo had managed to crawl into the loft by now. He looked at Zara, trembling and red-faced with rage. He reached over and hugged her. At first Zara didn't move. Then they were kissing.

Then they weren't.

"Mamá?" Lili called from below. "Lalo? Can I come up?"

"I'm sorry," Lalo whispered, touching Zara's cheeks, her lips, her stark collarbone and paper-dry skin. "I'm sorry, I'm sorry, I'm so sorry—"

Zara dug her nails into Lalo's wrists, the clean one and the bandaged one. She left marks.

"I'm coming up, okay?" Lili said.

"Of course, cariño," Zara called. "Be careful."

Lalo's eyes were tight with pain. "Amor—"

"You're right, Lalo," Zara said. "I loved a phantom. Who knows who you are. Who knows who is even apologizing to me right now. You pretend to have principles, but *you* befriended that bastard in our kitchen."

"Now you blame me for trying to save my job?"

"Ha! Have you forgotten why you lost it? The indictment? The investigation?"

"I told you, amor, it was a smear campaign and I was an easy target." Lalo had repeated this so often over the last year that the words seemed to shine with righteousness. Even now, they eased him.

Zara paused. "I met her, you know."

Lalo opened his mouth, closed it again. He couldn't get enough air up here without his mask.

She continued, her lips a few centimeters from his ear. "I need to give Lili a chance. You have always made me be the better person, Lalo. I remember when we were younger, admiring you— it must be amazing to be an asshole, it must be a fucking thrill."

Lili jumped over the edge. "Why don't you let me curse if you get to, Mamá?"

Lalo and Zara pulled apart. Zara laughed. "Because I want you to have everything I didn't, Lili. I want you to have better choices."

Lalo looked at Zara for several seconds. No one said anything. Lalo turned to Lili.

"Butterfly, do you want to go to the roof with me? I have another present for you."

Lili looked at filter panels that lined the far wall, gritty and untouched. They hadn't even brought a replacement for the pretense. She didn't seem surprised. Lili looked to Zara for permission, who nodded. "Okay," Lili said, and took Lalo's hand.

"Thank you," Zara mouthed.

Lalo pressed his lips together and looked away.

Lalo unzipped the old seal in a dark corner of the loft and opened the tower door. The apartment was unfashionably close to the surface, but they had bought it for this wonder: storage tower access. Views weren't popular these days, but Zara loved it. As Lalo had, once. Lili ran up the first flight of stairs. The sound of her shoes on the rusting metal echoed up the long and lonely tower. Lalo turned on his flashlight.

"Where's your mask, butterfly?"

"I left it downstairs. You don't have yours, either."

Lalo sighed, looked back at the door. "We won't be long," he said, and they started up. They were silent for a long time, nearly to the top of the tower.

"When are you coming to the north, Lalo?"

Lalo gripped the banister and pulled himself up a few more steps. His breath whistled.

"In a few years, butterfly."

Lili took a deep breath, as though she were going to cry. Then she let it out and helped Lalo the rest of the way up the stairs. Lalo shoved open the old door, whose hinges had been old before and were now nearly immobile.

Lili hesitated on the threshold. "Jared doesn't like me coming here," she said. "Don't tell him, okay?"

"All right."

"Promise?"

Lili was frozen in a half-crouch, looking up warily at Lalo. "I told you I won't," Lalo snapped.

"It's just," Lili said, "sometimes you do what you want. No matter what you promised."

Lalo turned away. The evening air blew cool across his forehead. The smells of dust and pollen and smog were overwhelmed by the dozens of marijuana plants in neat rows, fat on carbon dioxide and doubled over from the weight of their glittering rose-tinted buds.

"These are Jared's?" he asked.

"He says that I have to be careful, because he's growing the money that will get us north."

Lalo nodded slowly. The sun was setting, spectacular, like all sunsets these days. The oranges and reds and cool yellows outlined the tall peak of Popocatepetl and the surrounding mountains—even now, on a clear day there was no place in the world that could match it.

"I'm not sure I want to leave, Lalo."

Lili was gripping him around the waist. Lalo pried her hands off enough to kneel down. Lili was crying, but like an adult, without any sound. "I'm not sure I want to leave you. Even if you disappear sometimes."

"It's only for a little while," Lalo said, empty.

Lili just shook her head and kept crying. Lalo unlatched his hip bag and drew out a small round basket.

"I brought something special just for you," he said. "They're still warm."

Lili opened the basket and unfolded the cloth and drew out a fresh white tortilla.

"You made them, Lalo?"

"For you, butterfly. For your birthday." He had begged them off of his girlfriend's grandmother the night before, but he had heated them up before he left and he liked the way Lili was looking at him now.

Lili burst out sobbing now and ripped it in half with her teeth, without even waiting for the salsa de molcajete that Lalo had stolen from the fridge that morning. She'd eaten them like that when she was little, he now recalled, fresh with nothing on them.

"I still love you. Mamá says it's right for me to love you because you're my father, even though you're not always the best father. She says that you won't try to be better, but she doesn't understand. It's just how you are. And *I* know—you've always been this way."

"I'll come in a few years," Lalo repeated, though he was remembering Lili's judgmental cries as a baby, when Lalo would stagger home drunk just before dawn and Zara would be up, red-eyed, with the breast pump. "We'll be a family again."

Lili looked at her over her half-eaten tortilla. "It's okay. You don't have to lie."

Lalo looked down at the tortilla he was holding and saw two drops spatter on the brown-flecked surface. It was late August, and it hadn't rained one day since May.

"Do you remember, abuelita used to say that nothing tastes better than a tortilla when you're crying."

"She did?" Lalo took a bite, then another.

"It's delicious, Lalo," Lili said, but she wasn't looking at him. She was looking at the sunset. In the distance, a barrio church launched fireworks for some dried-out saints, which had once been, a long time ago, gods. There had been a Tlaloc judging him on the wall outside the gate this afternoon. The gods didn't need blood these days; they needed tears.

"It's delicious," Lalo agreed, swallowing the nixtamal of a poisoned earth and the salt of his poisoned body. He felt hollow, he felt like a figure of dust motes and light that the breeze would blow away. Jared had been one of the corporate consultants in charge of breaking up the university. He'd been sympathetic when

that girl in Lalo's The Radical Imagination class had posted her
denuncia. Sure, she and Lalo had fucked a few times during the
semester, but it was all consensual, and hadn't he given her a ten
for the course? The problems came afterward, when that ignorant village girl had somehow gotten it into her head that *theirs*
was the exploitative power dynamic. She'd demanded an apology.
He'd gotten angry. He'd yelled. He'd been drinking—it was possible that he had in fact struck her as she claimed. Certainly, he
remembered her on the floor. Her roar of inarticulate rage still
lifted the hairs on his arms when he recalled it. For a second, his
perspective had snapped and he had seen himself as she did. As
the coco ate him this past year, he wondered if she had cursed
him, paid a village chamán to send down a mal aire, for wasn't he
now turning into that very monster she had made him out to be?
Jared had tried to help Lalo—even then he'd had eyes for Zara—
but the conditions were a public apology and mandated anti-
harassment therapy. Lalo had refused. Zara found out, of course.

And now he was gone—how had he gone already—hadn't
he tried to be a good person—hadn't he had a chance—where
had he gone?

"Lalo?"

Was it Lili's or Zara's voice? They were both so sweet. He
had been loved once, but they didn't even know. You *can* love a
mirage, he would tell them, you can love a mirage, but too bad
for you when it all just blows away.

Reconstruction

(For Susie King Taylor)

In January of '63, my boys shared camp downriver from Beaufort with the 54th Massachusetts, who had among them a gunner of an intellectual disposition. Having been born free, he'd learned his letters young and read diligently of whatever improving literature he could find. He helped me teach the men their letters that winter, as we celebrated the passing of Lincoln's Proclamation into law. He had developed what he termed a taxonomy of anger. The gunner, called Flip, liked to expound upon his theory on watch or when we stayed up late on cold nights, drinking moonshine whisky and blinking back smoke from a damp fire of Spanish moss and live oak. As a woman, nominally the company laundress, I never warmed myself after a turn at the pickets with Flip, but I did spend a part of most nights around that fire, so that even all these years later, I have only to smell a bit of brackish marsh and burning pitch to remember more vividly than my present time, the men laughing, and Flip saying in his serious young man's voice, "The first, and best, is righteousness, that anger which speaks divinity."

You could pick the officers from the infantry by noting the slow, considering nods which greeted this observation. Their heads dipped before the fire, grimly pleased at their unexpected reflection. They had long since learned to harness that purer flame, these veterans of many engagements who knew they must face yet further.

Flip had primary care of the sow the men called Piggy, a guinea hog of pneumatic mammaries who had come to us as an adolescent and now behaved in camp like an oversized dog. Clarence, a drummer boy for the 1ˢᵗ South Carolina, had been known to ride Piggy into evening praise meetings with Flip leading the charge, much to the general hilarity of the men, and the ire of Billy Brown, a corporal in the 1ˢᵗ South Carolina who was fixing to become a preacher when the war ended, and took to the praise meetings as though he'd already been ordained. I had reason to know the hopping choler of "My Father" Brown, as he had kept his eye on me all spring and summer of '62, believing it my womanly duty to reward his attention with my favors. This ranked fourth in Flip's schema, as "affront, that which pricks at one's pride but not one's dignity"—though it seemed to me that this unduly privileged Billy Brown's perspective on the matter. His second and third—fury and vengefulness—switched places often over the course of that long, still winter. After some rebs snuck past our pickets and killed ten men in their sleep, Flip joined the retaliatory mission led by Sergeant Major Whittaker, a young black officer of mysterious origins who had come to us early that summer and whom Colonel Higginson quickly came to hold in much esteem. All that fall, Beau Whittaker had taken to picking the herbs I liked whenever he found them outside camp, but he returned that winter night with nothing in his haversack but a rattle of teeth, cracked and bloody at the roots.

"We did for them," he said, observing a molar seamed black with abscessed caries. Some reb's jaw had hurt like hell, but not anymore—in dying he had passed that burden, some-how, to my kind-eyed soldier. "Twelve, hiding in the mud by the estuary, white rats. Brought two slaves with them—Flip has them now."

And days later, the 1ˢᵗ South Carolina's two newest soldiers were drinking the sweet nectar of freedom—which had, in this case, the salutary burn of contraband whisky. Zollie and Guil-laume were brothers, natives to these waterways, though their mother had been a creole from Baton Rouge. They were laugh-ing, good-natured boys, eager to share our fire and our stories, and nodded when Flip elevated vengefulness to the grim honor of second place.

"But those Johnny Rebs," said the younger one, Guil-laume, "they got plenty of vengefulness too. They'd string us up quicker than a Christmas turkey—" He gave his brother a conspiratorial glance, and Zollie finished: "—if they could catch us!"

Flip's back stiffened. "Anger that grows in the soil of depri-vation is a holy fruit, while that which is sewn in the soil of overabundance grows crooked and full of poison. It is beneath our consideration."

Third, still indispensable, he ranked fury: "that berserk-ing wrath which bursts forth after long confinement." Flip was a freedman who had never known a day's bondage, but with this he named and mapped the power that made the Negro regiments the terror of Johnny Reb. I felt it, too, when I stared dead-eyed at the stinking midden of disarticulated flesh out-side the medical tent—a devil and a sawbones had carved my heart clean of pity and horror, and at first only fury filled that empty cavity.

But in my later years, it has been that fifth, overlooked anger who has abided and kept her step with mine after all the others fell aside. After Beau died, and Grandma came to help me with our baby, I felt her: a canker, a hard stone beneath a camp-stitched wound, turning. *Ten dollars, Seneca Stone Company*, read the check from the men who had killed Sergeant Major Beau Whittaker for the savings of a scaffold repair, and made me a widow at twenty-three.

"Gall," I heard Flip say that night, across the chasm of all my deaths and four hard years, "the fifth, and the least. That bitter medicine, the grime of commonplace indignity which collects in the soul day by day and grows there, like a cancer."

"There is a peculiar kind of sadness," declared Beau Whittaker one morning just before dawn, when we were still wrapped in one another in the tent the boys had given me for myself at the edge of camp, "in the starting of the spring."

I wrinkled my nose. "The return of the birds? The blooming of new flowers? Spring greens for the pot? What's sad about that, Sergeant Major?"

He smiled and blew out a soft breath, foggy in the morning air. I saw him as though through a shroud. "I believe," he said, "they call it melancholy."

I had forgotten Beau Whittaker's spring melancholy by the summer, when we had moved camp to Branwell plantation and all the talk was of rousting the rebels from their position at Fort Wagner. I was bristling, tetchy as a flea-bitten mule. I snapped at the boys I nursed through varioloid and taught their letters; I kicked at the racket-ribbed camp dogs that sniffed my cook pot.

"You'll break apart, holding yourself so tight, Sally," Beau would tell me after some snarling fight that left nothing in our jaws but rot. I chose not to hear him. I lingered over Flip's taxonomy as though it were the last hard tack of a long winter march. Had I not every right to my anger, its pettiest excesses? Had I not been born to slavery, like most of my boys? If I noticed the slight resemblance I bore to Billy Brown, I did not linger over the knowledge. After I refused his affections, he had loudly declared his intention to maintain his "purity" far away from the "wicked Jezebels out to tempt a holy man," and I was happy to leave him to it. He and all the other men who'd looked at me hopefully had given way with surprising ease when Beau Whittaker came to my tent. The resentment I felt toward my boys—was I only a human, a fellow in this bitter struggle for our freedom, when I had been claimed by a man?—I folded inside my other angers like a baby in swaddling. Affront was my meat and milk that summer, though it curdled, though it teemed with flies.

The first day of June I went out at the dawn's low tide to wade into the shallows and collect whatever wriggling bits of life mother water had seen fit to gift us: clams, mostly, and one small eel trapped in a tide pool. I picked it up by its tail and cracked it like a whip against the back of a hunching stone. My breath was heavy, my eyes stung with salt. I dropped the eel in my basket.

Across the water was Hall Island, a strip of rock and sand covered in bitter panicgrass and scraggly saw palm. Rebel pickets had been spotted there, and Colonel Higginson had ordered us to stay clear. Guillaume and Zollie flouted this order with impunity that summer. "There's sweet shrimp in the rocks, Beau," Zollie had said, more conciliatory than his brother, who had told Beau Whittaker that he was free now, "at least that what y'all told us, and ain't no white man giving me any orders now—at least none that I'm taking, Sergeant Major."

I looked the other way. I knew the hell these boys would soon face, and go back to god facing.

I returned to camp with a basket of clams and an eel too smashed for eating. I thought Beau Whittaker would find me, and I had a few words I'd been saving for him. I anticipated the fight more than the clams in my basket: *What do you care for me, when you can't be bothered to come back to the tent before midnight? You never bring me herbs anymore, you don't wait for my cooking, you come in and out like a ghost, like you're afraid of me.* And he would just look at me, sad as an old dog with death in its eyes, before I pushed him too far. But Flip found me first, that angular, serious face filled with an energy that dropped my guts and twisted.

"Orders?" I asked. "Fort Wagner?"

Flip shook his head. "Going up the Edisto River. Colonel Higginson thinks we can destroy one of the railway bridges to Savannah."

"Not just that."

Now Flip smiled. "The plantations."

Up the river, isolated among the waterways and islands of the Carolina coast were dozens of plantations filled with slaves whose masters had marched them behind the rebel lines before Lincoln's navy took Hilton Head. They would be freed if our boys could get to them.

"They won't be left behind, Sally."

"Both companies are going?"

"Just volunteers. Sergeant Major Whittaker is with the colonel. He says not to wait."

I waited. Baked the clams and fried up two mess pans of cracker dowdy in a bit of lard and then kept it all warm on the coals as the sun climbed up and back down again. As the moon rose in a sliver above the stands of live oak just beyond Hall Island, I took some dried herbs from my satchel and cast them upon the smoldering embers.

I sat on my makeshift bench—an old stump with a little rise at the back, as though the tree had been thoughtful in its falling—and drew a raw breath: blue rosemary, pale scrub sage, and a small crumbly leaf the color of the bayou before a storm. Grandmother had named them all, like Adam lonely in the first garden, but that last she had baptized with a word from her mother's people in their place across the water. I burned it when the moon laid her ancient light upon our fragile human endeavors, when none but Flip or Clarence or Piggy might see me. Beau Whittaker was too modern of a man, too favored by the generals, to approve of my rootworking. He would collect herbs for me—or he had—but he refused to wear a sprig of life everlasting in his cap when he went to battle.

He would be going back into battle soon; he always did. "Affront," I whispered to myself. My anger hadn't evaporated, it had merely undressed. There it was, shivering and gulping in the moonlight: melancholy, a fresh ghost.

That July night I whispered the chant my great-grandmother had taught me while she clamped an old clay tobacco pipe between her teeth as though it were the bone of an old slaver. I had only been four years old, but I hadn't dared forget. She had lived to eighty-four by her reckoning, a mythical age to the child that I had been. I still did not know what the chant meant, only that it was to keep me and mine safe, to remember us to the old spirits although we had traveled so far beyond them. And as at the time of that bloody summer I had no living children to pass into the spirits' sight, I commended to them, instead, my fine boys of the 1st South Carolina and 54th Massachusetts. I sent waves of that blue and fragrant smoke through the camp that night. I wanted my boys to have a taste of that other place behind their tongues, something they could recall, perhaps, in the noisome stink of the battlefield. And if the worst happened, a quiet space, drifted with holy incense, in which to pray and wait for death.

Beau came to my fire after mother moon had climbed into her house and Piggy lay slumbering by the embers of my fire, with Clarence snuggled beside her. I was smoking a bit of hoarded tobacco that Flip had given me with quiet solemnity before he went to his tent. I felt at peace for the first time in months, as though I had made myself the smoke of offering.

Beau ate my cracker dowdy and baked clams in reverent silence, even though the dowdy had long since turned to rubber. The clams were still good, and I seasoned them with a sprinkle of my scrub sage and sea salt. I will never forget how he looked up at me from his place by the fire, smoke in his eyes. How out of place, how inevitable, that spring melancholy in the redolent bloom of summer. He and the boys would be off tomorrow at dawn. Some would return, and some wouldn't. We would all go back to the earth in our time.

"You back, Sally?" Beau asked.

"I never left."

"But you were hiding."

Beau pulled down the collar of my dress and kissed down the tiny bones of my neck, twisted and sore from years of looking down at everything white men needed doing. For the first time in my nineteen years I was learning what I might do if I looked up. Now my former masters were just Johnny Rebs and we of the 1ˢᵗ South Carolina were united in what consideration they deserved. The world was not what it had been when I was a girl. I'd been summoned to the bed of Mr. Wentworth's son whenever he was home on holidays from school. I had been all but twelve when it first started. Mr. Wentworth's taste ran to the high yellow house slaves, so I suppose that I had counted myself lucky that the boy only claimed me for a few weeks out of the year. I had long since ceased to consider myself an innocent by the time Beau Whittaker crowned the company laundress with Spanish moss. I had watched my mother sold away when I was ten. I knew as well as any former slave the danger of cleaving to any but God (and take care, even with Him). Yet I found myself there: the sand-blown beaches of the Carolina islands were my own Eden and Canaan, a promised future in a reclaimed past. I didn't know it until I had left it, so foreign was such tenderness and childlike exploration to my experience of the world. With Beau, I learned to breathe, to take his hand, to say: I am, here, yours. And he, fresh-faced, milk-fed and free, saw nothing wrong in me.

He fed me the last remaining clams. They tasted of salt and smoke.

"When this is over, will we be free?"

"You're free now. Mr. Lincoln signed the proclamation."

It had not freed him. Though he put about a tale of being freeborn in Delaware, in reality Beau Whittaker had escaped from a Baltimore lawyer's household and made his way down the coast in order to join the 1ˢᵗ South Carolina. Mr. Lincoln's

Proclamation only applied to former slaves like myself from the rebellious south, not to those enslaved in states that still cleaved to the Union.

"No, no . . . free of this . . ."

"What?"

Like poisoned water you're too thirsty not to drink, like a thick maggot in a juicy apple, like that tar baby stuck fast to your hand, never shook loose again. (Grandma, ten years after Beau, dying to get free of some old and evil thing: *What's this worming its way up in me? What's this I can't get out?*)

I regarded him until his cedar brown eyes lit in shared despair, warm as his palms, house-slave-smooth, on my cheeks. We laughed like two babies crying, and looked again, past the embers of the fire to Piggy and Clarence snoring in counterpoint, and then to the spare gray tents of the men. They looked insubstantial in the moonlight, like a daguerreotype on silver; I loved them, but they—we all—were already ghosts.

The boys returned a week later. Their ranks had swelled so with the new freedmen from the plantations upriver that it was hard to spot the missing faces. Only two, this time, men who I only knew by sight and whose deaths inspired, to my great shame, nothing more than a swell of relief. Colonel Higginson, flush with pride over the mission, retired to his tent immediately to write a report for the generals at Fort Walker. They had only destroyed one of the two critical railroad bridges, but the liberation of the plantations inspired even Beau Whittaker to join in the celebrations upon return. The praise meeting began at midday and did not end until midnight, though the newest ranks of freedmen all spoke the Gullah tongue of these backwaters, and our mutual understanding was a painstaking endeavor.

Flip I saw when he entered camp, carrying two babies beside their ailing mother, and not again until after midnight. I only listened to Billy Brown fulminating during prayer meeting while I helped find the newcomers places to sleep for the night and attempted to ease the half-dozen who were already sick from the dreaded swamp fever. I prepared gallons of sassafras tea to fortify the blood and gave it to all the soldiers and the newcomers who would take it. We couldn't afford an outbreak among us. Not with orders set to come down any day for that final assault on Fort Wagner. Past midnight, I finally found time to squat on my heels in the sand and eat some crumbled hardtack and the last of the pudding I had whipped up from condensed milk rations and the eggs the newcomers had brought with them.

Flip walked back into camp as I finished eating. I thought he was Beau until his red breeches stopped a proper six feet away and I could make out the dirt and powder stains typical of a gunner. I took a deep breath of warm, salty air and looked at him through my swimming eyes.

"You want something too? I'm just as tired as you boys, and I've still got your messes to clean up."

Flip took a step closer. "What have I done to offend you, Sally?" His quiet voice was weary as mine.

Anger rose up in me and buckled like a broken leg. I rubbed my eyes. "Nothing," I said, "nothing. Just living, it seems." I held out the pudding.

He squatted beside me and ate it with the silent quickness of a soldier recently disgorged from battle. When he had finished, he turned, lifted his hand, as though we had been speaking this whole time and he could not keep himself from hitting this last mark:

"It's not the war that will kill us all, not bullets or cannon or implacable fever." He drew himself into his weedy height, filled with a spirit. "No," he said, "it is disillusion that delivers the final blow."

"And the bullet? The cannon? The gangrene?" I asked. I could not help myself. My grandmother had always chided me for my boldness in praise meetings; I would have questioned Moses at the bottom of the Red Sea, she always said.

Flip nodded with august grace. His eyes fixed on me. I wondered who he saw. "Mere affront. The means of delivery," he said, and then tipped his cap. "Be seeing you, Sally."

Flip was captured in the second raid, a spontaneous action spurred on by the praise meetings and the drunken jubilee from the success of the first. This expedition up the river to Poco-taligo was under the command of Sergeant Harry Williams, making it the first all-black mission of the war, and Sergeant Williams was warmly celebrated upon his return. It was Clarence who brought me the news, as the men were preparing, at last, for the assault on Fort Wagner.

"He might come back, though, Miss Sally," Clarence said, clacking his drumsticks in a nervous rhythm that had Piggy twitching her head, waiting for the trick. "He was living when last I saw him."

No one was young in this war, not even a drummer boy of thirteen, and certainly not a laundress of nineteen. We both knew what the rebs did to any free Negro soldier who fell into their hands. Abomination, that was what, abomination in the eyes of the Lord. But for a born freeman like Flip—I would rather he have died. I went to that spot by the river where I had last seen him and screamed until I swooned. Beau Whittaker was not in camp; he was off rushing Fort Wagner, where he was spared by the grace of our mysterious God. The returning soldiers found me there, weedy in the rising tide. The company doctor rolled me over a barrel to get the water from my lungs, but a cough lingered. Perhaps I let it; in those gray-rimed hospital days there were times when I was sure I heard Flip's filling voice, reciting verses of our own, newer testament.

The men and women we freed in those raids went on to the contraband camps in Mitchelville and around Beaufort, unsteady with deliverance. A few dozen of the young men stayed on with the 1st South Carolina and 54th Massachusetts and so were among the first into the field when we sallied the rebs at Fort Wagner. Nearly all of them died, along with the 54th Massachusetts's own Colonel Shaw; nearly a thousand in all, so many that in the years that remained to the war, when I would walk from Camp Saxton to Fort Wagner, the path was littered with the skulls of those men, rebs and Union alike, grinning in the thickets of saw palms, and we never did know which was which. Perhaps that meant they had died in vain. Perhaps it meant that they had died facing Canaan. *The Lord is generous even in our grief,* Flip whispered to me amid the screams of the men dying in the Beaufort hospital. *They would not be left behind. Is it disillusion, or illusion? Our lives on earth, our bondage, our freedom. But what, my Lord, of our liberation, our liberation, our liberation on judgment day?*

I fell down in a praise meeting after the rout at Fort Gregg. We were stationed on Cole Island that fall of '64, and I felt my own life's flame as a cold and lonely pricking in the dark. Beau Whittaker was even more improbably alive, and it was his steady warmth, more than any doctor's treatment, that kept me above the earth in that time. That evening we were singing "Where, oh where are the Hebrew children" in honor of Billy Brown, who had just been planted, as the boys would say, in the mud of the levee behind them. I tossed stinging jokes around with the boys that at least now Jesus could keep him away from "those Jezebels" and one threw back, "Oh, knowing Billy, he's negotiating a few for himself right now." My laughter was a giddy, bitter thing, which I hid behind another joking observation that he would be spared the affront of the drummer boys riding Piggy into meetings. One replied that "Her Pigship" would meet him soon enough in heaven.

"Clarence must miss her," Young Moses said, so solemnly that our laughter dried like mud. Our last drummer boy had been rolled by swamp fever three months before.

How do you bear that which cannot be borne? It could have been Flip, whispering to me again in my delirium. That is the question asked by the slave, as her eye catches the steady light of the north star, of the mother who has lost her child, and of the child roughly stripped of her mother's embrace. Where, oh where are the Hebrew children? Away! Over in the Promised Land!

Someone moaned, "Lord, take me there! Surely by now we have earned our reward?"

I rolled my eyes heavenward, but instead of the star-whorled sky I saw our boys, red breeches stark as a cardinal's crest against the charcoal of a recently-burned field. There were so many dead I could not count them. Water lapped against the causeway, and above us turkey vultures swung in slow-descending spirals.

It was Beau Whittaker who woke me. My hair was wet and my eyes stung. I squinted up at him and the milling faces above.

"Sally?"

"What happened?"

"The spirit touched you."

I had spoken in tongues, they told me. I had an aunt who was always touched by the spirit during praise meetings, but I had never been one for the holy shakes. Beau Whittaker took me back to our tent and held me while he cried. I was coughing again.

"You promised to marry me, Sally."

"If we win." My voice was hoarse and without conviction.

He wiped his eyes and gave me a tired smile like he had once given me a crown of Spanish moss. "If not, we'll jump the broom in the Promised Land," he said, "with Clarence and Flip and Piggy as witnesses."

I slept to that lullaby, and did not remember until morning that Piggy had not yet gone on ahead, and I still lit a flame with Flip's name on it some nights after Beau Whittaker had gone to sleep, and prayed to the spirits to light his way home. I worried at my vision like a sore tooth; I could not make sense of the burned field, the wide causeway, the salty tang of marshland in that cold dawn air. What battle had that been? Fort Wagner for the bodies, but I knew the lay of that battle very well and could not place my vision among those fields where saw palms cradled vulture-cleaned bones. I told Beau of my worry as I scrubbed the long johns of a few dozen soldiers. I had to pause for breath in my telling of it, but he just helped me move a pair to the wringer and planted a soft kiss in the nap at the back of my head.

"That's just war, Sally. Folks die in the fields and the crows come for them. There's nothing easier to predict."

"But what if something's coming, Beau? A big one, like Fort Wagner?"

He whistled lightly through that gap between his front teeth. "They all the big one if it's your turn to go on ahead. Flip didn't even see Fort Wagner."

I nodded like a scarecrow in a breeze. A deep breath of carbolic and Beau Whittaker was not enough to stop it: ambulance wagons rolling into the field, the squelch and pop of those great wheels rolling over the dead, the sweet green smell of plantation fields after a rain mixing with the sour aftertaste of blood, they called me their mother, their woman, the ones still alive, who would die soon enough—

Beau took me by the shoulders and held on. "Finish your washing. General Saxton came in to see Colonel Trowbridge this morning. I think they're fixing to send us out again."

"Sherman?"

"They're still not sure where he is. Those rebel pickets up by Port Royal Ferry, my guess."

We'd been trading bullets like jokes with the rebs up north on Port Royal Island ever since I enlisted as company laundress. "Now?"

Beau's laugh was a bleak, fleshless thing. "Johnny Reb's still there, ain't he?"

The news washed through camp like a summer rain, and the boys made a show of it. Young Moses wove a bonnet of dune grass for "Her Pigship" and paraded her through camp that evening. I made myself smile and then felt a tiny release, a soap-bubble burst of joy. Piggy was still alive, and so was

Beau and so was I. Zollie's bones littered the fields of Fort Wagner, but Guillaume was still with us. He played bullfighter to Piggy's snuffling entreaties for the dried shrimp she could smell in his pockets. The boys laughed as tears streamed from their eyes.

The next morning the sun shone the yellow of clabbered milk upon the rows of long johns and undershirts hanging blessedly clean upon the line. I met Guillaume as he was climbing out of the channel from the Stono River, a striped bass the size of my forearm speared on a stick topped with an old Indian arrowhead. He struck a pose when he saw me, his beard beaded with water and his naked torso streaming. He looked like a painting in one of Mr. Wentworth's books, the ones I would read in his study when granted house duty. An old white man with a trident and sea-tangled beard. But this vision was no white man's god; here was mother water's son, guardian of the deep, black and free.

"The colonel has you boys running drills today, Guillaume," I told him.

He squinted past my shoulder to the even rows of company tents and planted the butt-end of his spear into the ground. The sea bass trembled. "The colonel can get himself planted, Miss Sally."

The force of his diction rocked me back like a hot wind. "Colonel Trowbridge has been very good to us."

He spat. "He's one just like the others, the ones that got Zollie killed. Like I said, they can *all* get planted. Johnny Reb and Billy Yank. They can just leave us be."

"Guillaume," I said, carefully, "those are dangerous words in wartime."

He pointed to my rucksack and basket. "Ain't those con-juring herbs, Miss Sally? If you go talking to the dead, be sure to tell Zollie that I won't—I won't—"

"I won't be telling Zollie anything, Guillaume!"

His eyes lingered on me, empty as a pine box. "They'll pay, the ones that did this to us."

"You can't revenge yourself upon the whole Union army."

But at that he just laughed and took the path back to camp, whistling. I watched him, unsettled, until he passed out of sight.

I tried to put Guillaume's request from my mind. I knew that thirst for vengeance, and I did not agree with Flip on this point, after all. Righteous or not, all vengeance bore poison fruit.

I took the little skiff we kept on the west side of Cole Island across the creek and made the half-hour trek to the cypress forest on Snake Island. Beau Whittaker would be drill-ing with the boys for most of the day, and a soft hand had touched me in the night, bringing with it the smell of speaking herbs. It was a relief, at last, to know what to do.

Dandelion greens, edges ridged like the inside fold of Beau Whittaker's ear, which I would touch while he slept. A beauti-ful clutch of chicory roots that would serve for coffee in the morning, the greens still fresh enough for the pot. Peppergrass and red clover and shepherd's purse, each heart-shaped fold of its leaves the size of my first baby's fingernails.

There are herbs for the dying—that's rootworking—and herbs for the dead—that's conjuring. A bit of flame, a bit of smoke, and a few thumbs of moonshine whisky to whet the haunted earth. I had no use for goopher dust here. The story went that some thirty years ago a contraband slaver was spotted by a federal sloop a few miles out from the Charleston harbor and so ran up the Stono River for cover. The federals caught their trail, though, and the slaver captain realized they would soon be discovered. To hide the evidence of his crime, he pushed all the Africans on board into the deepest part of the river, their hands and feet bound and weighted with wooden yokes and steel chains. The locals had it you could still hear the old Africans groaning, rattling their chains and cursing that old slave captain in their mother tongues. The mud of this place would be all the grave dirt I needed. Then my herbs: John the Conqueror, five-finger grass, camphor, and a pinch of a sage so old the wide, gray-green leaves had crumbled to a powder the color of ashes. My fingers trembled as I sprinkled this over the rest. It had come from far away, from a place I had sworn I would never see again but that I would miss, as a wounded soldier misses a limb. With my cooking knife I cut my left index finger, and let the blood fall onto the conjuring.

I waited. The sun was tangled in the branches of the cypress to my right, casting an eleven o'clock shadow over the conjure bowl and the gray muslin of my skirts. The leaves jumped and shook, clamored in the clean breeze that hummed of salt sea and steel ships, danced their way between my ragged hemline and the tarnished silver of my bowl. Just a little longer now. I had brought that bowl with me when we took off from Mr. Wentworth's plantation. I figured I was stealing myself, so I might as well steal a little something else besides. I had always liked that bowl: it had held the soup I gave Mr. Wentworth's son the night my first baby was born.

I never gave that baby a name. Martinique sent me back to quarters from the kitchens and told me to "take care of it" before dinner. The baby came out with no one to catch her— Grandma had bought her freedom the year before. She died in the time it took me to reach for the bloody straw where she lay, limp and twisted. She was red, but I knew she would have been light if she lived; she had my nose and great-grandma's mouth. I buried her in the herb garden with that bloody straw for a shroud, beneath the sage and the sorrel. I washed myself in the trough and pinned back my hair and made it back to the big house in time to serve Mr. Wentworth and his son, back from school for the first time in six months. I laced his soup with a generous dose of mayapple tincture that Martinique handed me without a single shared word or glance. Just our fingers, passing rebellion. He spent that whole visit purging himself fit to die. I cleaned his chamber pot and slept on the truckle bed beneath his, and not once did he importune me. I considered killing the boy; it would have been easy to do, and in his state, no one would have suspected me. I passed nights sweating with desire, sweating the poison out of me. The boy lived. Above my girl's head flowered a riot of sage, sorrel flower, knobby bushes of peppermint that no winter could kill.

The shadows slid neatly over themselves and left me alone among the trees. I dug up a handful of dirt, black as pitch, and blew.

"O spirits, o Great-grandmother, who resides in heaven with our Lord and Savior, I am weary and sore of heart. O Mama, I am willow-twisted and cracked in the roil and storm of this war. The nearer we are to freedom, the farther from peace. Justice smells of life everlasting and copper coins, and her voice is not a song, or a prayer, but a cry."

Remember, the spirits blow back.

I heard her in the breeze, the mouthy leaves, a sudden gust of whisky and pipe tobacco.

"What do you ask of the dead, my daughter?"

My great-grandmother had been a great conjure woman in her day. It was said she could fly, but she would always return to the plantation for her babies, and her babies' babies, and, eventually, me.

I was afraid of her, of my audacity in asking, but I was possessed of such bravery that is the bitter reward of despair.

"Keep my boys here," I cried to the trees flaunting their drapery of Spanish moss. "Let them stay, at least a little while longer. A few more weeks, just a few more weeks . . ."

A perfect stillness settled over the noontime. My labored breath was the only air that moved in that place. I did not see her, but I remembered her, more sharply than any painting: the dark of her skin, the bone whites of her eyes, her lips, which never frowned and rarely smiled.

"I have heard you, my daughter. I will do as you ask. Will you bear it?"

I tasted the pact as copper on my tongue. "I will."

An autumn rain, brief as a peal of laughter, blessed my conjuring. I lay upon the earth, pouring whisky down my throat as black water leeched through my petticoats. I thought of my daughter whom I never knew, of the earth where she and my great-grandmother rested, of my boys in the 54th Massachusetts and the 1st South Carolina, those who had been planted and those who still lived to face shellfire.

I heard the man approach before I saw his face. He moved as one with no fear of these woods, of Johnny Reb or old African ghosts. But this was no white man. I knew that, too, by his weary footfalls on this land that had never been, but might one day be, his. I turned my tear-streaked face south and waited.

The man limped, and an old straw hat covered his face with shadow, but I could no more mistake the weary grace of his approach than I could forget the poetry of his voice. He wore mere rags on his feet, a pair of rebel breeches, and a slave's homespun shirt.

I sat up and my head spun. He removed his hat.

"I heard you, Sally. I followed your voice as a beacon, as the shepherds followed a light to God." Flip took in the conjure bowl, the nearly-empty bottle of whisky, the knife. He held out his hand.

"Let's leave this place, Sally. It smells of blood."

Piggy did all of her tricks when she saw Flip and would not leave his side all the riotous night long. The morning after Flip's miraculous return to camp, the white officers of the 1st South Carolina were, to a man, gripped by a bloody flux of the bowels. Guillaume, it seemed, had made a great show of cooking that fine striped bass and passing out the choicest morsels among the officers. He had disappeared by the next morning. I wondered, had it been his vengeance or my conjure? Had the spirits made him do it, or had they merely found in him an instrument suited to the purpose? The sickness spread down the ranks. Beau Whittaker was among the few who didn't fall ill, but he watched me as one watches a feral dog, and came to our tent late, when he came at all. As he had predicted, the whispers in camp were all about the possibilities of a siege of

Gregg Landing, a strategic position in the north of Port Royal Island where the rebels were still quite firmly entrenched. We all speculated as to the unknown whereabouts of General Sherman, who had left Atlanta with 50,000 men weeks before. A week later, a white officer died; the healthiest among our boys were dispatched to carry the body back to Hilton Head for full military honors. *Will you bear it?* that old woman had asked. *I am bearing it,* I thought now, shivering through long nights, *as I have borne everything else.* The night Beau returned from Hilton Head he held me hard against him. "It's no use, Sally," he whispered. "We're at war. There's no honor in avoiding our duty, like Guillaume."

"Are they so sure his fish was poisoned? It could have been the shellfish, anything else they ate that day."

Beau shrugged. "It's all the same, now. A white officer died. If they find him, it's the court-martial. No, Sally, have done. You can't stop it."

"I only wanted you to stay. For a little longer."

He sighed my name and we said no more.

Days later, word came down from Fort Walker: those of the 1st South Carolina healthy enough for the journey would go to Port Royal Ferry on the first of November to lay siege to Gregg Landing until such time as the rebs there surrendered. Sergeant Major Whittaker would help guide the advance of his regiment. Flip, due back to the 54th Massachusetts, had still not been cleared by their company doctor, and would stay in our camp while his regiment went out on other maneuvers. A little more than half of the men were getting ready for the attempt on Gregg Landing.

I knew the place. In the early summer of '63 we had passed a jolly three weeks among the plantations and cypress woods between the muddy Coosaw and the wide shell road to Charleston. They were days of endless picnic and praise, the boys and I at turns giddy with freedom and snarling at ghosts. We ate like King Reb, like the unrighteous, angry men we had once called master: wild boar, venison, goat, turkey—Zollie found something for the barbecue every night, though the Lord knew where he got it, as none of the Negro regiments had been paid a penny in wages, and hard tack was a poor prospect for barter.

Zollie was gone, now, and his brother a hunted man. Beau Whittaker would lead his regiment over those fields that had witnessed our first season of joy as free men and women, and he would cover them, as was his duty, with blood and shellfire. At least the terrain of that place was far enough from my holy vision to ease my nerves on that count.

The boys left under cover of night, guided by those of our men who had grown up in the sea islands. Guillaume should have been among them. If I found him first, I'd hide him, and so would many of his former brothers-at-arms. An icy rain descended as they left, sliding through the mist on their flat-bottomed boats like baby Moses through the reeds. I locked eyes with Sergeant Major Beau Whittaker until he was lost to the water. It was more than likely we would never see one another again. (I was sharpened steel in those days—I did not flinch, and I did not expect, yet when Beau Whittaker truly left me I was as soft as old meat, disarticulated by the blow. We had allowed ourselves to dream a kind of safety, but I have never since made this mistake.) As soon as they left, the rebs took advantage and began to shell the half-deserted camp. We were saved from evacuation only by the timely arrival of one of our gunboats in the rear.

I took cover with the boys from the medical tents in a shallow dugout. A brief lull in the chorus of artillery fire brought Flip running from the sandbagged fortifications by the landing to tell me of what I would have to now bear for my fortnight's reprieve. General Sherman's army was nearly to the coast, and he had sent messengers ahead asking for reinforcements to meet them on their march to Savannah. The remaining soldiers of the 1st South Carolina would join the 54th Massachusetts and a half-dozen other colored regiments to capture the confederate rails outside Savannah. I knew this would be no lucky battle. I had seen it, had I not? The Lord had granted me a vision.

I regarded Flip with speaking fear.

"Have they no pity? The men are still recovering. You only just returned."

"What grows tall in springtime is threshed by autumn."

I rubbed a salty grit from my eyes. "You are men. Not bales of cotton!"

"No," he agreed, thoughtful. "This time, we keep our harvest."

Flip went with his regiment; I could not convince him to spare himself. He told me that God would decide.

I hated them all. I brimmed with rage. I would kill them if I could, Johnny Reb and Billy Yank alike, for what they had taken from us, and would continue to take, until this war was over and they might let us be. A scent came to me on the keening wind: the stink of blood and afterbirth on green straw, the sweetness of basil and the sharp sweep of peppermint. We were birthing a new world in these killing fields, but I cried without any hope of it. Her flowers, her colors, her scents: all that she would ever be. (Is it guilt, Grandma, what holds fast when our chance for vengeance goes away? I didn't even know she was there until she was gone.)

The boys of the colored regiments were cut down like threshed grain two days later in the battle of Honey Hill. They wore sprigs of life everlasting in their caps and they were left in the cold and ice in the thousands upon the burned broom sedge field and the marsh. The scouts of the 56th New York caught Guillaume five days later trying to sneak past their pickets by the Savannah railroad. The firing squad was made of our own men and neither he nor they flinched as they shot him down at Fort Walker on Hilton Head.

We started at dawn on the causeway through the marshes that would take four full brigades plus cavalry, over the course of a few dozen hard-footed miles, to the rebel railway between Savannah and Charleston.

It will not be long now, the song ran its lonely track between my ears, *it will not be long, my Lord, till we reach the promised land.* So much joy, oh they were near to dizzy with it, but I could hardly lift my voice to sing. Was I not free, here among my people? Were we not, at last, fighting for what the Lord himself had promised us? But I carried my vision like a weight against my eyes; I dragged my guilt like blistered feet over a hot road. I hurt just the same as my boys, but my heart was filled with rocky soil, it could not grow my pain into righteousness.

The fighting began at ten the next morning, an ambush along the causeway to Grahamville. We never did make it to the tracks. We were marching along that wide avenue, bayonets swinging, the men's deep-voiced chorus enough to startle the egrets from their morning hunt. Long-necked birds lifted and then wheeled higher for a better look at the sight of my boys in their red breeches and blue shirts, shining in formation. They were a wide and easy target. General Hatch had not expected enemy engagement for another dozen miles yet. Rebel cannon had a clear view down the causeway and they loosed their fire with the desperate precision of cornered animals. The marsh on one side of the causeway offered little cover, though a few soldiers fell into the muddy shallows in their desperation to escape the shelling. Many drowned there, and their blood painted the water red.

In the back of the army train with the supply and ambulance wagons, we were spared the worst of it. We dove into the broom sedge on the other side of the causeway. The dry weeds were taller than the horses' heads, and I quickly lost my way in the maze of them, as though I were a flea trapped in a fur blanket. I didn't dare shout for the others in case the rebs were near. I had come with Lois Thompson, the wife of a soldier in the 102nd US Colored troops, but I could not find her, nor anyone else. From the front I heard the wounded screaming and generals bellowing to rally the men. My breath expelled in short white gasps. The air reeked of spent gunpowder, brackish water, sweet hay. The sun was well in the sky by now, but it had not done much to banish the night's chill. What a day for winter, I thought, and wondered where Beau Whittaker might be, if his breath, too, painted this quiet moment's chill or if his lips had stilled to clay.

The quiet held me tight. A wind rolled through, bringing with it the acrid burn of more shellfire, the reek of blood and shit—oh, we were in it, now!—and parted the sedge like a comb through oiled hair. For a curled peel of time, I caught sight of a reb officer, stiff blue collar gummy with ash, putting a torch to the sedge. Our eyes met and the wind lifted. We vanished from one another's sight.

I turned, lifted my skirts and sprinted back to where I reckoned I had left the wagons, the sun over my left shoulder. "Fire!" I screamed, heedless now of Johnny Reb. Let him do for me, if I could save even a few of my boys. "Fire in the field!"

The fire drove out most of our boys back to the causeway, where they were once again easy targets for the straight-shooting cannons of the rebel lines. By the time we formed our lines again and General Hatch managed to advance upon the rebel fortifications at Honey Hill, the tall broom sedge had been reduced to smoldering char that choked the wounded left behind. Lois Thompson and I sat with the boys as they waited their turn in the surgeon's tent. We made them tea sweetened with the tins of condensed milk that sat in their neat rows by the dozens in the supply carts. I pitied Lois, her earnest relief and renewed horror as she scanned each man's face to see if it was her husband lying there, crying out for succor.

The surgeons did not do much doctoring in that war; they carved them up like meat, white and black boys alike, still alive and screaming for it, until they fainted from extremity. There is a limit to pain. This came to me, eventually, as a comfort. I took down names and plucked their last notes from their breast pockets and wrote a few for those who did not have their letters. I watched them die and I watched the bodies moved for the next group of blood-soaked soldiers to be brought in and cut to pieces and then left to die quickly or die slowly or—if they were very lucky—live out their lives in the constant absence of some vital part.

General Hatch sounded the retreat that afternoon. What was left of the brigades marched straight back to Boyd's Landing. We loaded the wounded into the ambulance wagons to be taken back to the hospital there. Lois went with the first group, hoping to find her husband hale, or at least still standing, among the retreating troops. I wished her luck warmly, but she could see the littered field behind us as well as I; in her eyes I saw cracks, a light shining through, that other kind of pain hatching like a new snake. What is it to be left behind? I have known it too many times, and yet I can never accustom myself. The sharp lash, the empty space, the words that haunt your breath like moonshine.

I walked that field and marsh until the moon was a high sliver in the indigo sky. Nubs of charred sedge crumbled and crunched beneath my shoes. A few other lights bobbed in the field, and I never knew if they were Negroes or whites, women or men. We did not speak, beyond the too-rare call for help when we found one alive. There was not much to do for them. If they had not received help by now, no art of man might keep them from going on ahead. I held my lamp ahead of me, a flickering globe of light that caught the shine of frozen blood and glassy eyes. I had never been more aware of my own flesh. I felt a just and fearful kinship with these fleshy houses who had been men in the morning. Like the ferryman, I crossed the waters with my light and my burden. Unlike the ferryman, I did not take the coin in their pockets, which all the black boys had duly placed there before marching.

"I won't be left behind," I sang, knee-deep in the marsh. "I won't be left behind, my lord." There was a boy ahead of me who had crawled upon a muddy hillock and curled upon himself there, bayonet clutched in his remaining hand. In the lamplight he still seemed to possess a fading life.

He opened his eyes when I touched him. He smiled. His arm had been blasted off above the elbow and a piece of shrapnel had lodged itself in his gut. Above the hole in his flesh, I made out the edge of a homespun bandage wrapped tightly around his upper torso. He breathed sharply, and I turned my gaze to his face.

"Are you . . ." I wasn't even sure what to ask.

The soldier's smile deepened, and I realized that she saw *me*, not some lost mother or ministering angel. "Wanted to fight," she said. "Our secret."

I squeezed her remaining hand. Neither of us could speak. We had always been fighting this war right alongside them, though the boys chose to pretend otherwise. How had she hid herself for so long? Who had loved her, who had protected her, who had made her want to support our bloody course for freedom not with the succor they called our duty, but with bullets?

I tried to give her water, but it dribbled from her lips. So I held her and hummed some old childhood memory until I realized that my heart was the only one beating in that place and the sun, that old traitor, was turning the night into day.

"But what is it that makes us stay," Flip asked, the night of my wedding to Beau Whittaker at the end of that war, "when everything in our quailing hearts is telling us to run?"

I thought of that woman I found in the marsh outside of Honey Hill. What had made her seek the water instead of the sedge? What had kept her alive for so long, as though she had waited to die for the sight of me?

Beau Whittaker kept his hand around my waist. His other was in a sling. He had caught a musket ball at Port Royal Ferry. It had passed clean through the muscle and spared him the rest of the fighting. I would have kissed that reb's musket if I could.

"It's courage," said Moses. Our drummer boy had carried a musket instead of the drumsticks into the 1st South Carolina's last battle. "We just got a man's courage, that's all."

We had a cask of ale for the occasion, a gift from Colonel Trowbridge, but Flip was nursing a ration cup of moonshine whisky as though we had never left Cole Island. I drank the same. I did not quite know what to make of this end of the war. We were in a guest house above the Charleston Harbor, requisitioned from the defeated populace. If glares had been muskets, the white people passing below us would have riddled me like a deserter on my wedding day.

"I don't know about the white boys," said Beau Whittaker, who was properly drinking the colonel's fine ale, "but you know that we Negroes had the fire at our backs before we ever got to the front."

"Not all of us were born slaves, Beau," said Flip, for now that Lincoln had extended his Proclamation to all of the newly reunited Union, my husband had no need to hide his Baltimore origins.

Beau Whittaker shrugged. "And any day of the week a Boston slave catcher could have trussed you up and sold you down the river to some good ol' South Carolina plantation—hell, maybe real downriver, around Hilton Head—and it would have been as though you never existed, Flip."

Flip gulped down the rest of his tin cup.

"Is it only courage, Moses?" I asked. "Because I've spent four years cleaning the mess you boys make in your britches at the start of battle."

My husband snorted and raised his glass to me. "I'm sure you've never had to clean mine, Mrs. Whittaker."

Moses's chin trembled as he shook his head. "That's just fear. Fear and courage, they can live together in a man."

"Indeed," said Flip, recovering from the specter of slave-catchers, "you could say that one is necessary for the other."

"Oh, sure," I said, "you boys have plenty of courage. But I'd say it ain't courage that grows alongside fear, that nurses from the same teat. It's fury."

"What would you know of a soldier's fury, Sally?" asked Flip.

There was something in my heart that evening that wished for a musket. But for a lack of opportunity, or perhaps imagination, I would have had one.

"Do you not remember what you said that winter of your taxonomy? The soil of deprivation is fertile for a righteous anger? What deprivation have I not felt, right alongside you boys?"

"The role of the female of our species," said Flip, "is to offer succor and companionship to the embattled male."

I had cleaned muskets at Camp Saxton and Cole Island. I had loaded and fired each one into the marsh to check them, imagining with each bone-jarring ricochet that a tiny ball of lead shot had infiltrated the white flesh of a man who would enslave me. I had imagined their screams, their dying cries for aid, and I had felt pleasure, bone-deep.

"So it's only fury to throw yourself in the path of bullets? It's only courage to fight? My mama ran when I was eight years old. They brought her back after the dogs had gotten to her. My grandma and I brought her back to life, only for our master to sell her off to a tobacco plantation a year later as a trouble-maker. Do you not think I prayed to the Lord to let me fight that man? Do you not think I would have wept for the chance? There is as much anger in my heart as yours, Flip. There is more fear. It takes courage to wait, to sit still as death's witness. I pray you boys never discover how much."

Beau Whittaker pulled away from me now to look into my eyes. I do not know what he saw there. "Sally," he said.

I stood and walked to the railing that overlooked the harbor. Union navy boats were docked beside the blackened husks of Confederate ships that had been burned, like much of the rest of the city, by the rebs themselves when they fled Sherman's army. The colored troops had done what we could to save the city and its residents from the fire, though our reward had been the uniform antipathy of a populace eager to burn their noses to spite our race.

To my side, the three men shifted uneasily, shared significant looks. I had always known the grave limitations of their view of me. Deprivation is no even soil—the rich fruit of my anger was unknowable to these men with just a little more to hold onto. Even Beau Whittaker could only understand so much of what had driven a woman like me to follow my boys till the end of the war. And the southern white man's anger, that fruit of unholy overabundance? It was no mirror to our righteousness, only a poison that burned everywhere it touched.

"But we're free now," I said. The boats, living and dead, rocked with the rising tide. Sherman was cleaning up the last of the rebs in Virginia and scuttlebutt had it Lee would surrender any day now. Even Charleston had fallen; I had taken it as a sign from our Lord and married as I said I would. The breeze from the harbor reeked of char and brine. There was no blood, but I smelled it anyway; I always would.

Moses sat up. "That's the truth, Miss Sally. We can go wherever we please, now. We can buy land and grow our own crops and live just as well as these white men been living. No more slaves, and no more masters."

We turned to Flip as though he had pulled our gazes to him, though he was as unassuming as ever: slight, straight-backed, sloe-eyed.

"We died for this," he said, one month before a bush-whacker, still seething at the end of the war, cut his throat in his sleep. We waited.

"Is that it?" Beau said, laughing.

"I worry about Piggy. I hope those rebs didn't catch her. I want to take her home when we're discharged."

"To Boston!" Moses said. "Her pigship won't last the winter."

"We're free," Flip said, his eyes as distant as that land across the ocean.

It was Moses who found Piggy happily wallowing on Cole Island and brought her with him to Hilton Head. He settled in Mitchelville, which had been a contraband settlement, and is still living there, though her pigship died of natural causes five years after the war.

I moved to Boston a few years after Beau died. I raised our child and supported myself for years with my own school for

Negro children. At first the work was a balm, a way to make real that future we had all prayed for in our days on the sea islands. One particularly brutal winter, hard even for Boston, I realized that the demands of those beautiful children, who had never known slavery or war, felt like shrapnel in an old wound. To them, we had not done nearly enough. They were embarrassed by our disillusion. There was no one left to care for; Grandma had died some years before. I closed the school in the spring. Alone, I have had much time to think.

I am the only one alive who holds their memories: Beau, Flip, Guillaume, Grandmother, Great-Grandmother, my little daughter. I am afraid, the true mirror of that young woman's rage—afraid I have become unworthy of their memories. I speak this incantation as I did long ago in the cypress woods of Snake Island: O Grandmother, Great-Grandmother, bring her back to me. The woman Sally, company laundress of the 1st South Carolina, who loved Beau Whittaker and shared the gunner Flip's visions, who never once doubted to what end her anger. Let this worming thing inside of her be cast out, to writhe and wither, at last, on rocky soil.

And do they speak?

O Daughter! Will you refuse to see until you are a corpse, wide-eyed at the glory of the sky? That which torments you cannot be cast from your flesh, for it is the selfsame; what worms through your veins is your very blood. Would you cast yourself aside? Would you curse your own heart?

Remember, remember, and when you cannot, speak it to the sky and to the stars and to our children, so they may make you whole—

Remember?

"There is the fear of the bullet, and the fear of the noose. The fear of watching one you love march away and never return. And then that other, stranger fear. Not of losing everything but of everything twisting away from you; the promises made and received distorted like a reflection in muddy water, recognizable, but wrong. The fear not of death, but of sickness. An affliction that mimics life but removes, with merciless intent, its foundations."

Acknowledgments

Like many writers who came of age before the widespread use of electronic submissions, I for a time cultivated a collection of self-addressed, stamped envelopes, all of which contained folded inside a small note of rejection. They eventually filled a medium-size desk drawer; mostly "Dear Author" but a few "Dear Alaya" or "Dear Ms. Johnson" sprinkled among them, like drops of amber in Cretaceous rock. I bid farewell to that collection several moves ago, but for the many years that it kept my desk drawer company, the letters served as a perverse kind of inspiration. You paid your dues, they said. You were no wunderkind, blessed with talent whose exercise required little sacrifice. Much of the struggle was mine—the painstaking, never-mastered process of taking words and creating spaces with them that fill not a page, but the imaginations of unseen others. But it must be admitted that the atmosphere into which I submitted my first stories was actively hostile to a writer like myself. There were so few Black writers of speculative fiction that we were regularly mistaken for one another—once, memorably, in the pages of *Locus*, the industry's magazine of record. Rejection letters treated my non-white main characters as strange specimens whose identities aroused suspicion and had to be justified, thoroughly, for the white gaze. Writing my work in that environment was an act of defiance, and submitting that work even more so. Still, I can see with some embarrassment how that hegemonic white gaze crept into my early stories. Decolonization must be approached at a societal and individual level, in tandem. I am not exempt from its corrosive effects, and my stories certainly aren't. As my fiction gained traction, I gained confidence. My experiments in content and form grew bolder, my willingness to question myself and the received wisdom of the imperialist power structure more robust.

The stories in this collection span my first published science fiction story in 2005 at the age of twenty-three to stories that I finished this year, at the age of thirty-eight. There is a fascinating dissonance in confronting these pieces again as a science fiction writer living in their future, one in many ways bleaker than my imagination. Some seem remarkably prescient, others like faded photographs of discarded timelines of the past, improbable but hopefully charming. The science fiction short story is an open, forgiving medium with a long history, one more than able to transcend some of its more unsavory antecedents rooted in upholding historical oppressions. I am indebted always to those brilliant Black writers who welcomed me in my formative years in New York City and in conventions around the country. These writers challenged me, expanded my vision and my ambition, and allowed me to feel for the first time that I truly had a place in the genre I so stubbornly clung to: in particular, K. Tempest Bradford, N. K. Jemisin, Carol Burrell, Doselle Young, Nisi Shawl, Nalo Hopkinson, Terence Taylor, the late, great L. A. Banks, Jennifer Marie Brissett, and Andrea Hairston. I always try to pay your generosity forward.

———

Short story anthologies edited by masters like Gardner Dozois, Ellen Datlow and Terri Windling gave me an early and heady taste of the genre. Getting to meet these editors in person drove me to create work that would be worthy of their eye. The motley members of my inimitable writing group, Altered Fluid, are not only some of my favorite people on earth, but the ones who found a lonely writer in the city and gave her a place to hone her craft—and complain about the local Irish pub while stealing everyone else's French fries! It is interesting to me how much speculative fiction can be understood in its social context; the scene in New York City in the aughts and teens of this century was dominated by the twin fixtures of the NYRSF and KGB reading series, which exposed me to countless new writers and works of short fiction. I will not name the dozens of New York friends who have enriched my life, as I have thanked them all elsewhere. Even though I left town six years ago, I think and dream of you all often, and with much love.

I wrote most of these stories in New York City in a very specific window: post–9-11, pre–President Trump. These stories are a map of a time and a place and a person as she was then. This is to say that they are not perfect, but they are very much themselves, and very me. Together, they paint a picture that I regard, I must admit, with a great deal of fondness.

Alaya Dawn Johnson
Oaxaca, Mexico, 2020

Publication History

These stories were previously published as follows:

"A Guide to the Fruits of Hawai'i," *The Magazine of Fantasy & Science Fiction*, Jul./Aug. 2014.
"They Shall Salt the Earth with Seeds of Glass," *Asimov's*, January 2013.
"Their Changing Bodies," *Subterranean Online*, 2011.
"The Score," *Interfictions 2*, 2009.
"A Song to Greet the Sun," *Fantasy Magazine*, October 2009.
"Far and Deep," *Interzone* 221, Mar./Apr. 2009.
"Down the Well," *Strange Horizons*, Aug. 2008.
"Third Day Lights," *Interzone* 200, Sep./Oct. 2005.
"The Mirages" and "Reconstruction" are published here for the first time.

About the Author

Alaya Dawn Johnson (alayadawnjohnson.com) is the author of seven novels for adults and young adults. Her most recent novel for adults is *Trouble the Saints*. Her young adult novel *The Summer Prince* was longlisted for the National Book Award and *Love Is the Drug* won the Norton Award. Her short stories have appeared in many magazines and anthologies, including *Best American Science Fiction and Fantasy*. She lives in San Pedro Amuzgos, Oaxaca, and received a master's degree with honors in Mesoamerican Studies at the Universidad Nacional Autónoma de México for her thesis on pre-Columbian fermented food and its role in the religious-agricultural calendar.